"A pleasure to meet you, Aura."

He offered her a hand, and Aura shifted the bag of peanuts to her left in order to shake it. Her fingers must have been slightly greasy from the roasted snack, but Eduardo hardly seemed to care as he gave her hand a gentle pump and lingered for a few seconds with their hands tangled together.

There was nothing truly improper in it, not really, but Aura felt herself suffused by a curious heat that had nothing to do with the patch of sunshine on the back of her neck. Was her life really so solitary that a simple handshake could make her knees quiver as though they'd been filled with flan?

Or maybe it wasn't the handshake at all, but the light in his eyes as he gazed down at her, his lips slightly parted. His cheerful charm had sharpened into an intensity that snatched her breath away even as it made her want to step closer, all the better to bask in his admiring scrutiny.

Author Note

When I was around eleven or twelve years old, I got it into my head that I was going to learn how to sew.

I was obsessed with anything historical from a very early age, and movies like *A Little Princess* and *The Secret Garden*, which had come out in the early '90s, were in heavy rotation in my white-wicker-furniture-filled bedroom. I was determined to make myself dozens of frilly white nightdresses with satin ribbons at the neckline—to start with.

Needless to say, I did not have the attention span for all that. (Though my dolls got spectacular wardrobes.)

I still don't have what it takes to sew well or consistently, but my obsession with the craft hasn't lessened. So when the time came to give Eduardo Martinez his heroine, I decided on a fierce, prickly dressmaker who is thoroughly unimpressed with his easy charm.

I had such a good time writing Aura and Eduardo's story that I can only hope you will enjoy yourself as much when you read it!

UNEXPECTEDLY WED TO THE HEIR

LYDIA SAN ANDRES

HISTORICAL

H Harlequin®
HISTORICAL

ISBN-13: 978-1-335-53966-3

Recycling programs for this product may not exist in your area.

Unexpectedly Wed to the Heir

Harlequin Enterprises ULC
22 Adelaide St. West, 41st Floor
Toronto, Ontario M5H 4E3, Canada
www.Harlequin.com

Printed in U.S.A.

Lydia San Andres lives and writes in the tropics, where she can be found reading and making excuses to stay out of the sun. Lydia would love to hear from her readers, and you can visit her at lydiasanandres.com or follow her on Instagram and TikTok @lydiaallthetime.

Books by Lydia San Andres

Harlequin Historical

Compromised into a Scandalous Marriage
Alliance with His Stolen Heiress
The Return of His Caribbean Heiress

Look out for more books from Lydia San Andres coming soon.

Visit the Author Profile page
at Harlequin.com.

To my friend and writing buddy Lory Wendy,
with so much gratitude for all the advice,
encouragement and support.

And to my sister, who knows when to untangle
plot threads and when to pick out all the stitches.

Chapter One

San Pedro de Macorís,
1910

Aura Soriano had been living in San Pedro for a little over two years and she could count on the fingers of one hand the number of times she had attended a Sunday concert at the park.

The summer's oppressive heat had begun to lift, and it was late enough in the afternoon that the sunlight had lost some of its intensity, though most of the fashionable ladies in attendance still held silk-fringed parasols with polished wooden handles. A shame because Aura had really been hoping to get a glimpse of their hats.

In her capacity as a dressmaker, Aura was used to studying the latest fashions in the fashion plates and illustrated magazines she subscribed to. Today, however, was different—with her new store opening in less than a week, Aura was making note of the ribbons and trimmings favored by the fashionable crowd in order to tailor her next order of merchandise to suit their needs.

Most of the benches around her had been claimed by matrons, but the younger set had preferred to stand, all the better to show off their opulently trimmed frocks. Young trees cast dappled shadows on the crisp whites and soft ivories that had been in vogue all through the past decade, now adorned with sashes and ribbons in bright sherbet colors.

The small notepad and pencil in the embroidered handbag hanging from her wrist went unused as Aura tried not to be too obvious about scrutinizing the women who had gathered to hear the sprightly tunes being played by the municipal band. She could always sketch out anything that caught her eye once she returned home.

The stock she had purchased from abroad—several dozen yards of machine-made lace, carved mother-of-pearl buttons and embroidery threads in a wide array of shades— was already on its way to San Pedro. She'd agonized over what to order, hoping to strike just the right balance between new and unusual materials and colors and the safe standbys that would count for the bulk of her sales.

It had been mere optimism that had made her step out today to try to anticipate what she would add to her next order.

Optimism—and a slight wistfulness.

It wasn't that she was lonely, of course. Aura was far too busy to even acknowledge such a possibility. But as she sewed late into the night, ignoring her stinging eyes and aching back, she was all too aware of the silence that permeated the house where she now lived alone.

In any case, the music was welcome and she had spied some—

One of the men in the crowd turned and Aura's stomach sank as she recognized the features under the brim of a panama hat.

Rafael Marchena had been an associate of her father's when the latter had still been alive, and he'd made a pest of himself over the past three months. She should have been flattered by his solicitousness—Aura didn't know why it made her so uncomfortable, save that she didn't particularly wish to talk about her father now that he was gone.

At the moment, Aura's sole focus was on her store—on her survival. She did *not* have the time, or the patience, to fend off questions about how she was holding up.

But Aura was not a coward and she most definitely did not shirk her duties. So when Marchena spotted her and began heading her way, she squared her shoulders, commanded her lips to turn up into a semblance of a smile and prepared to endure the next several minutes with as much good grace as she could muster.

Her gaze wandered for just a second—long enough to see a little boy slip his fingers into a man's pocket and emerge with several folded banknotes.

Marchena forgotten, she charged forward, saying sharply, "You there!"

Appearing not to hear her through the music, the little boy disappeared into the crowd. Acting on sheer instinct, Aura bounded in the boy's direction—and was forced to come to an abrupt stop when the man whose pocket had just been burglarized stepped in her way.

"It's all right," he said quietly. He wasn't particularly large, though he was almost a head taller than Aura herself, but his lean body filled her field of vision so completely that Aura might as well have been stopped by a brick wall. "Let him go."

"But he—"

"I noticed. And it's all right. I only had a few pesos in my pocket and he likely needs them more than I do." The man nodded toward the peanut seller. "I've seen the two of them before—I think they're siblings. She's fearfully proud, wouldn't take an extra few cents when I paid her for the peanuts, though I insisted. I feel better knowing her brother is more...shall we call it *enterprising*?"

His warm laugh trailed over Aura, who tightened her grip on her embroidered handbag. She was used to agonizing over every cent—letting someone make off with the contents of one's pocket was an incomprehensible folly.

"That's certainly an odd way of going about doing acts of charity," she remarked. "Aren't you concerned that you're just encouraging him to pick someone else's pocket?"

"I hadn't thought of that," the man admitted, before lifting his shoulders into a shrug. He had the kind of smile that Aura suspected would make most people automatically break into a smile of their own just to look at it. "Whoever they encounter next will have to handle that particular moral quandary. Would you like some peanuts?"

"Would I—"

She must have still been a little dazed by what had just happened, because instead of politely declining and going on her way, Aura found herself accepting the small brown bag. The aroma rising from it made her mouth water.

Aura was reasonably sure she had never met this man before, but he had such a friendly demeanor that she found herself smiling back at him as she popped a roasted peanut into her mouth.

It wasn't just his demeanor, or even his infectious smile, that she found attractive. Practiced as Aura was at divining a person's shape through their garments, she could tell that he had the lean, athletic build of a sportsman. This impression was corroborated by the reddish tinge on his dark brown skin, which spoke of plenty of time spent outdoors.

His dark eyes were bold, and only the humor in them saved them from being impertinent as his gaze swept over Aura and his beautiful lips spread into another bright smile.

"Didn't I meet you at one of Paulina de Linares's dances?"

Aura shook her head. "I don't believe so."

"Then it must have been at the horse show hosted by Julián Fuentes and his wife."

"I don't go out into society much," Aura told him. And definitely not the kind of society he seemed to belong to—if the obvious quality of his fashionably cut suit hadn't given him away, the easy confidence in his voice and the way he moved revealed plenty about his privileged background. "I doubt you would have come across me, señor, unless you're in the habit of patronizing ladies' dressmakers."

The latter came out with just a tinge of defensiveness. But if she expected that knowing she was far from the society woman he had mistaken her for would dampen his obvious interest in her, she was wrong.

"A dressmaker? The way you were prepared to charge after the pickpocket, I would have taken you for an undercover member of the Civil Guard."

Embarrassment flooded Aura.

"Don't get me wrong," the man continued before she had a chance to say anything, "I thought it was delightfully brave of you to want to protect a grown man from a little boy."

Part of Aura wanted to bristle at his teasing tone, but there was something almost affectionate in it, as if they were already acquaintances who could take the liberty of gently ribbing each other without repercussions.

She cocked her head. "I wouldn't have tried if you hadn't looked like you needed protection."

He burst into laughter. "Dressmaker, protector of innocents and a wit—is there anything you can't do?"

"Resist a roasted peanut, evidently," she replied, holding out the small brown bag, which was much lighter than when it had been pressed into her hands.

He surrendered his claim to it with a gesture. "I don't really like peanuts. I only made the purchase to help the girl."

Aura couldn't help but think it was foolish generosity, when so many other people in the park were patronizing the girl's cart. Still, she *was* enjoying the peanuts. She'd scrimped and saved for so long in the interest of getting the funds together to open her store, she'd fallen into the habit of denying herself even the smallest treats.

"I hope you don't think me too forward for asking," he continued, "but I'll need to know your name for when I write to the captain of the Civil Guard with a recommendation to hire dressmakers to fortify his ranks."

She laughed, and said, "It's Aura."

"Laura?"

"Aura," she corrected. "Short for Aureliana, though no one ever calls me that."

"That's an interesting name," he said curiously. "I don't think I'd ever heard it before."

"It's an amalgam of the two things my father loved best—my mother, Ana, and gold." Aura felt her lips twisting wryly as she thought about her father's inability to hang on to either of those things.

As if sensing a need to distract her from her own thoughts, the man shrugged. "Much more interesting than my own name. Which is Eduardo, by the way. A pleasure to meet you, Aura."

He offered her a hand, and Aura shifted the bag of peanuts to her left in order to shake it. Her fingers must have been slightly greasy from the roasted snack, but Eduardo hardly seemed to care as he gave her hand a gentle pump and lingered for a few seconds with their palms touching.

There was nothing at all improper in it, but Aura felt herself suffused by a curious heat that had nothing to do with the patch of sunshine on the back of her neck. Was her life really so solitary that a simple handshake could make her knees quiver as though they'd been filled with flan?

Or maybe it wasn't the handshake at all, but the light in his eyes as he gazed down at her, his lips slightly parted. His cheerful charm had sharpened into an intensity that snatched her breath away even as it made her want to step closer, all the better to bask in his admiring scrutiny.

Whatever magnetic pull had ensnared them shattered as seven sharp chimes came from the nearby clock tower. Aura stepped back with a short gasp, almost dropping the paper bag she'd been clutching. She pressed it back into Eduardo's hands, instead, berating herself for having let the afternoon get away from her when she still had a commission to finish and deliver to a client by that evening.

"I'm so sorry," she told Eduardo, "but I really have to go."

"Can I do anything to persuade you to stay?" he asked, flashing her a smile that seemed designed to make her knees fail altogether.

The accompanying gleam in his eyes made it clear that he knew exactly what effect that smile had on other people—and that he was not above deploying it to get his way.

She answered it with a wry look. "You seem like the kind of man who rarely hears no for an answer. Unfortunately, I'll have to disappoint you."

His fingers tightened on hers, but she was already slipping them out of his grasp.

"I'm sorry," she said again. "It was nice meeting you."

"Likewise, of course, but—"

Aura didn't let him finish. She had too many things to do, and no time to waste on silly flirtations that would lead nowhere. Tossing him one last, distracted smile, she hurried along the path back out into the street.

Maybe it was an intrinsic part of his personality—or, more likely, a skill he had honed over twenty-six years of being in the exact middle of a large brood of cousins, all of whom had very strong and very distinct personalities— but Eduardo Martínez had long been designated the official peacemaker of the family.

So it was no surprise when, at the first sign of strife in the front room of Martínez & Hijos, the shipping company owned by his grandfather, his cousin Gregorio let out an exasperated sigh and looked up from his ledgers long enough to wipe his spectacles and ask Eduardo, "Will you handle it?"

"I always do," Eduardo replied, setting down his pen and stretching lightly.

He'd only come into the office they shared to pen a quick note to the dock administrator. Repairs were being made to the dock, which made it necessary to use rowboats to unload the larger freight steamers of the shipments they carried. The administrator had only two at his disposal, but that was all right because Eduardo had three in San Pedro and three more in Santo Domingo, and he was willing to loan them out in exchange for an unspecified favor at a later date.

Gregorio could revel in his ledgers and price lists. What Eduardo most enjoyed was dealing with people and putting his considerable resources toward helping things run smoothly.

Folding the note and passing it to the messenger, Eduardo followed the sounds of an argument to the front of the office, a large room crowded with desks and the sound of six or seven clerks clattering on typewriters. The source of the altercation seemed to come from one of the desks, where a clerk was impatiently explaining something to a woman standing with her back to Eduardo.

"What seems to be the problem?"

The woman turned, and Eduardo almost let out an audible gasp. He suppressed it just in time, but he couldn't hold back a delighted smile as he took in the high cheekbones, bold eyebrows and the eyes that snapped with inner fire. She'd run away from him before he'd had much of a chance to ask the important details, like her last name and whether she wanted to see him again. Eduardo had talked about it at such length at dinner the night before that both Gregorio and their other cousin María del Mar had threatened to stuff Eduardo's serving of roast chicken down his own shirt if he didn't change the subject.

And here she was.

The irritated clerk, whose name was Ruiz, stepped out from behind his desk, suddenly much more accommodating than he had been a moment before. "Don Eduardo, this is *la señorita* Aureliana Soriano. She—"

Eduardo didn't let him finish. "It's you. I was hoping to see you again."

The clerk cleared his throat, as if to recall Eduardo to the business at hand.

Ignoring him, Eduardo asked, "What seems to be the problem?"

Ruiz immediately launched into an explanation, but Eduardo held up a hand and looked at Aura.

"I put in an order for a great quantity of merchandise for the store I'm opening," she said. "Sewing notions and fabric, mostly. It was meant to arrive today—I received confirmation that it did—only, when I went to inspect the crates, there was nothing there."

Eduardo nodded. "Things are a bit of a shambles right now, as the facilities at the docks haven't been able to keep up with the demand for imported items. We're petitioning the public works office to build a new warehouse for the inspection of new arrivals, but in the meantime we're forced to deal with the confusion. I'm sure that if we send someone to search more thoroughly—"

"You misunderstand me," she said crisply. "My crates are here. They're just…empty. Well, not empty—they're full of rocks."

"Rocks?" Eduardo frowned. "But that makes no sense. Unless—"

"Whoever took my things wanted to make sure that the theft wouldn't be noticed until it was too late."

That was deeply troubling. It was one thing for a crate or two to go missing, quite another to think that at some point between them being unloaded from the ships and inspected by customs officials and their receipt by Martínez & Hijos's own warehouses, someone had been able to access their contents.

Replacing them with rocks was a clever idea, admittedly. The burly men he employed to transport the crates would have noticed if a crate was too light. But why would anyone go to all that trouble just to take fabric and sewing things?

Unless they thought that Aura's crates contained something else? Martínez & Hijos did plenty of business with prosperous merchants, some of whom imported wines and liquor and other objects of great value.

"I have no idea how this happened," he told Aura, "but believe me, I mean to find out. You'll have your things before you know it—I promise you."

Eduardo had a reasonably good idea of the kind of response he could expect when he was at his most charming—young women swooned, matrons were reduced to giggling behind their fans and gentlemen of all ages began pounding Eduardo on the back and proffering their undying friendship.

Which made Aura's reaction all the more surprising. Her chin rose, her eyes narrowed slightly. "I don't need promises, Don Eduardo," she said, and he winced at the polite, distancing honorific. "I just need to know that the matter will be looked into."

"It will. And I'll write to the suppliers on your behalf, if I have your permission to do so. The mistake might have occurred on their end."

She gave him a curt nod.

Eduardo couldn't figure out what he had said, or done, to make her so cold toward him. Hadn't she seemed to find him amusing the day before? Had he inadvertently insulted her?

Then again, she had just cause to be annoyed.

"In the meantime," he said, "is there anything else I could do to help?"

"No," she said immediately. "I don't need help."

But he had seen the look of dismay on her face when he hadn't come up with an immediate solution to her problem.

Affecting nonchalance as he discreetly removed his checkbook from his pocket, he moved to one of the desks to fill out an empty check. "We have a policy of refunding our clients for losses incurred while employing our services."

She glanced down at the check but didn't make a move toward it.

"Is it company policy to refund clients with personal checks?" she asked quietly.

"It is when your family owns the company," Eduardo told her, giving her his most charming smile—which she received with a frown.

"I appreciate the gesture, but it won't be necessary. I'm

sure my things will turn up. Maybe you'd like for me to write out an inventory of everything that was in the crates."

Eduardo waved her toward the empty desk, which he knew was supplied with pen, ink and paper. "Please do. And don't forget to add a way for us to contact you."

She nodded in a way that made it clear she was dismissing him. From his own office, no less. Aura Soriano wasn't just bold in the face of diminutive pickpockets; she was fearless in ways that Eduardo had only begun to glimpse. She had a smile that could rival the sun—and that couldn't hide the sadness lurking in the depths of her dark brown eyes.

Eduardo had never met anyone who intrigued him as much as this young woman did. And that was saying a lot, because Eduardo had always been outgoing and he had a knack for meeting new people that often astounded the more reserved Gregorio. Aura was like no one he had ever met, and Eduardo was determined that this shouldn't be the end of their acquaintance.

Chapter Two

A s if that day had not held enough disappointments, Aura returned home from Martínez & Hijos to find Rafael Marchena hovering by the front door. She'd completely forgotten him at the park, where he had clearly decided against approaching her as she fell into conversation with Eduardo.

Her pleasure at coming across Eduardo again hadn't just been dimmed by the day's events. Their meeting at the park had been too brief for her to get a good sense of his character. Today, though, she'd been able to put a stop to the daydreams that had occupied her mind since the past afternoon.

Eduardo was just as handsome as she remembered. The only problem was that he was a little too dashing, a little too free with his promises. Hardly the kind of man Aura needed in her life.

Especially not now that her plans seemed to be crumbling before her very eyes.

The empty crate was not only a puzzling mystery and an inconvenience. It was nothing short of disaster. More than two months had passed before Aura had enough money to replenish her savings after her father had spent them, just before dying. She didn't have another two months. She barely had two days. The contents of her cupboards had dwindled to almost nothing, and most of the payment for the dress she had just finished had gone toward settling her accounts. The amount she had left was just enough to feed her for a couple of days—if she was careful.

She'd try to get another commission, of course. There might be something she could finish within a week. It would mean knocking on doors, but that was nothing she hadn't done before.

A wiser, or perhaps shrewder, person would have taken Eduardo Martínez up on his offer. He was clearly in a position where replacing a hundred pesos' worth of missing merchandise wouldn't make much of a dent in his company's finances. Why shouldn't his company bear the cost of their own mistake?

Why couldn't Aura take a helping hand when it was extended to her?

She might not have been a pickpocket or even a peanut hawker in need of charity, but neither did she have to refuse the one offer of help she'd ever received.

Stifling a sigh, Aura reached the front door. "Don Rafael. Is there anything I can do for you? I was just—"

"I need to have a word with you."

A little startled at the man's unusually brusque tone, Aura inclined her head into a nod and reached into her handbag for her keys. "Of course. Please, come inside."

She had closed up the house before leaving, and it took a few moments to prop the door open and unfasten the shutters covering the windows. Once she had let light and air back into the room, she turned back to Marchena, who had perched in the upholstered armchair she had set out for her dressmaking customers.

"May I offer you a glass of water?" she asked, trying not to sound too reluctant.

It was the height of rudeness to limit her hospitality to

water instead of suggesting a cup of coffee or some fruit juice, but Aura did not want to encourage him in the slightest. She hadn't even offered to take his hat, which he'd placed awkwardly on his knee.

"Thank you, but no," he said curtly. "I can't stay long."

That was a relief. "Oh?"

Marchena lifted his gaze to hers. "I'm afraid there's no easy way to say it. Before his death, your father solicited a very large sum from me."

She'd been afraid of this. Her father hadn't just been reckless with money; he'd been reckless with his friendships as well—she couldn't keep count of how many people had declined to continue their acquaintance after her father had requested loans that he'd later been unable to repay.

Aura clasped her hands together. "Don Rafael, I—"

She was forced to subside as he held up a hand. "He offered the deed to this house as collateral. As I said, it was a very large sum."

Slowly, Aura sank onto the square platform where her clients stood to have their skirts hemmed. Purchasing the house was the only prudent thing her father had ever done. Aura had insisted on it, after one of his infrequent windfalls had left him with just enough funds to acquire the small, two-story house. She'd been using the front room to receive her dressmaking clients, though she did most of her sewing upstairs, and she'd already arranged the two display cases in preparation for the opening of her modest store.

"Out of my esteem for your late father and my respect for your grief, I have waited what I believe is a prudent time." Marchena looked faintly apologetic. "It pains me to have to ask you—"

"Don Rafael, I couldn't possibly repay the loan, not at this moment."

"I am aware of that, my dear. Which is why I must ask you to vacate the house."

He continued talking, something about how it was much better for a woman to be with family rather than on her own. Aura was no longer listening. No stock and no house meant no store and *that* meant no income. And no income meant...

Aura straightened her back and interrupted Marchena with a single word. "No."

If the situation hadn't been so serious—or so dire—Aura would have been tempted to laugh at Marchena's comically startled expression. He clearly hadn't expected her to challenge him. "I'm not sure I understand," he said stiffly.

"I won't vacate the house. Not right away—I want a month, at the very least," she said, lifting her chin. "As you can see, I'm just about to open a store, right here in the front room. It will take me at least that long to turn a profit. Once I do, we will be able to arrange a repayment schedule that will suit both of us."

"But—"

Aura stood. As rude as she knew she was being—again— she couldn't give him a single moment to reject her proposal. "Don Rafael, you have no idea how much I appreciate your understanding. I know that my father would have been deeply appreciative as well."

Though obviously disgruntled, Marchena had no choice but to get to his feet. He jammed his hat on his head and let her usher him to the door.

Aura closed it firmly behind him, not giving in to the urge to slam it. And then she drew in a deep breath that did nothing to calm the storm of anxiety surging inside her chest. Spending most of her savings on one of his reckless schemes hadn't been enough—she should have known her father would leave her with all kinds of debts.

And without a home.

He'd promised her the world, and he hadn't been able to give her the only thing she'd ever wanted. The only thing he *had* given her was the certainty that she could rely on no one other than herself.

Aura strode to her desk, on the opposite side of the room from her worktable, and found the address book where she kept meticulous records on all her clients. She would write out a list of women to approach—those who paid well and promptly, and whose social life was busy enough to warrant a new frock. She would take an hour or two to sketch out some ideas, and then she would pay a call to every single name on her list.

This wouldn't be the first time she'd found herself having to start from scratch. Aura dipped the tip of her pen into a pot of ink. If she had any say in it, though, it would be the last.

Aura bolted out of bed before she had quite figured out what had awoken her.

The night was fairly quiet. Aside from the pulse roaring in her ears, the only sound was the faint music of frogs and crickets and the even fainter roar of the sea in the distance. Her bedroom was still dark, though the lightness pressing against the half-drawn curtains led her to think that dawn wasn't too far away.

A cat yowled on the street below, and Aura felt herself relaxing. That must have been what she'd heard.

Lifting a hand to cover her yawn, she began shuffling back to bed—and froze as she heard another, more distinct sound, come from directly below her.

Without pausing for thought, she seized a pair of embroidery scissors from the top of her bureau and scrambled barefoot out into the hallway.

Her father had installed iron bars on the windows of the ground floor—a silly precaution she'd thought at the time, since they rarely had anything worth stealing. She was fiercely grateful for them tonight, though knowing they existed didn't make her any less apprehensive as she crept downstairs.

She reached the front room in time to see one of the windows, whose shutters she'd fastened before heading upstairs for the night, shake as if someone were pushing it from outside. As she watched, something that looked like a narrow saw slid in between the shutter's two leaves.

"Who's there?" she asked sharply. "What do you want?"

The saw retreated instantly. Aura's heart was still racing as she reached the window and flung the shutters open with one hand, gripping the scissors in the other.

There was no one there—the intruder must have fled as soon as he heard her voice.

She made sure that the door was still bolted, then repositioned her armchair to have a clear view of both door and window and curled up on the embroidered cushion. Her grip on the scissors was so tight her knuckles ached, but she didn't dare set them down in case the would-be intruder returned.

Her eyes were burning as she fought to keep them open for what felt like an eternity. Slowly but surely, the panic that had coursed through her began to ebb and Aura fell into a shallow doze right there on the chair.

With all the shutters closed and firmly fastened, Aura couldn't tell how much time had passed before another noise awoke her. She fumbled for the scissors—and realized with horror that she must have dropped them in her sleep.

A quick scan of the tiles underfoot revealed that the scissors must have skidded under some piece of furniture. Her momentary panic turned almost instantly into anger. Anger at herself for being so scared, and at the intruder for choosing a week already piled with misfortunes to disrupt her peace.

Scrambling out of the chair, Aura raced for the empty vase on a nearby side table and hugged it to her chest as she unbolted the door.

"Who is it? What do you want?"

She was reaching for the doorknob when it began to turn. As the door swung open, Aura heaved the vase at it with all her strength.

Her aim was off. The vase smashed against the doorframe.

Whoever was at the door jumped back with a deep exclamation, but the flying shards were clearly not enough to deter him. Aura took a step back as the door flew open the rest of the way, casting wildly about for something to defend herself with. The big shears she used for cutting fabric were at the far end of the room, too far from her grasp to—

Eduardo Martínez stepped cautiously into the doorway, his forehead creased with wariness. "I'm not sure what I did to deserve such a greeting, but I probably—"

That was as far as he got before Aura burst into tears.

The tense night must have frayed her nerves more than she'd realized, because Aura *never* cried. Neither did she find it easy to lean on someone else in times of trouble, but as Eduardo gathered her into his arms, murmuring something that was clearly intended to be soothing, she found herself sinking into his embrace. Gently, he stroked her hair, his capable palm roaming over the loose strands that fell over her shoulders and upper back.

Aura had always been strong. And she would continue to be strong. Just for a moment, though, it felt so easy and so right to let Eduardo try and comfort her.

She drew back a moment later, appalled by her momentary weakness. Exhaustion was no excuse. Not to mention, she was still in her thin cotton nightgown, without even a shawl to cover her exposed shoulders.

"I'm all right," she said quickly, brushing away some of the moisture that had gathered under her eyes and crossing her arms over her chest. "It's only that I didn't sleep well and…"

She drew in a shuddery breath.

"You'll forgive me for being so frank, but it looks to me like you haven't slept at all. Did something happen?"

Aura nodded. "Someone tried to break in last night. And when you came in just now, I thought—I thought—" She bit down on her lip for a moment, willing herself to stop trembling. Falling apart wouldn't help her. It took several moments to regain her composure, but her voice was markedly steadier when she started over. "Someone tried to break in last night. I heard a noise just before dawn and when I came down to investigate, I saw that the shutters on the window had been broken."

Eduardo's eyebrows rose. "You came down to investigate? On your own, in the middle of the night? I don't know whether to admire your bravery or be appalled at your lack of self-preservation."

"Trust me, it was neither of those things. I was just…" She shrugged. "Half-asleep, I suppose, and acting on instinct. I called out, and I think I scared off whoever had been trying to come in."

"And you spent the rest of the night on a chair in case they returned?" Eduardo asked, nodded toward the armchair. "You really are fearless. Foiling burglaries, confronting intruders... I'd have hidden under the covers myself."

Aura met his attempt to cheer her up with a slight smile. "I doubt that."

"Which window was it?" Eduardo asked, moving toward it when Aura pointed it out.

She took advantage of his distraction to turn to her worktable. The only material left in it was a folded length of embroidered tulle, left over from the gown she had just completed. She slipped it around her shoulders, holding it close to her chest with one hand.

"The shutters aren't just broken—the iron bars were sawed almost all the way through," he reported, turning back to Aura. His gaze skipped down to the filmy fabric swathing her upper half, but he didn't remark on it. "I don't think it likely that a petty thief would have taken the trouble unless he was assured of finding something valuable."

"There's nothing of real value here," Aura said, gesturing around the room at the dressmaker dummies lined neatly behind her worktable, the painted screen that shielded those from the entrance, and the empty display cases that should have been housing the ribbons and lace and buttons that had failed to turn up. "I've a sewing machine, but I keep that upstairs, and I doubt anyone would try to cart away something so heavy and unwieldy, even in the dark of night. And the store hasn't even opened, so there's no reasonable expectation of finding money here."

Eduardo was frowning. "Would you like me to report it to the Civil Guard?"

"No," Aura said, more out of habit than because she had any real objection to the Guard. After all, her father was no longer around to scornfully condemn them—and another possibility, this one connected to her father, was beginning to occur to her. "I…it's all right. I'm sure whoever tried to break in won't attempt it again."

Aura had never known how to ask for help. But she was quickly finding out that Eduardo Martínez didn't need to be asked.

"That may be true," he said doubtfully. "But if you feel in any way unsafe, you're more than welcome to stay at my house tonight—my cousin María del Mar will be home for the next several days, so there should be no impropriety in it."

Everything in Aura was straining to leap gratefully on his offer and say yes. It was horrifying—this man was practically a stranger, and she knew better than to think she could rely on anyone else for security.

But he was also the closest thing she had to a friend at the moment. And it needn't be for long.

"Your cousin? Not your wife?" Aura asked, though she had already noticed the absence of any rings on his fingers.

"A wife, me? I'm the consummate bachelor. The envy of all my married friends." As if sensing that she was wavering, Eduardo added, "At least stay with us until the window and bars are repaired. I know someone who does good work with iron if you need a recommendation."

All too aware of what little remained in her coin purse—and the fact that she might have to turn over the house to Marchena soon—Aura shook her head. "Do you do this for all your clients?"

"Only the ones who throw vases at me," he said, so cheerfully that Aura couldn't prevent her lips from turning up in an answering smile.

"My apologies for that, though I am grateful it was you. Why *did* you come?"

Eduardo shrugged. "I just wanted to confirm something from the inventory you wrote out for me. Your handwriting was a little illegible in some places."

"My handwriting," she replied, raising her eyebrow, "is perfect. I used to win prizes at school for having the neatest penmanship."

"Are you trying to ask me if I made up an excuse to see you again?" he asked teasingly.

His easy smile filled Aura with longing—and the desire to ask him what it was like to go through life so free of anxiety and concern.

Tilting her head, she said, "It would be silly to ask when the answer is so clear."

She couldn't remember the last time she'd engaged in lighthearted flirting. Or any flirting at all—embarrassment over her father's exploits had led her to keep to herself for far too long. Even though anxiety was still fluttering inside her, Eduardo's easy demeanor was making some of the weight lift from Aura's chest, which allowed her to think more clearly. She'd take Eduardo up on his offer and stay with him for the night while she tried to formulate a plan to raise enough money to placate Marchena.

Twenty-five years of being her father's daughter had taught her that great quantities of money never arrived when one most needed them—or at all. But that didn't mean Aura was ready to admit defeat.

She didn't know what Eduardo saw in her face that led him to say, "I pr—I can assure you that I don't intend to make a pest of myself. If you'd rather I send a messenger next time, I will. Though I don't think any of the company's messengers have my quick reflexes—I might have to ask you to refrain from greeting new arrivals with porcelain vases."

Aura buried her face in her hands. "I'll never live that down, will I?"

"Why would you want to? I thought it was spectacularly brave of you."

"Not brave, just foolish." Drawing in a quick breath, she added, "If it won't be any trouble, I think I will take you up on your offer. I'll spend the night at your house."

Chapter Three

Even with Gregorio and María del Mar and the countless people he employed mostly to fill up his too-large house, Eduardo had always put off coming home at the end of the day.

Sunset often found him sharing a companionable bottle of rum with his clerks or some of the men who worked at the company's warehouse, or attired in an evening suit as he made pleasant conversation with one society girl or another. There were always races to attend, and dances, and any number of amusements at the social clubs he belonged to.

Still, there really was no need for Gregorio to tease him when the clock in their office struck the hour and Eduardo almost knocked a pile of ledgers off his desk in his haste to shove his arms through the sleeves of his jacket.

Or for their housekeeper's eyes to widen when she walked past the front room to find Eduardo laying his hat on the entrance table while the sun still shone through the louvered sidelights on either side of the front door.

The faint sound of conversation led him to the upstairs parlor, where María del Mar had evidently brought their visitor.

"You needn't worry that he's after something. This is just the kind of person Eduardo is," he heard María say to

Aura. "Earlier this year, he helped a pair of his friends hide from the law for—"

"Discretion is not among my cousin's good qualities," he told Aura with fond exasperation as he finished striding into the room. Nudging a pile of journals and sketchbooks out of the way, he added, "Tidiness, either."

"Will you please stop slandering me in front of my new friend?" María del Mar retorted.

Taking a pair of small scissors from a side table, Aura snipped the thread connecting her needle to María's skirt and stepped back.

Eduardo surveyed them with a raised eyebrow. "Should I ask?"

"I popped a button doing calisthenics and Aura here was kind enough to fix it."

"And I'm sure we're all grateful for it," Eduardo said, turning to Aura. "The last time she popped a button, she fixed it by poking a hole where the button used to be and tying the whole thing with a piece of twine."

María shrugged. "I was in a rush. In fact, I'm in a rush now—I've got to finish writing some letters before we sit down for dinner."

Thanking Aura again, she hurried away at twice her usual speed.

As Aura settled into an armchair, Eduardo headed toward the sideboard where they kept a tray full of bottles and decanters. "Would you like a glass of *jerez*? Or I could have someone make you some fruit juice if you'd rather something more refreshing."

"*Jerez* would be fine," she said. "Are you always this prepared for guests?"

"We're a big family." Eduardo uncovered a small bowl of the roasted peanuts she'd seemed to enjoy so much at their first meeting and set it on the side table by Aura's chair. "We're always coming in and out. And we're a sociable bunch—there always seems to be at least a guest or two staying with us. The staff is always prepared for unexpected arrivals."

"Will your parents be joining us for dinner?"

That would have been difficult, considering that they had lived in New York for the past fourteen years. And considering that they had sent Eduardo away at the first sign that he was finding it difficult to adapt to the change in environment.

Not that Eduardo still smarted over having been all but discarded by his parents when he was little more than a child. He'd had a good life here, thanks to his grandparents.

Eduardo turned his back to her as he reached for one of the bottles on the tray. "I was raised by my grandfather. He and one of my uncles oversee the main branch of the company in Santo Domingo. Gregorio—that's my other cousin, you'll meet him at dinner—and I are in charge of operations here."

He handed her a small cut-crystal glass, half-full of Spanish sherry, and instead of sitting, gestured for her to join him on the balcony.

The room was positioned in such a way as to provide a clear view of both the Higuamo River and the Caribbean Sea. At that hour, the sun was beginning to make its descent toward the horizon and the glinting waves were studded with sailboats as the fishermen finished out their days.

Eduardo leaned against the railing and paused for a moment to savor both the sherry and the view—bathed in late afternoon light, Aura was a study in contrasts, her eyes and hair very dark against her white blouse.

That morning, swathed in some filmy fabric, she'd looked

like some sort of vision emerging from a cloud. Anyone would think that her everyday clothes would make her look ordinary, but Eduardo thought she looked even more like a vision as she leaned against the railing, holding the small wineglass by its stem. Light shone through the etched glass and the amber liquid within, casting vibrant reflections on her blouse and smooth brown skin.

Less than ten hours had passed since he had walked in on her, alone and barefoot and trembling with fear, and already she seemed to have regained every bit of the fearless approach to life he had noticed in her.

What had her life been like, for her to have become the kind of person who went after pickpockets and confronted intruders?

He wanted to know everything about her but didn't want to overwhelm her, so when she noticed him looking, he limited himself to asking, "I trust the staff have made you comfortable?"

She answered with an enthusiastic nod. "The room is lovely—and has very sturdy windows." Her lips twitched. "I'm sure I'll get a good night's sleep."

Eduardo had made sure she'd been given the room next to María del Mar's, on the other side of the house from his and Gregorio's. He was well aware that for a woman on her own, being invited to spend the night at the house of a near stranger wasn't just unconventional, it was fraught with all kinds of danger, and he'd wanted her to feel comfortable.

"It's a beautiful house," Aura added, circling the rim of her glass with a fingertip. "So elegantly furnished."

"And full of clutter," Eduardo added, laughing. "María del Mar brings back so many things from her travels. Last month she brought back a stuffed crocodile, and insisted it be kept in the parlor for the edification of our guests.

And Gregorio will never admit it, but he's a catalog fiend. He orders every kind of gadget imaginable, none of which ever work, of course, and gets annoyed if any of us say a word about discarding them. It's been worse since he got engaged last year—he's been ordering carpet sweepers and lemon squeezers and so many housekeeping gadgets that I finally had to persuade him to take over a section of one of the warehouses."

"Is the wedding soon?" Aura asked with bright interest.

Eduardo held back a wince, rolling the stem of his wineglass between his thumb and forefinger. "Well, that's somewhat of a sore point at the moment. The date hasn't been set yet."

Gregorio had denied it, but Eduardo had long suspected that the main reason he refused to set a date was because Gregorio knew how hard Eduardo would have found it to remain at the house by himself.

María del Mar whirled through the house like a sentient hurricane, making her presence felt in every corner, but she took to the open seas often enough that she hardly counted as a resident of the household. And Eduardo was quickly running out of friends and family to invite to the house on long visits.

Eduardo's chest tightened every time he saw Gregorio with Celia, their longing looks, their lingering touches, knowing that he was the reason they weren't living in newly wedded bliss. He had suggested they both move into the house after the wedding, but Celia was the youngest child of aging parents and she preferred to remain at their side. Gregorio liked them enormously and didn't mind living with them—but he just wouldn't leave Eduardo.

He had remained unmoving on that point, no matter how much Eduardo had tried to persuade first Gregorio, and then Celia, that he would be more than fine on his own. They were right not to believe him. The one time he'd tried being on his own had been a disaster, and it had ended with him following Gregorio to university in Madrid.

Not for the first time, Eduardo wondered if he should just get married himself. The faster Eduardo found someone else to stay with him, the faster Gregorio could move on to his new life.

He didn't say any of that to Aura, though. All he did was shrug and say, "Large families are complicated and Gregorio is far too loyal for his own good. You know what it's like."

She shook her head. Was it his imagination, or did she look a little wistful?

"I don't, actually. It's been just my father and me for a few years now." She seemed to catch herself. "It's just me now, I suppose."

"Ah, the father who loved nothing more than your mother and gold," Eduardo said, and she gave him a quick little look, as if surprised that he had remembered what she'd said upon telling him her name. "I'm sorry for your loss. Is it recent?"

She lifted her shoulders into a shrug. "Three months, more or less. Sometimes it feels like an eternity, sometimes I can scarcely believe it hasn't been longer."

Her shoulders were drooping, as if she felt the weight of her loss on her body.

"I can't imagine how much you must miss him."

"Some days are harder than others," she said. "But I've plenty to keep me occupied."

"Like your work," Eduardo prompted. "And the store."

"For all *that's* worth," she said with a wry smile that she then followed with a toss of her head. "Not that I'd let an insignificant detail like not having anything to sell in it keep me from following through with my plans."

Eduardo laughed with delight. "You really are formidable, Aura. I know you don't need it, but I hope it goes without saying that you have my support in this endeavor."

She turned to face him then, her expression falling into serious lines. "I truly appreciate everything you've done for me, Eduardo."

He gave her an easy shrug. "It's as María del Mar said—I don't find it a burden to help anyone who needs it. And even those who don't. I have so many resources at my disposal, it doesn't feel right to keep from doing everything I can."

She raised an eyebrow, though he saw the smile lurking in the corners of her lips. "You certainly know how to make a woman feel special."

"Oh, you don't need me for that," he said softly. "You are extraordinary all on your own."

"You know that from two days' acquaintance?"

He'd known it from the second he first saw her, lunging after the pickpocket. He didn't say so out loud, though, merely shrugged and grinned. "You may be extraordinary, but I'm extraordinarily perceptive, as everyone who knows me will tell you."

Aura gave him a mischievous look. "I'll have to ask María del Mar if she agrees with that assessment."

"What assessment?"

He glanced behind him to see his cousin standing in the archway that led out into the balcony, looking amused.

"Far be it from me to interrupt a fascinating conversation that is obviously all about me, but dinner has been on the table for two and a half minutes, which means that Gregorio has grown impatient. We'll have to hurry if we want to eat anything more than a single slice of ham divided three ways."

Eduardo turned to look at Aura. "We had better go fight for our fair share of dinner. I swear, sometimes it feels like I'm living in a zoo rather than a house."

Gesturing for Aura to go on ahead, Eduardo took her wineglass and followed her back into the house, pausing only for a moment to leave it alongside his on the sideboard. María del Mar was already bounding toward the stairs, evidently having decided to leave them to their fates.

They had almost caught up with her when Aura slowed to a stop at the head of stairs and glanced back at Eduardo. "I'm glad it was you who walked through that door," she said simply.

He nodded, trying not to think about what would have happened had it been someone else. If there was any comfort to be drawn from his presence, he hoped it was enough.

"So am I," he told her.

For all María's talk of solitary slices of ham, dinner was a lavish, if intimate, affair. Aura was presented with a succession of courses, all cooked to perfection, and all a far cry from the humble plate of plantain and local white cheese she'd grown used to. There was wine, too, just as good as the sherry she and Eduardo had sipped before heading downstairs.

Eduardo and his cousins were generous in their concern for her. It was almost overwhelming—Aura had never been around people who cared so deeply and so thoroughly about a near stranger. She didn't quite know what to do with all that generosity save make unspecific plans to repay it some day, in some way.

After several hours of conversation and cards in the upstairs parlor, where a cool breeze blew in through the open archways that led out into the balcony, Aura and the Martínez cousins retired for the night.

Aura half expected to fall right asleep as soon as she nestled into the luxuriously plush mattress. As exhausted as she was, however, she found herself invaded by a curious restlessness.

None of the clients she had visited had shown any inclination to avail themselves of her services, so she had kept herself busy that day by turning scraps of organdy and silk into petals she would later assemble into flowers for trimming gowns and hats. It was meticulous work, and fairly tedious, but at least it had kept her mind on something other than her misfortunes.

The work was better suited to daylight, though, so she left her sewing case inside her small valise and went instead to the tall window on the other side of the room. As she had noticed when she'd first arrived and María del Mar had conducted her upstairs to freshen up before dinner, the window overlooked a small side garden. Surrounded by hedges on three sides and containing only a small white wrought iron table and two chairs, it was clearly intended to be private.

Despite the moonlight that flooded it, it took Aura a moment to realize that Eduardo was sitting in one of the chairs. He noticed her almost a second later, and waved up to her.

"Can't sleep?" he called.

She shook her head.

"Come join me. Go down the small staircase at the end of the hallway, next to the grandfather clock."

There were plenty of reasons why she shouldn't go, not the least among them the fact that she should be taking advantage of the safety of her surroundings—and the opulent comfort of her bed—to get some much-needed rest.

And yet.

The memory of the way Eduardo's eyes had softened earlier when he'd called her extraordinary was enough to override all her good sense.

She did hesitate next to her valise, where she had folded some fresh clothes for the next day. It took her only a moment to decide against getting dressed—after all, it wasn't as though Eduardo hadn't seen her in her nightdress.

The smile he greeted her with when she stepped through a pair of shuttered doors and into the private garden was bright enough to shine in the moonlight.

"The breeze is nicer upstairs, but I've always liked this garden. Can you smell that?"

Aura closed her eyes as she inhaled, the better to appreciate the faint floral scent washing over them. "What is it?"

"Arabian jasmine."

At Eduardo's beckoning, she perched on the other seat, feeling the coolness of the iron through the thin cotton of her nightdress. "It's lovely. This entire garden is."

Eduardo nodded. "My grandfather's an amateur botanist and he's almost as fond of his exotic plants as Gregorio is of his catalogs and María del Mar of being a hellion. I'll have to show you around when it's light out. In the meantime, you really must try one of his latest acquisitions."

"Oh?" Aura asked warily.

Eduardo gestured toward a tray that was resting on the table, which held a small bowl and cutlery that glinted in the moonlight. Aura couldn't see its contents very well, but Eduardo's vision must have been better than hers because he confidently used a fork to spear a piece of something and guide it toward her mouth.

"Oh!" she repeated in a much more different tone as a piece of fruit, delicately flavored and bursting with juiciness, filled her mouth. "What is it?"

"Pitaya," Eduardo said, sounding pleased. "Or dragon fruit, I think it's called in some places. Comes from a most unusual tree that looks like an overgrown aloe plant. My grandfather had two or three crates shipped over from somewhere in South America—Guatemala, I think."

"It must be so interesting having access to things from all around the world. Like something out of a fairy tale."

"Only instead of a genie granting wishes, it's a grandfather with an entire fleet of ships." Eduardo laughed. "I think I'll give him a lamp for his next birthday. Would you like another piece?"

He fed her again instead of handing her the fork. Aura bit down on the fruit, and felt a trail of juice running down her chin. Eduardo swiped it away with his thumb, and every fiber of Aura's body strained toward his touch.

He was still wearing most of the clothes from earlier, though at some point he'd shed his jacket, necktie and vest and had rolled up his sleeves. His suspenders bisected the pale expanse of his shirt in two dark lines that followed his torso all the way down to the waistband of his dark trousers.

Even surrounded by the garden's moonlit glory, Aura found she could hardly keep her gaze from those two lines.

Eduardo didn't seem completely unconscious to where her attention was focused, and amusement colored his voice as he made light conversation and alternated taking bites from the bowl of fruit with feeding some pieces to Aura until the bowl was empty.

"Is this what you do when you can't sleep?" she asked. "Eat fruit by the light of the moon?"

"Well, no," he replied. "There are plenty of drinking

establishments open throughout the night that offer a little more entertainment than this. But I didn't want to leave you alone, not after the night you had. I thought you would feel safer if I was here."

"I do feel safe." Safer than she had any right to feel in the home of a stranger. And in her nightdress, no less. "And I'm gr—"

"If you tell me you're grateful again, Aura, I'll be forced to do something drastic."

"Like what?"

Eduardo shook his head. "Give me time to think of something suitably horrifying."

"Should I be scared?" Aura asked, tilting her head.

She was flirting deliberately now, and it was making her pulse race.

"I can't think of anything I'd dislike more than for a woman to be scared in my presence," Eduardo said softly. "Not when there are far more pleasant emotions she could feel around me."

"Will you be providing examples?"

"Far be it from me to tell a woman what she should feel," he replied, with a hint of his usual humor. "Especially not one who seems to know her mind so well."

It was impossible to keep her guard up in the face of his relentless cheer, and Aura felt hers slipping even as she asked, "At the risk of sounding suspicious… I was wondering why you took me in."

Eduardo shrugged. "It's what anyone would do, under the circumstances."

"Anyone?" Her eyebrow arched. "I doubt even you believe that's true."

"Well, it sounds better than the truth, at least," Eduardo

said, laughing outright. "Much less selfish than saying it makes me feel good to be needed."

There were worse reasons for helping someone, Aura supposed. In the half dark, she couldn't quite tell if his expression matched the lightness in his tone.

"How do you know this isn't some elaborate scheme to gain your sympathy and your confidence before defrauding you?" she asked with mild exasperation.

"I suppose I don't. If it were, it would only mean that you were in a position dire enough to warrant resorting to elaborate schemes, so I'd help you anyway."

"I do believe you actually would."

Eduardo didn't strike her as naive. And yet, Aura had never met anyone with such a trusting nature as Eduardo Martínez.

He laughed again. "Besides, I like people and I like you. Why wouldn't I want to make myself as useful as possible?"

She had to ask, "Perhaps because someone in your life might take objection to your going around town rescuing damsels in distress?"

"I've no romantic attachments, if that's what you're asking. I'm the consummate bachelor, envied by every married man of my acquaintance. And you might be in distress at the moment but you, Aura, are no mere damsel."

His hands, which were resting on the table, were so close to her own that a mere twitch would have brought them together. She wanted to do more than twitch—she wanted to give in to the waves of desire coursing through her and ride them all the way to their inevitable conclusion.

Instead, she cocked her head. "What am I, then?"

"A mystery."

Inside the house, the grandfather clock in the upstairs

hallway struck the hour, filling the garden with the faint ringing of chimes.

"You won't disappear again, will you?" Eduardo's voice sounded hushed in the silence left over by the chimes. "Like you did last Sunday? I thought I would never see you again."

Aura traced one of the iron whorls on the table's surface with the tip of her finger, imagining what it would be like to do the same on Eduardo's skin. "It's not such a large town. We would have come across each other again before long."

"Then I'm glad we didn't have to wait—I've never had much patience."

Their fingers touched in the lightest of caresses, making Aura shiver.

"I'm not very patient, either," she admitted. "And I…"

And she wanted so much. She wanted to take a seat on Eduardo's lap and trace the lines of his suspenders with her fingertips. She wanted to press her lips to his and drink in some of the brightness in his smile.

But most of all, she wanted to make sure that she had a roof above her head and enough work to get her through the days, and that would never happen if she wasted her precious time flirting with young men, however handsome they were.

Aura tore her gaze away from Eduardo and saw, in the half dark, how close their fingertips were. She stood. "And I think it's time I went back upstairs. Thank you so much for the fruit, Eduardo. I hope you sleep well."

Chapter Four

Holding her keys in a tight grip, Aura scrutinized the outside of her house before unlocking the front door. Save for the iron bars that had been sawn through and the window the would-be intruder had broken, everything looked undisturbed.

She couldn't say the same thing for herself. The longing that flared to life when her fingers brushed Eduardo's had followed her to bed, where she'd spent a restless handful of hours. As the bright light of morning started to flood the guest room, however, the moonlight, the night-blooming flowers, the sultry air that had caressed her through the thin layer of her nightdress, all began to feel like a dream.

She'd written Eduardo a thank-you note and, instead of staying for breakfast as he had suggested before they parted for the night, she hurried home.

The house had never felt as large and empty as it did that morning after Aura locked the door behind her and double-checked to make sure the latch had caught properly. Shooting frequent glances toward it, she cleaned the front room with her usual swift efficiency.

That one little bit of normalcy relaxed her enough that she was able to go upstairs to bathe and dress. By the time she had made herself a cup of strong, sweet coffee—larger than normal to make up for two sleepless nights—Aura was well on her way to feeling like her usual self.

Still, when she returned to the front room, she hesitated over the locked door before deciding to leave it hospitably propped open.

It wasn't as though she was expecting anyone that day. In fact, she would be incredibly fortunate if one of her regular clients decided to drop in unexpectedly. As for Eduardo…

Just because he'd been kind to her, it didn't mean…well, it didn't mean anything at all. Even if he were inclined to chase after a visitor who'd chosen to slip out of his house without waiting to thank him in person, he had his own work to do that day. He'd go to his office, not to Aura's house, and it was utterly ridiculous of her to even think that he would abandon his responsibilities for the sake of doing something as nonsensical as spending the day with her.

And yes, of course, thinking about his appealingly warm smile was a pleasant diversion to the worry that had plagued her for the past several days. But as she'd told herself the night before, mooning over a man wasn't going to solve any of her problems.

Like her sadly depleted pantry. While her coffee was brewing, she had taken careful stock of its contents—the oatmeal canister was almost empty, as was the one that held the flour. A few onions, three or four ripening plantains and a handful of rice and dried beans were all that remained. She wouldn't worry about it, not today.

Today, she had work to do.

Neatly piling up several dozen squares of organdy on the clean surface of the table, Aura grew quickly absorbed in the painstaking process of shaping each square of fabric into a perfect, gently curving petal. It reminded her of spending hours as a child doing the exact thing. Only then she'd worked alongside her two sisters while their baby brother played with on the floor. Their mother usually sat across from them, stitching quickly through the piles of sewing she took in to pay the bills whenever Aura's father was haring off after some get-rich-quick scheme.

The memories brought a lump to Aura's throat. Not for the first time, she thought about trying to seek out her mother and siblings. A woman had to be with her family—that was what Rafael Marchena had told her. Aura would have done anything to find them again, though she was the one who had declined to join them when they had left. She was the one who had let her self-righteousness—and her loyalty to her father—get in the way after the inevitable divorce.

With her attention so fiercely focused, the morning hours unspooled more quickly than Aura would have thought possible. The midday sun was scorching on her hands and forearms when her hunger pangs grew too insistent to ignore. Stretching lightly, she made one last petal.

Earlier, she'd spied some long scraps of ribbon that she could turn into rosettes. Maybe she'd be able to sell those along with the organdy flowers—to trim hats, perhaps, or even to make hair ornaments for little girls...

Aura swept the finished petals into a basket to keep them from blowing away and, still deep in thought, went to water the potted fern she'd placed on the plant stand by the front door to replace the vase she'd broken the day before.

She couldn't have said what drew her gaze to the open door. A slight sound, perhaps, or a moving shadow that broke the midday stillness around her. The small flame of hope that burst into life in her chest at the thought of a potential client was quickly extinguished.

The man whose shadow was darkening her doorstep was definitely not one of her usual clients.

"Señorita Aureliana Soriano?"

Aura gave a cautious nod, already moving to grasp the edge of the door. "How may I help you?"

"I've a message for you."

When he made no move to reach for a note, Aura's grip on the door tightened and she began to swing it closed. "A message from—"

She didn't have time for more than a sharp intake of breath before the man was roughly pushing his way inside, putting himself between Aura and the exit.

"Where is it?" he demanded, crowding her so that she was forced to take a step backward. "Where are you hiding it?"

"I don't suppose you'd care to enlighten me as to what 'it' is?" Aura's fear lent an edge to her voice that she hoped would pass for irritation. "Or as to why you have the temerity to barge into my home—"

There was a second man at the door. The wild hope that Eduardo *had* decided to avoid his responsibilities for the sake of spending a few hours with her after all bloomed and withered within the space of a second as Aura caught a glimpse of his face.

It wasn't Eduardo.

And neither was it someone who'd come to her aid.

Deliberately, the second man turned his back to the room in a gesture that made it clear that he was there to guard against that very thing. He might as well not have bothered—there *was* no one to come to Aura's aid.

She drew in a sharp breath that did nothing to steady her frayed nerves. Then she turned to the first intruder. "If you'd at least *tell* me what you want—"

"You know what I'm looking for," was his reply as he ruthlessly overturned the basket of petals on her table and trampled over them on his way to the mirrored wardrobe.

Aura couldn't hold back a wince. All those hours of work, utterly wasted. Her aching fingers, her stinging eyes… Anger burned away some of the fear coursing through her, and Aura welcomed it.

"I don't have any valuables—or the desire to watch you wreck my things. Leave my house at once, or I *will* scream for the Civil Guard."

He barely spared her a glance. "A daughter of Alfredo Soriano's, going to the Guard for protection? He'd hate to see it."

Aura's stomach sank. So this *did* have something to do with her father. She'd suspected as much, though she'd still harbored the faint—now demolished—hopes that he'd been honest about reforming. That was what he'd claimed just before his death, when he'd rasped out, *Cambié*. "I changed."

The singularly most heartbreaking thing about Aura's father was that in spite of all his protestations to the contrary, he never did change. He might not have even been capable of it.

"My father," she said icily, "left me nothing but trouble."

"I heard otherwise."

The man threw open the doors to the wardrobe and began systematically flinging out the lengths of fabric folded on its shelves. Aura couldn't fail to see how he shook each out first, before tossing them over his shoulder. Whatever he'd been expecting to find was on the smaller side, then. Money? It wouldn't be the first time her father had run out on a debt, or even the first time he'd left Aura to deal with the consequences—though of course this time he hadn't done so intentionally.

Aside from the leftover fabric, the only thing the wardrobe held was a crate full of clay figurines, which her father had purchased just before dying for some moneymaking scheme or another that of course hadn't worked out.

The anger and fear boiling inside her were joined by another emotion—frustration. At the way this man seemed to be determined to tear her front room apart, for one, and also at her father's terrible habit of keeping her in the dark.

Half expecting the intruder to overturn the crate, Aura watched as he shoved it aside with his foot in order to knock on the back of the wardrobe with a large, hammer-like fist. The thin wooden panel broke apart with a splintering noise and Aura, acting on instinct and indignation, launched herself at him in protest.

He flung her aside with one sweep of his powerful arm.

Aura fell backward with a bone-jarring thump. The man at the door must have glanced behind him to see what had happened, because he didn't issue a single word of warning before a reassuringly familiar voice was asking, "What the devil is happening here?"

It was Eduardo, looking furious and every inch the businessman in his fashionably cut suit—and like he wouldn't hesitate to bring down the entire Civil Guard on the heads of the two ruffians. His progress into the front room was halted as the man at the door put out an arm to prevent him from coming any farther.

Eduardo looked down at the arm, then at the man it belonged to. "Get that out of my way if you wish to keep it," he said icily.

The man at the door responded with insolent amusement. "And who are you?"

Eduardo glowered at him. "Her fiancé."

Aura felt her heart clenching inside her chest. No one had ever claimed her that way before—not to protect her, not for any reason. Her urge to seek refuge in his arms was almost as strong as her desire to make him leave before he got hurt.

"I asked," Eduardo repeated, impatience snapping in his tone, "what the devil is going on here? Why is my fiancée on the floor and what do you mean by—"

The man at the door silenced Eduardo with a blow so sharp and sudden, it made Eduardo's head jerk backward. The man's mouth was twisted into an eager, malicious grin, as if he had been waiting for an excuse to employ violence.

The exchange made the other intruder frown. He was so intent on berating his associate that he took his attention off Aura for a split second, plainly not considering her a threat.

It was enough. For better or for worse, Aura *was* her father's daughter, and she knew how to take advantage of someone's momentary distraction to get the better of them in a brawl.

Scooping up her metal watering can from where it lay tumbled on the floor, Aura surged to her feet and tried to slam it into the man's head. Unfortunately, her long skirts got in the way and she stumbled, clanging the watering can against his shoulder instead.

The intruder reared around, ready to swat Aura aside as one might an annoying mosquito. But she'd already jerked up her hem and delivered a swift kick to his kneecap. Her sturdy, sensible shoes connected with an audible noise, which was quickly followed by a bellow as the intruder half collapsed, still reaching for her. Pain made his breathing harsh and his swing wild—he missed her by mere centimeters.

Aura couldn't spare a glance toward where Eduardo was grappling with the other man, though from the grunts and breathless curses that came from that side of the room it was clear that the fight was ongoing.

Gasping out expletives, the intruder staggered toward her. Aura stepped nimbly back, putting her chair between them. This gave her enough courage to say, "This might be a good time for you and your associate to leave."

The words were hardly out of her mouth when the back of her heel scraped unpleasantly against the crate and she tumbled back, her arms windmilling wildly as she sought to keep her balance.

The intruder lunged, knocking the chair out of the way and landing half on her, the bulk of him so heavy that she felt the breath knocked out of her.

"Where is it?" he asked in a low voice, pressing his forearm against Aura's throat. "You might as well tell me— we won't let you have a moment's peace until it's found."

Another loud noise, and suddenly there was Eduardo, pulling the man off her.

"The lady told you to leave," Eduardo ground out. A trickle of blood was seeping slowly from a cut on his eyebrow. "I'd listen to her, if I were you—if for no other reason than because I sent my coachman to fetch the Civil Guard and they'll be here at any moment."

The man who'd struck Eduardo was nowhere to be seen. The remaining ruffian took calm stock of the situation and opted to make his retreat.

"No need to get excited, *señor*," he said, baring his teeth at Aura in what he might have thought resembled a smile. "You'll remember what we talked about, won't you? And you'll have it for me when I return?"

It was a clear threat, made no less effective by the fact that Aura was frustratingly in the dark as to what they had been hoping to find. Still, she held herself in stiff, quiet loathing as the man strolled out of her house with infuriating nonchalance.

Only then did she run for the door, almost slipping on something round and bright pink that was rolling underfoot. A pitaya, one of two that Eduardo had evidently brought with him. A slightly hysterical laugh bubbled out of her as she threw her weight against the door and bolted it.

"Is it true?" she asked wildly. "Are the guardsmen coming?"

Eduardo offered her a crooked smile because apparently not even a split eyebrow could make a dent in his unflagging good cheer. "I came alone."

Flooded in equal parts dismay and distress, Aura went to kneel beside him. "What if they hadn't believed you? You could have been seriously hurt."

"I was more worried about you being hurt." Eduardo's fingertips skimmed a spot just below her collarbone, making her shiver, even as she glanced down to see a rip in her blouse.

"I'm all right," she said, and she knew she sounded as if she was trying to convince herself as well as Eduardo. Clearing her throat, she tried again. "I'm fine."

"Well, so am I. So it all worked out in the end." Eduardo's words would have been more reassuring if they hadn't come accompanied by a wince.

"You'll excuse me if I don't take your word for it," Aura said, reaching into the pocket of her skirt for her handkerchief, which she then offered to Eduardo. When he dabbed it just right to the cut on his forehead, she took it back from him and pressed it gently to the shallow wound.

"Not that I'm not thrilled to see you…"

"But you're wondering what brought me here?"

Each of his easy smiles seemed to act upon Aura like a fortifying sip of spirits, allowing the shock of all that had transpired to recede even as her jaw unclenched and the cast of her shoulders lost their rigidity.

"Well, I didn't think you'd come to propose marriage," Aura replied lightly, unable to forget the way his face had looked when he'd informed the ruffians that he was her fiancé.

Eduardo's hand rose to cover hers. She shivered again when his fingers grazed her wrist, and quickly withdrew the hand, pretending that she had lifted the handkerchief to check if the blood that had been welling from the cut had been stanched.

"I would, you know," Eduardo said seriously. "If it meant keeping you safe from those two."

Aura must have been more shaken than she'd realized, because she was suddenly overwhelmed by how much she wanted Eduardo's offer to be real. By how much she wanted to lay her head on his shoulder and let him continue to help her.

Her pantry was still bare, she was still on the verge of losing her home, and the merchandise for her store was still missing. And she was still alone.

"I mean it." Eduardo was looking at her. "It needn't just be a convenient fiction. I'd take care of you."

"I know you would. But I…" But she couldn't let herself depend on anyone, not even him. Aura cleared her throat. "What was the real reason you came?"

"You seemed to enjoy the dragon fruit so much last night, I thought you might want more." Eduardo's lips twisted as he seemed to recognize the excuse for what it was. "And I wanted to make sure you were all right."

"I was," she said quickly, before he could mention that morning's abrupt departure. "Though I really expected a better excuse from you—you've had plenty of time to practice."

"I'll be sure to work on it for next time."

"Do you expect there to be a next time?"

"There might be if you continue to be besieged by intruders and ruffians. I gathered they were looking for something? Something important enough they were willing to hurt you over it?"

Aura could guess what he was thinking—what could a simple dressmaker be involved in that would warrant such intrusion into her home? None of the conclusions were particularly flattering to her character. Neither was the truth, she supposed.

She wouldn't go as far as to call her father a criminal, but whatever he had been involved in just before her death had now become her problem.

Aura's expression wavered. Eduardo wouldn't have blamed her in the slightest if she had dissolved into tears— the situation she found herself in more than justified falling apart, and he wasn't sure that he would be entirely sanguine himself if he'd just witnessed two ruffians intrude into his house to conduct what could only generously be called a search, and had received some rough treatment in the bargain.

If Eduardo had learned anything about Aura, however, it was that she was used to facing the kind of adversity that would have made any other person crumble.

As he'd witnessed her do once before, she drew in a breath and subtly squared her shoulders. "I suppose I owe you an explanation."

"You don't owe me a thing," Eduardo said, adding carefully, "though of course I wouldn't find it a burden to listen to anything you might wish to tell me."

For a second, Eduardo thought that Aura was twisting

her hands in her lap. Then he realized that she had put away her handkerchief and was winding stray strands of thread she had picked up from the floor into a small, neat bundle. There was a spare, economical quality in the way she used her hands that Eduardo recognized as efficiency. This was a woman with plenty to do and no time to waste. It appealed to him almost as much as her soft, slightly pouting lips.

"I truly don't know what those men were looking for, only that it had something to do with my father. I can only guess at what nefarious business he was involved in before his death. But the fact is that he *was* involved in something nefarious, if not outright illegal. It's bound to be complicated at best, dangerous at worst, so I'd understand if you'd prefer to avoid getting entangled in it any more than you already have."

If Aura resented her father for his role in whatever was happening, she didn't show it. In fact, she didn't show much of anything save for a toughness of spirit that made him ache to clasp her to him and offer what comfort he could.

Instead, he allowed a grin to slip over his face.

"I thought you knew me better by now. I cherish complications. I *crave* danger. And I…" And he remembered that Aura hadn't responded to the cockiness that seemed to charm everyone else. He spread his hands, opting instead for simple sincerity. "I'd despise myself if I were to let you face all of it by yourself. My help is yours, if you want it."

She glanced up at that, a quick, uncertain gesture as if she were reluctant to admit that she did want it. Then her mouth firmed. "We'll have to start a list of all the things you're helping me with so I can properly repay you when this is all over."

Eduardo's relief showed itself in the form of another grin. "Don't worry, I've already put it on your account."

Aura, who seemed to be relaxing by degrees, seemed to recall something that put a frown between her brows. "They thought I knew," she said. "Whatever they came here hoping to find, they thought I knew what it was or where it was."

"Your father didn't confide in you?"

She shook her head. "He knew I disapproved of the things he did." Aura made a slight noise that sounded distinctly like exasperation. "He tried to tell me he'd changed. People never do, you know."

"Never? That's a cynical position for someone so young."

Aura lifted a shoulder. "I'm not that young. Don't tell me you're an idealist."

"Where people are concerned, yes, I believe I am. I think people do the best with what they have, and redemption is within everybody's grasp."

She shook her head at him, as if appalled by his naivety. "I can only imagine that you're frequently disappointed."

"Occasionally," Eduardo allowed. "Doesn't mean I don't still believe in people." He shrugged. "I trust my instincts, I suppose. And they've never led me too far astray."

The small noise she made was enough to communicate her disbelief. "Well, in any case, my father didn't change. And now I've got to figure out what those men wanted."

The rest of her sentence might have gone unspoken, but it hung heavy in the air between them: *before they come back*.

They'd as much as promised they would—it was only a question as to when that would be. And how many more associates they would bring along.

If Eduardo had any say in the matter, Aura would not be here when they did.

Her teeth descended briefly on her lower lip. "He seemed to think that my father had left me something. But what would that be? Funds that he owed them? If he had any money, I certainly didn't know about it." She made another one of those expressive little noises, only this one signaled something akin to amusement. "I can't decide if I'm angry at him or grateful to him for having kept me in the dark."

"I don't see why you'd have to limit yourself to one option. Most doctors recommend holding several emotions at once—especially if two or more of them are in direct conflict to each other."

"Is that how you contrive to be so cheerful all the time?"

"Not me. I gave up emotions for Lent one year and never picked the habit back up."

Aura laughed at that, a rippling sound of unrestrained delight that eased some of the tension that had gathered in Eduardo's limbs from the moment he'd realized that she wasn't going to respond to his—admittedly rushed and unromantic—proposal of marriage.

He'd done it for his own benefit as much as hers. Sitting with her in the garden the night before had been a revelation. She'd looked so right there in her nightdress, sharing his bowl of pitaya as if it was something they'd done every night for years. He wanted more moments like that with her, if only because he'd discovered it was a good distraction against the panic that started hammering against his insides whenever darkness found him alone and in silence.

"Maybe you'd like to conduct a search of your own," Eduardo suggested. "A more decorous one. In the meantime, I'll help you put the room to rights."

Aura nodded and disappeared briefly down a short hallway, returning several moments later with a broom and a dustpan. Eduardo, who had righted the overturned chair, held out his hand for the broom and began awkwardly gathering some of the debris.

He had a moment to wonder if her silence was due to his staggering incompetence with a broom before she spoke up again.

"I'd hate for you to get the wrong idea about my father. He wasn't a bad man, not really—he never tried to defraud anyone on purpose. All he wanted was to provide his family with everything he never had. It's just that he went the wrong way about it." Aura's soft inhalation sounded like someone stifling a sigh, though of course it might have been a reaction to the lengths of fabric that had been thrown to the floor. "There was no malice to the things he did, just… enthusiasm gone awry, I'd say. He'd get an idea for a moneymaking scheme in his head and nothing anyone could say would dislodge it. Until it had proven a failure, of course, and then he'd be so mired in debts that he'd grow convinced that another brilliant idea was all it would take to acquire enough funds to repay them…"

And then the whole process would begin again.

It made a certain sense, he supposed, that the circumstances of her upbringing had conspired to make her as talented at brawling as she seemed to be at sewing. Not to mention, so fiercely independent.

"Did his schemes ever work out?"

"Oh, yes," she replied, lighting up as she made quick work of refolding the fabric. "Very infrequently, but we had some lovely times when they did—and silk stockings and lace and fine, imported chocolates. Of course, our lives were mostly bread and avocado and hiding from creditors."

"Sounds eventful," he remarked.

"I used to think that was how everybody lived." He caught a glimpse of Aura's lips twisting up wryly before she turned to place the pile of folded cloth inside the wardrobe. "Imagine my surprise when I found out that wasn't the case." She peeked around the wardrobe's open door. "What was your life like when you were small?"

Before or after he had been discarded by his parents?

"Very similar to what you first described, only neither Gregorio, María and I had much interest in silk stockings," Eduardo said lightly. "We did a great deal of sailing, and there were frequent parties aboard Abuelo's ship."

"Ship? I thought he had dozens of them."

"For transporting cargo, yes—my cousins and I weren't really allowed to play in those, though María and I snuck aboard one once and were halfway to Portugal before we were found. But that's a story for another time." Eduardo allowed himself a small smile, as much at the memory as at the satisfaction that he had successfully distracted Aura from the thoughts responsible for the deep indentation between her brows. "He kept only one ship for his personal use, and we used to have all sorts of romps in it, sailing up and down the coast—and, on one occasion when María managed to persuade the captain that she should have a turn at the wheel, almost *into* it."

The broom he was still using in a fruitless attempt to sweep up the filmy petals knocked against a crate full of clay figurines, most plagued with hairline cracks.

"What are those?" he asked curiously.

"My father's latest scheme," Aura said. "His last one, I should say. I think he intended to pass them off as the work of some famed sculptor and sell them for exorbitant prices. In New York, I think—he'd booked passage on a steamer that was supposed to sail on the day he died."

"New York?" Eduardo echoed.

Aura ran the tip of one finger over one long crack. "They're worth even less now than they were before. I should throw them out."

Eduardo was in the act of nodding when he caught sight of the clock on the far wall. The hour made him swear under his breath.

"María del Mar is hosting a confounded garden party at the house, and I promised that I would be there to occupy some of the matrons she couldn't get out of inviting."

Aura bit her lip. "You should get going, then."

"I wasn't intending to leave you alone." Eduardo didn't know many young women who lived on their own—or anyone at all, for that matter—and he had no idea how Aura had managed it for so long, intruders or no intruders. "You can't stay here, Aura. Not by yourself, and not after what happened today. Don't you think you should come back to the house?"

"Don't you think you ought to consult your cousins before you start issuing invitations?" she shot back.

"I already did," Eduardo said calmly. "That's the real reason I came today—we'd assumed that you would stay a little longer and when you disappeared before breakfast, we were concerned. María del Mar insisted I tell you that if it makes you feel better about accepting our offer, she has trunks full of garments that could use your expertise with a needle."

"Are you sure, Eduardo? Because I'd hate to impose more than I already have."

He made his tone brisk and matter-of-fact. "The house has been something of a safe haven for all three of us. It could be one for you as well, if you wish it. If you'd rather not, will you allow me to hire you a guard, and perhaps some household help to assist you in finding whatever it was your father left behind?"

"Definitely not," she said swiftly, then her teeth descended on her lower lip.

"You don't have to decide now, but it would make me feel a great deal better if you came with me to the party. If for no other reason than there will be a great many society ladies in attendance—the kind who commission two dozen gowns per season—and I will make sure to introduce you to each and every one of them."

She glanced down at herself, perhaps noticing, as Eduardo had, the smears of dust and stray threads that clung to her dark gray skirt. "I'm a mess."

"So am I," Eduardo declared, gesturing to the cut on his forehead, which had mostly stopped throbbing. "Not much I can do about it, but you can tidy yourself up. As quickly as you can—María won't hesitate to do me considerable violence if I'm late to her party."

Aura placed her hands on her hips. "Has anyone told you that you're extremely bossy?"

"All the time," Eduardo said cheerfully. "And also that they like it."

Looking highly skeptical at this last remark, Aura went upstairs.

While she dressed, Eduardo occupied himself with putting his clothes back to rights in front of the full-length mirror in the corner. He was dabbing at the cut with the dampened corner of his own handkerchief when he caught a glimpse of movement behind him and turned to see Aura reemerging from the narrow hallway.

Her hair was once again neatly arranged, and she had exchanged her plain skirt and shirtwaist for a dress of muted lavender with black trim. For all it was mourning attire, even Eduardo recognized it as modish and well-made.

With a flourish, he extended his arm to her. "Shall we, mademoiselle?"

Shaking her head with faint exasperation, she handed him one of the two valises she carried and went to the door on her own. "Let's go."

The house Eduardo had inherited from his maternal grandparents was never more beautiful than when he or one of his cousins was hosting a party. It wasn't just the decorations, though the household staff always did a splendid job in the way of flower arrangements and the brightly polished silver and crystal.

What filled Eduard's heart were the people crowded into the parlor and the terrace, spilling out into the garden's brick paths. María del Mar's guests were perhaps a more eclectic collection than could be found in most of society's drawing rooms, but Eduardo found them a lovely sight just the same as he gestured for Aura to enter through the open double doors ahead of him.

Spotting one of the housemaids, he handed her Aura's small valises with instructions to bring them up to the guest room Aura had occupied the night before.

In the cacophony of music—María always insisted on hiring musicians—and the chattering of his cousin's guests, Aura didn't seem to hear Eduardo's offer to fetch her something to drink. He gave her arm a quick pat to get her attention. She'd been doing such a good job of concealing just how jumpy the attack had made her that Eduardo was taken aback at the intensity of her reaction when she started at the light touch. She whirled around to face him with equal parts fierceness and fear in her dark brown eyes, already surging forward as she trapped his wrist in a surprisingly strong grip.

She stared at him for a long moment, breathing hard.

Eduardo was similarly arrested by the intensity of her

gaze, but he managed to remain calm. "Would you like champagne or fruit juice?"

Whether it was the banality of his question that did it, or her mind clearing as the rush of fear ebbed away, Aura seemed to notice that she was still holding on to him and abruptly released his wrist.

"Fruit juice, please," she said, and began stepping back from him just as a trio of young women crossed behind her.

Eduardo reached out for her, pulling her toward him just in time to avoid a collision. For the second time in as many days, Aura stood pressed against him, a hand against his chest and her warm breath trailing over his neck.

"Are you all right?" he asked in a low voice.

He felt more than saw her draw in a deep breath. Her shoulder straightened and she stepped back again, more carefully this time, her features arranged into something that he would have believed to be a smile if he hadn't seen the real thing. "I'm all right."

He lifted an eyebrow and her smiled deepened.

"I will be," she said, more convincingly this time.

"That's a shame," Eduardo told her.

It was her turn to raise a questioning eyebrow. "Is that so?"

"Well, yes, because if you had felt the slightest bit out of sorts, you would have been guided to a comfortable seat and plied with champagne and cake and ice cream and regaled with all the best stories from my misspent youth. But you're all right, so go ahead and find yourself a chair or an unoccupied corner and I'll see if I can find you a glass of..." he shrugged "...something. Dishwater, perhaps."

The rigid cast of her shoulders softened as she shook her head, clearly trying not to laugh. "I'll do my best to oblige you later. For now... I really am feeling fine."

"Your loss," Eduardo said cheerfully, trying not to let her

see his concern as he skimmed his gaze over her. Fighting against his every instinct to hover and lead her to a chair himself, he waved her toward an empty arrangement of seats in the terrace and told her he would find her in a moment.

He had asked one of the maids for two glasses of juice when he turned to see Gregorio and María del Mar looking at him from across the room.

"I thought Aura was going home today," Gregorio remarked when Eduardo joined them.

"She did," Eduardo reminded him, knowing that Gregorio's nose had been buried so deep in a catalog during their conversation over breakfast that he likely didn't remember what they'd all decided. "There was an abrupt change of plans, courtesy of a pair of would-be robbers who pushed into her house. You don't mind, do you?"

"I certainly don't," María del Mar declared, echoing her sentiment from that morning. "It'll be nice to have the company of someone with brains around here, for once."

Abandoning his usual stoic dignity, Gregorio made a hideous face at her. "Says the girl who hasn't cracked open a book since 1889."

"Children, children," Eduardo said mildly, hiding his smile. "I expect you both to be on your best behavior in front of her."

Gregorio adjusted his spectacles. "You do realize you just gave María all the motivation she needed to stick to Aura like a burr for the rest of the day?"

Eduardo groaned. "Aura's had a very long day—the last thing she needs is for you to plague her."

María del Mar was already moving in Aura's direction. "I make no promises," she called. "And I take no hostages!"

Eduardo laughed, and shook his head. "Something she heard in a play?"

Gregorio confirmed it with a nod. "Most likely," he said, but he sounded like he was already thinking of something else. As he must have been that morning at the breakfast table when Eduardo and María discussed the possibility of having Aura to stay for a few days.

Patiently, Eduardo reminded him of the conversation that had taken place in front of him. "She's in trouble, Gregorio, and she could use our help."

His cousin spread his hands. "I don't mind. It won't be the first time you've brought home a bird with an injured wing."

"Aura isn't a bird," Eduardo protested.

"But you want to take care of her all the same, don't you?" Gregorio didn't wait for an answer. "I don't mind her staying here for as long as she needs to. Just…don't grow too attached."

"I would never," Eduardo told his cousin with a grin, trying not to think too deeply about the fact that he already had.

Chapter Five

"Say the word and I'll rescue you from this hellion," Eduardo said, interrupting the perfectly pleasant conversation that Aura had been having with his cousin.

"I think you've done enough rescuing for today," Aura replied with amusement.

"Then allow me to offer something else instead." Eduardo held out a glass to her.

"Ah, the promised dishwater."

"Lime juice, unfortunately. And an introduction to one of my dearest friends, who just so happens to be a fabulously wealthy heiress and in need of some traveling clothes, as she and her husband are leaving soon for a stint in Europe."

Eduardo's friend sounded so much grander than Aura's usual clients that she almost begged off the introduction. But his promise to get her new clients *had* been what had convinced her to return to the house. So she allowed him to tug her away from María del Mar and toward a slight, brown-skinned woman with laughing eyes and an audaciously cut afternoon dress in the exact shade of pale orange as the tarts being offered by the uniformed waiters.

"Aura Soriano, allow me to introduce you to Lucía Troncoso."

Aura quelled the little start as she recognized the name from the gossip columns.

"It's Lucía de Díaz now, and you of all people should know it." Chuckling with obvious affection, Lucía turned to Aura. "My husband and I had a very small wedding some weeks ago, and Eduardo and my sister comprised the bulk of our wedding party."

"As it should have been," Eduardo said. "Seeing as you would have never reconciled if not for my generous invitation to spend a fortnight at my grandfather's estate."

Aura followed Lucía's gaze across the terrace, where a man with powerful shoulders was deep in conversation with a taller, leaner man, who looked rakish and windblown in spite of his perfectly tailored suit.

"As grateful as we were for your invitation, I have a feeling we would have found our way regardless," Lucía told Eduardo, then turned to Aura. "I thought I had met all of Eduardo's friends by now. Are you another recent arrival from exotic travels?"

"No. I—I'm just a dressmaker."

"A very good one, I might add," Eduardo said.

Lucía glanced at him. "I'm not sure I would consider you an expert on women's fashions. But Aura's dress is testament enough to her skills. You did make that yourself, didn't you?"

Loath as Aura always was to spend money on herself, she'd always been aware that a seamstress's best advertisement was her own ensemble. The dress she had chosen for Eduardo's cousin's party was, if not as lavishly trimmed as those of the women around her, cut and constructed to the best of her considerable abilities.

She should still have been wearing black. She'd planned on it, in fact. But when she'd gone to lift her one nice black dress from where it was folded in her wardrobe, some impulse that had more to do with Eduardo than with a pressing need to look less dreary for the party had her reaching for another dress.

The fabric, which had once been white, had taken the mauve dye beautifully. All she'd really had to do was pick out the trim and replace it with black ribbon and a small quantity of jet beads that echoed the darkness of her own hair and eyes.

Before long, Lucía had drawn several other women into orbit around them both. There was her sister Amalia, a voluptuous woman in a dress striped with bands of lace. A friend of theirs, Paulina de Linares, whose saffron-colored sash accentuated her advanced pregnancy. Another woman, introduced to Aura as Gregorio's fiancée, Celia, joined them with curiosity etched into her pale features.

These were women who benefited from the budget to indulge in expensive materials and immaculate workmanship, and they all offered Aura unstinting praise at her style. And not only that, they were eagerly discussing the new fashions they had seen in their overseas travels, filling Aura with so much inspiration that she half wished her pencil and notebook weren't tucked away in her luggage.

Holding out her arm so that Lucía's mother-in-law could examine the broderie anglaise on her sleeve, Aura caught Eduardo's eye.

I told you, he mouthed, before turning his attention back to the gray-haired matron he'd been shamelessly flattering, if the look in her eyes was any indication.

He had told her indeed.

Maybe it was the tartly refreshing lime juice that was making her feel buoyant, or maybe it was the fact that all five of the women had expressed their interest in having

Aura supply their wardrobes with new pieces. Either way, Aura all but floated down to the garden when their conversation ended.

Eduardo only needed one glimpse of her face to say, "I gather it went well?"

"You could say so."

Aura had never tended to gush, but she could hear the excitement in her own voice as she told him that she had several prospective new clients. She had never liked counting her coins before they were safely in her pocket, but if half of the offers that had been extended to her materialized into concrete orders, she would soon find herself back on track.

The prospect made her feel steadier than she had all day, more capable of taking on whatever else life chose to throw her way—though she did hope there would be no more surprises forthcoming.

Eduardo was looking down at her, his expression inscrutable. "Will you come with me?" he asked suddenly. "There's something I'd like you to see."

His hand half lifted, as if he'd been about to offer his hand to Aura before thinking better of it and converting the motion into a beckoning gesture that she complied with obligingly.

"Is it more exotic fruit?" Aura asked.

"Unfortunately, it's not. Though if you'd like, we could pay a visit to the kitchen and see if any new shipments have come in."

Aura tilted her head in curiosity. "Wouldn't you know?"

"Not always. My grandfather rarely sends word ahead of time when he's on his way here from Santo Domingo—we usually find out by the crates of fruit that precede him. Or even trees, as he's always ordering new seeds and experimenting with grafting different species."

Eduardo's warm way of referring to his grandfather was in stark contrast to how he'd stiffened when Aura had mentioned his parents the night before. Her only possible conclusion was that they had perished in tragic circumstances and his grief was as raw as her own. Sympathy swirled through her, tamping down the small part of her that was faintly envious that he had his grandfather and his cousins—what sounded like a great deal of cousins, actually—to help him weather the blow.

"Your grandfather sounds fascinating."

Eduardo turned to give her a smile. "He really is. I hope you'll have a chance to meet soon."

Aura was conflicted at the way her heart swelled at his words. There had been a time when she would have loved nothing more than to be part of the Martínez's large clan, to feel herself sheltered in their warmth and power. Under the current circumstances, though, all she could think about was whether she was endangering them with her mere presence in their home.

Not knowing what those men had been looking for, or what her father had been embroiled in...

Aura would never have faulted him for leaving her with little in the way of material possessions or funds in the bank. That he had left her with so many problems instead sent a pang of bitterness through her that she tried hard to push down as she followed Eduardo through the garden and toward the house.

Their progress was halted every handful of steps by people who wanted to either thank Eduardo for a favor he'd rendered them, or to ask him to intercede in their behalf on matters that seemed to range from business to personal. If it hadn't been obvious before, it quickly became apparent to Aura just how trusted Eduardo was—how needed.

Knowing she wasn't the only one made her feel a little less anxious and embarrassed about relying so heavily on his help, even though he'd offered it willingly. He was giving her no more or no less than he had given what seemed like half the people in the garden.

She also didn't seem to be alone in her desire to bask in his attention. Everyone seemed to want to linger in conversation, some shooting Aura curious glances but most content with Eduardo's introduction of her as a family friend.

Aura had to be grateful for their presence, if only because it served as a reminder that she ought to behave. That she shouldn't allow the intoxicating sensation of being around Eduardo to go to her head, even as a small—tiny, minuscule really—part of her wondered what it would be like to have him all to herself.

Aura could see how easy it would be to get swept into this glittering world of Eduardo's, full of all the warmth and comfort and abundance that hers lacked. The brightness of his smile alone, flashed at her from across a crowded room, could be enough to light up all the shadowy corners of her world. If she let it.

It was tempting, if only because it provided such a welcome reprieve against all the troubles knocking at her door and the anxiety that flared inside her every time she thought about returning home. But she wasn't likely to succumb, not when she still had such a long way to go before she could achieve her goals.

Skillfully extricating himself from a man who appeared to be desperate for an introduction to the docks' administrator, Eduardo ushered Aura into his grandfather's study.

He closed the door firmly behind them and gave Aura a conspiratorial smile. "I thought they'd never let me go."

Aura wasn't used to being around good-looking young

men. That must have been why prickles of awareness were chasing themselves over her chest and thighs as she found herself alone with Eduardo.

Or, more likely, she had been through a great deal over the past several days and she was finally on the verge of succumbing to a nervous condition.

She crossed her arms over her chest. "What did you want to show me?"

Beckoning her to follow, Eduardo led her to the double doors and into the enclosed garden where they'd shared the bowl of fruit the night before.

"I thought you might like to see the garden in the daylight. There's a certain beauty to it in the dark, but I doubt you would have been able to see my masterpiece."

"Your masterpiece?" Aura glanced down at the flower bed in front of her, where long stalks of wire rose from among the brightly colored birds of paradise. "Are those... bees?"

Eduardo nodded, sliding his hands into his pocket. "My grandmother and I made them when I was a child. She taught me to leave small bowls of sugar water out for the real kind at certain times of year, and to make sure they and the birds had places to drink from on hot days." The charming smile he had worn throughout the party had worn away into something softer, more wistful that made Aura gather her skirts and crouch down for a better view.

The bees in the flower bed had been fashioned out of twisted wire, their outlines studded with buttons. All kinds of buttons—the kind that belonged on the shirts of little boys, beautifully worked ones that had to come from a lady's gown, inexpensive pewter ones that showed the effect of more than a decade in the sun and rain.

"I had no idea you were such an artist," Aura teased as

she touched a fingertip to one stiff wing, unaccountably delighted with the thought of a young Eduardo carefully fastening buttons to wire.

"There's a lot you don't know about me." Eduardo crouched down beside her, offering her his hand.

He pulled her to her feet as he rose, and Aura felt as momentarily weightless as if she herself were a bee, borne aloft on a gust of wind.

Her fingertips landing briefly on the front of his starched white shirt. It was a light touch, one that lasted only long enough for her to regain her balance. There was nothing improper in it, and certainly nothing that would cause Eduardo to draw in a sharp intake of breath.

Unless he'd been struck, as she had, by a lightning bolt of desire.

In the dazzling flash that followed, Aura saw it clearly—Eduardo was as affected by her as she was by him. The realization unbound something inside her and her prized restraint fell away. She could kiss him. He wouldn't object—far from it. And maybe one kiss, a mere meeting of lips, was what she needed to prove to herself that she could remain in control even in the face of so much longing.

"We shouldn't," he murmured, correctly guessing what was going through Aura's mind. A crooked smile gave an irresistible curl to his lips. "But we will, won't we?"

His dark eyes were sparkling in the sunshine, as if he found what would inevitably come next a delight and not the mistake it so clearly was. Aura made it anyway.

She placed her hands on Eduardo's arms, her touch even lighter than before. And then she leaned in.

Aura had always thought of kisses as small offers that she could accept, or not, as she deemed fit. It wasn't until her lips met Eduardo's and his mouth parted open that she realized that kissing was a conversation. Each graze of their lips was a call and a response, a question and an answer.

And when the tip of his tongue swept a scorching path over the seam of her lips…it spoke more eloquently than anything they had allowed themselves to say.

The bright, fresh scent that Eduardo had perceived in Aura's atelier was even more prominent now, intriguingly so. He couldn't claim that he had ever paused to wonder what a ladies' dressmaker would smell like—if he had, he might have thought of something floral, perhaps, faintly dusty like fabric that had spent too long folded inside a wardrobe. But Aura's scent reminded him of a warm wind rising from a river and whistling through grass. Of lazy afternoons whiled away plucking wildflowers from the ground and nibbling on freshly picked fruit.

It took a great deal of effort—and all the discipline at his command—to keep his lips from roaming over her neck. Sneaking a kiss in the middle of a party was one thing. There was no need to let it get out of hand, no matter how much he strained to dive into the hollows of her collarbone and follow the light aroma wherever it might lead him.

Then again, what had just transpired between them felt like so much more than a stolen moment or one of the covert, mischievous dalliances that Eduardo hadn't indulged in since he'd been young enough that the prospect of whisking a girl into a private corner for a kiss or two had been the height of excitement. It felt…

Like a path that was better left untrodden.

Even so, he and Aura clung together for a long moment after he broke the kiss, lips touching, breath intermingling. Eduardo didn't know about Aura, but it wasn't mere reluctance that kept him from releasing his hold on her—it was that he suspected he wouldn't be able to stand up straight on his own.

He let out a groaning laugh, pressing his forehead against hers. "I hope you don't think that's why I convinced you to come here—to the garden, or to the house."

"I didn't think so," she said a little breathlessly. Taking short sips of air, she recovered much more quickly than Eduardo. She stepped away, looking like she was casting around for a topic of conversation banal enough to dispel some of the tension still crackling between them. "So tell me. Are you still devoted to the craft?" She nodded toward the bees. "If so, I believe I may have some buttons I could contribute."

Yes. Conversation. Something Eduardo was perfectly capable of.

"You'll laugh, but collecting buttons for the bees was such a big part of my childhood that I can't quite seem to quit the habit," he said, reaching into his pocket. "I picked this one up a few minutes ago—it must have been dropped by one of the guests at the party."

To his surprise, Aura snatched the button from his palm with a frown. "This is mine."

He hadn't noticed anything amiss with her dress, but then again, short of it hanging off her shoulders he wasn't sure he *could* have noticed anything other than her smile and her figure and those eyes of hers. "Would you like one of the housemaids to help you—"

Aura shook her head. "No, I mean that this is one of the buttons I ordered for my store—the ones that should have been in my crates."

Eduardo peered at the tiny thing in her hand. The button was made out of mother-of-pearl, and it had been carved

into a flower. He had no doubt that she recognized it, but…
"You're sure it's one of yours?"

"It was a special order—I asked for a camellia specifically. I suppose it's entirely possible that they could have
made the same design for someone else."

"But not likely?" Eduardo guessed.

"I don't believe so. You know what this means, don't
you?" In her noticeably growing excitement, Aura didn't
let him answer. "Whoever stole my crates must be here."

There were any number of explanations as to why the
button had turned up in Eduardo's home, but far be it from
him to dash her hopes when there was a chance she might
be right. "If they are," he told her, trying to infuse his voice
with certainty, "we'll find them. At the very least, whoever was wearing the button will be able to tell us where
she got it."

Eduardo couldn't lie—there was a certain thrill to playing detective even if it was mostly an excuse to spend the
rest of the party at Aura's side.

Since she'd already been introduced as a dressmaker, nobody seemed to find it too odd when she went around the
garden and terrace, asking the women discreetly if one of
their friends had lost a button and offering to sew it back
on. Even with Eduardo there to smooth her way with a well-
placed remark here and a pleasant smile there, nobody took
her up on her offer.

"Maybe she realized she lost a button and went home,"
Aura murmured to Eduardo as they stepped away from the
group they had been chatting with. "Or maybe…"

Eduardo followed her gaze. A few meters away, María
del Mar was telling some sort of involved joke that seemed
to require a great deal of hand waving, and as she whirled
around to illustrate some point or another, he saw what

Aura must have noticed—there was a ribbon tied into a bow at an awkward point in her back, where a button should go.

Making up a smooth little lie about needing to borrow his cousin for a moment, he dragged the girl to a secluded spot in the garden, Aura at his heels.

"Is this yours?" he demanded, showing María the button that Aura was holding.

María del Mar blinked. "I don't know—is it? One of my confounded buttons came off earlier, but damned if I know what it looks like."

"It matches the ones on the back of your dress," Aura reported.

To Eduardo's surprise, his cousin looked relieved. "Good, then I can sew it back on before I give the dress back to its owner. You'd think I would have learned by now not to borrow expensive things."

"You borrowed the dress? From whom?" Aura asked eagerly.

María gave her a questioning glance, and when no answer came forth, she shrugged and said, "Perla de Marchena."

Aura's gaze sharpened with recognition. All she said, though, was, "I can fix the button for you before you return it, if you want."

"Would you? I tore the hem something awful, too." María kicked at the skirt of her dress to show the place where the stitching had come unraveled. "This is why hardly anyone lets me borrow their things."

"Just bring it to my room when you change," Aura told her.

Eduardo waited until he and Aura were alone again before saying, without any preliminaries, "You recognized the name."

She nodded. "Perla is married to Rafael Marchena—an

associate of my father's, if you'll pardon the euphemism."
She gave a little pause. "If she somehow got her hands on
my things…"

Eduardo followed her train of thought without too much
trouble—either Rafael Marchena or his wife was responsible for stealing the contents of Aura's crates. It didn't
take too much of a leap to guess the reason, or to reach
the conclusion that he was probably behind the intrusion
into Aura's home, which had likely come about as a result
of not finding whatever he was seeking inside the crates.

"Is he here?" Eduardo asked, looking out over the
crowded terrace and down at the garden.

"If he is, I'll find him," Aura said grimly, starting to
move forward. "And I'll—"

"Pretend to be utterly ignorant of whatever's going on,"
he suggested. "You don't want to give away your hand too
soon."

"What I want is to be left out of any criminal endeavors." There was little chance of that, and Aura seemed to
realize it at once. She let out a grudging breath. "I despise
intrigue, but I suppose that's exactly what it will take to
get myself out of this wretched mess."

"Is Marchena likely to be dangerous?"

"Not unless you're frightened of being bored to death,"
Aura said tartly before shrugging. "He tried to cast me out
of the house—in order to search it, I imagine. I refused,
of course, which must be why he escalated matters. Either
he wants what he's searching for badly enough to be unconcerned by a little violence, or he must be more annoyed
than I thought about my putting up any kind of opposition
to his trying to evict me from my own home."

"Does he have a real claim to it?"

"So he says—apparently, my father gave him the deeds

to the house in exchange for a large loan. Which is unfortunately plausible, though I have no idea what he would have spent the money on, especially since he'd already taken most of my savings." Aura rubbed a hand over her face. "Heaven knows there haven't been any silk stockings in a long time."

"I've known plenty of men who would have no compunction over taking out one loan in order to repay another," Eduardo told her. "If all Marchena wants with your house is whatever he's been looking for, helping him find it is probably your best bet to persuading him to leave you alone. Easier said than done, I know."

"Particularly since I have no idea what it is," Aura said with a sigh. "Though they all seem to be under the impression that I know what my father was up to."

Eduardo followed Aura as she strode toward the terrace railing and stood surveying the crowd milling around the garden. It took a minute or two, but eventually she pointed out an ordinary-looking man dressed in a dark suit and panama hat, like most others in attendance.

"That's him."

"Seems a little short to be the head of a criminal enterprise," Eduardo said critically, watching as the man sidled up to someone else and began conducting an intent conversation. The deep shadows cast by the hedge prevented Eduardo from seeing the other person clearly. "And I'd have chosen a better hat. Still, he does seem shifty enough."

He also seemed familiar, though Eduardo couldn't pinpoint the reason why. Though of course, if his wife was friends with María del Mar it was likely that Eduardo had come across him before.

"I can't say I care for María's taste in acquaintances," he continued. "Though to be fair, she's always been delightfully indiscriminate in her invitations and that always makes for a good time."

Aura was frowning. "He is acting shifty, isn't he? That doesn't seem like him. Do you think he's up to something?"

"If he is, we can hear whatever he's saying from Abuelo's garden. Come on."

Eduardo couldn't begin to imagine what María's guests were thinking as he and Aura hurried into the house and back to his grandfather's study, pausing only when they reached the leafy hedge surrounding the private garden.

They were in time to hear only the last fragment of a sentence, delivered in a hissing whisper that carried through the vegetation separating them from Marchena.

"—we'll have to use the *Leonor*."

The *Leonor*. The familiar name juddered through Eduardo with the impact of a shipwreck. Inside his grandfather's estate in Santo Domingo, there was a larger-than-life-size portrait at the head of the stairs that bore that very name, inscribed on a gold plaque. Her namesake, the site of Eduardo's childhood romps, was docked in the San Pedro harbor.

Knowing what little he did of Aura's father, it didn't take much for Eduardo to connect the conversation he'd just overheard with the rocks that had turned up in lieu of Aura's merchandise and come up with one likely explanation.

Smuggling.

Chapter Six

"You'd be doing me a favor, you know," Eduardo said.

Aura turned to look at him. Twilight was gathering in the garden below them where Gregorio and Celia strolled arm in arm, chatting in low voices. Up here on the balcony outside the upstairs parlor, however, sunshine still lingered. A patch of it touched Eduardo's profile, as if to highlight the lines that had formed between his brows.

Eduardo had been quiet for the past couple of hours. Aura wasn't sure if it had anything to do with the conversation they had overheard, or if he was reconsidering having invited her into his home.

"A favor?" she asked.

"If you married me." He gestured to the couple in the garden. "Celia has been waiting a year to marry Gregorio, but he refuses to set a date. Because of me."

"Why is that?"

Eduardo spread his hands. "Some misguided notion that I will turn into a wreck if he isn't here to keep order," he said, so lightly that Aura suspected there was far more behind his words than he was letting on.

She folded her arms against the railing. "And you'd do something as drastic as marrying someone just to appease him?"

"It doesn't seem like such a drastic step to me," Eduardo said, shrugging. "I happen to think that marriage can be as easy and uncomplicated as sharing an ice cream cone."

"How romantic," Aura said dryly. "Truly what every woman wishes to hear when being asked to join her life to someone else's."

"Would it help if I told you that I like you a great deal? That I think being married to you would be exciting and honestly quite a lot of fun?"

"I don't have time for fun," Aura protested. "I have far too much work to do."

"What if I told you that María del Mar would be eternally grateful? The aunts are plaguing her more than ever about ending up a spinster. You and me getting married might just be the distraction she needs to evade their lectures for at least another six months." He dropped his voice, and a certain intensity kindled in his gaze. "And if that's not enough to persuade you, think of how thoroughly and how often I'd be able to kiss you if we were married. Wouldn't you like that?"

Aura frowned in response to the heat that curled through her, though she didn't step away from Eduardo. "Would you be serious for a moment?"

She half thought that he would respond with another joke, but he surprised her by grasping her loosely by both elbows. His hands were pleasantly warm on the skin just below her ribbon-banded sleeve, and he was still so distractingly close that the scent of his eau de toilette seemed to waft all around her, surrounding her in a cloud scented with tangerines and lime, which mingled surprisingly well with her own perfume.

"I know you're used to fending for yourself, but you don't have to. Not anymore. And even though I will do everything I can to get you out of the mess you've found yourself in, I might not be enough. If we married, we'd have the entire Martínez clan behind us."

The pad of his thumb stroked a gentle back-and-forth on one of her forearms, and Aura wondered if he could sense that she was wavering.

"I need this just as much as you do. I'd even be prepared to compensate—"

Swiftly, Aura shook her head. "I could never accept your money, and I really wish you'd stop offering it. I've taken enough from you as it is."

"I can arrange for a bank loan in your name. For your store, Aura."

Now that she knew that Marchena had reasons for holding on to the deed to her house, Aura didn't think he would simply let her pay back the money her father had borrowed from him. But with a line of credit she'd never be able to secure on her own, she could rent a small space somewhere and open her store faster than she had anticipated—not to mention replenish her missing stock. With patronage from Eduardo's friends, she had a fighting chance of making her dream come true.

All she had to do was marry Eduardo.

A false marriage felt too close to her father's own deceptions for Aura to be entirely comfortable with it. She had spent most of her life engaged in some subterfuge or another—pretending as a child to be ill so that her father would be spared that month's rent, for instance. After being welcomed so readily into the Martínez household, the last thing she wanted was to lie to them all.

That alone should have been enough to cure her of any romantic notions she might have harbored. Added to the way her body seemed to burst into heated awareness at the mere fact of Eduardo's nearness, or the way her heartbeat sped up at the thought of potentially sharing a bed with him, she should have refused the proposal at once.

"I don't know," she said instead.

"It would be a partnership," Eduardo said. "Something easy and uncomplicated, with no wretched feelings to get in the way. Just a great deal of kissing."

"You're not worried that kissing could lead to affection?"

He shrugged. "It never has for me. And in any case, I haven't anything against affection—as long as it doesn't turn into anything more."

"Into love, you mean?" Aura pressed, not sure why that particular point felt so important. It wasn't as though she herself was in love with Eduardo after all, or with anyone else. And heaven only knew he was offering her enough that overlooking it should have been a simple matter. What did she care if Eduardo didn't wish to marry for love? "Why are you so scared of it?"

"Scared, me? I crave danger, remember?" The grin Eduardo shot her reminded her uncomfortably of the expression her father plastered on when he was determined to get his own way. "Almost as much as I crave to feel your lips again."

Her entire body would have thrilled at such an admission, if it hadn't come with the off-putting certainty that he was trying to distract her from her probing questions. She shifted, and the hands that still held her by the elbows dropped to his sides.

"That's more than enough to base a marriage on, surely," he continued smoothly.

"I imagine it is, in plenty of cases," she said, aware that her voice sounded a trifle stiff. "But…haven't you ever wanted more than a marriage of convenience?"

Eduardo held her gaze for a moment, then turned back toward the garden. "You mean a love match? Those are far more work than they're worth."

Aura waited, but when it became clear that he wasn't going to elaborate, she stifled a sigh. "Well, marriage does make a certain kind of sense. Especially since María del Mar told me she's leaving on another journey in less than a week and it would be unseemly for me to stay alone with two bachelors—and I don't think I can quite face going home again." Though she would have hated for Eduardo to think that she was contemplating his proposal solely for mercenary reasons, honesty compelled her to add, "And I can't deny that a bank loan would help me a great deal."

Whether she wanted to admit it or not, marrying him to keep herself out of danger, to be able to stay in his home, even to finally make her store a reality…it still seemed to her like a drastic solution and a terrible idea.

But none of her careful, practical plans had worked out so far.

Still, she had to ask, "Why me? I can't image there's any lack of women who'd be willing—even eager—to enter into such an arrangement with you."

"I can trust you to remain businesslike," Eduardo said with another careless shrug. "To not forget that this is a partnership, nothing more."

A partnership…well, she could certainly do that. Aura had never held much hope for a brilliant match, and in the past few years she had been far too busy to even consider the notion. Far too busy to let herself even dream about things like falling in love. If anything, she'd told herself that love would only hinder her efforts to become financially inde-pendent. Love would only make her vulnerable in all the ways she had seen her own mother been made vulnerable by her father's constantly changing fortunes.

Which was what made her partnership with Eduardo so ideal. While she had her doubts about there being anything easy or uncomplicated in this arrangement, there was friendship between them, and that was more than enough to help them see things through without any dangerous feelings to get in the way.

So why did she feel a shard of disappointment slicing its way through her chest?

Aura forced herself to ignore the feeling, and instead held out her hand. "Then yes, Eduardo. I'll marry you."

Eduardo had never imagined that he would seal his own engagement with a handshake rather than a kiss, but with Gregorio and Celia lingering below them and the household staff already milling around, putting the garden to rights, he didn't quite dare.

There was a moment when he'd been sure that Aura would tell him that she'd only agree to a wedding on the condition that they didn't kiss again, and though he wouldn't have rescinded his offer if she had, the prospect would have been crushing. She hadn't said anything about it, though, and the awareness that sizzled between them both made Eduardo think that she was looking forward to it as much as he was.

And honestly, that was all Eduardo could ask from his future wife. Easy and uncomplicated wasn't just the motto by which he lived his life—it was what he aspired to in every relationship he had ever entered into.

"It's a deal," he told her.

Her palm was still pressed against Eduardo's, and the contact was shockingly intimate. Finding the callus in her forefinger, he stroked it with the tip of his thumb, making her breath hitch.

She inclined her face toward his. A small movement, but one that put her lips conveniently close to his.

Maybe they *would* seal the engagement with a kiss, after all.

Her warm breath wafted out over his mouth and Eduardo was painfully, excruciatingly aware of the warm line of her body mere centimeters from his. He wouldn't even have to take a step to reach her lips or to line his body up with hers. All it would take was—

María del Mar burst into the upstairs parlor, holding a bottle of Veuve Clicquot by the neck. And while Gregorio and Celia followed at a much more sedate pace, their arrival signaled the end of Eduardo and Aura's conversation. But that was all right—they could hatch their plots later, after they'd broken the news to his family.

Taking the bottle from María before she could hurt someone with it, Eduardo took it over to the sideboard and poured them all a drink. Gregorio helped him gather the full coupes and hand them to the women, who had gathered into a loose knot on the balcony.

"Aura and I have something to tell you," Eduardo said.

María's mouth fell open. "You didn't."

"I didn't what?"

"Ask her to marry you." Without waiting for his answer, María clasped her hands together. "I knew it the moment I saw you together. Oh, I wish I wasn't leaving so soon. Aura, you'll have to write to me with news of all the wedding preparations."

"Actually," Eduardo said, clearing his throat, "we wish to be married as soon as possible."

"Tomorrow, in fact," Aura added.

"The aunts won't be happy that we'll deprive them of a wedding," Eduardo told his cousins, making a face. "Good thing they have yours to look forward to, Gregorio. Hopefully sooner, rather than later."

Oblivious to the piercing look Gregorio was directing toward him, Aura glanced down at the glass in her hands. "You don't think they'll…regard me with suspicion at how quickly it's all come about?"

Both Gregorio and María shook their heads. "No one who knows Eduardo will be in the least surprised," Gregorio said, and he felt himself tensing until his cousin added, "At least not when they become acquainted with how lovely you are, Aura."

She received his compliment gracefully and returned it by saying a few warm words about how welcome they had made her and how she was looking forward to getting to know Gregorio, Celia and María better.

Under the pretext of refilling their glasses, Eduardo drew María del Mar aside. "How do you know Rafael Marchena?"

"Who?" María asked blankly.

"He was one of the guests at the party." His cousin continued to look quizzical, so he elaborated. "His wife was the one who loaned you the dress you were wearing."

"Oh! Well, she's a second cousin of the Gonzalezes. I met her at a musical evening, but I'd never been introduced to her husband. As a matter of fact, I'm not quite sure if he came to the party—there were so many people that I was nearly run off my feet. Why are you asking about him? Is it a business matter?"

"Something like that."

Eduardo changed the subject. It had been Aura's decision to tell María and Gregorio about her troubles, but seeing as they now involved smuggling, he'd much rather keep them both out of it until it had been handled.

After several minutes, Eduardo had successfully steered the conversation toward María del Mar's upcoming voyage. Handing her the newly filled champagne coupes, he motioned for them to rejoin Gregorio and Celia, who along with Aura had drifted over to the armchairs. María perched on the arm of Gregorio's chair and immediately interjected herself in the conversation.

Eduardo took the seat opposite, waiting until he had caught Aura's gaze to raise a silent glass in celebration of their partnership. Looking only slightly overwhelmed, she acknowledged his toast with a nod.

Aura's crates being tampered with was concerning enough, both from a practical standpoint—the company couldn't afford to have their clients' orders go missing or being interfered with—and because the extraction of her things had to have been done in one of their warehouses, which implied an unforgivable lapse in security.

It would be galling, but not surprising, if Marchena and his accomplices were using or even attempting to use the *Leonor* to transport their smuggled goods, since a private passenger ship would be subject to less scrutiny than the company's cargo vessels, which went through a more rigorous inspection upon entering and exiting any port. If any illicit cargo were discovered by Customs, it would only implicate the Martínezes.

For better or worse, everything that had happened to Aura now directly concerned him.

If someone was using Martínez & Hijos to transport smuggled goods, he would simply have to roust them and deal with the matter before word of it reached his grandfather.

Chapter Seven

Even with the Martínezes' considerable influence, it took the better part of the following day for Eduardo to procure the marriage license and make the necessary arrangements for them to marry.

Having run out of organdy scraps, Aura retired to her bedroom after dinner and set about making rosettes out of short lengths of silk ribbon. It was going to take a dispiriting amount of rosettes to restore her fortune, small as it had been.

It wasn't that she didn't trust Eduardo's promise of arranging a bank loan, just that experience had made her cautious of believing in any kind of windfall. And as for promises… they rarely went unbroken. He had all the best intentions, she was sure of it, but all kinds of things could happen to keep him from going through with it—including his grandfather, who might take outrage at the fact that she was marrying into the family without his approval. And with a swiftness usually reserved for reasons of a scandalous nature.

Time would assure everyone that wasn't the case. But whether or not Eduardo's family and friends would become suspicious of her motives remained to be seen.

Aura's thoughts hadn't stopped her from continuing to skillfully twist ribbon into rosettes. But she did pause a moment later when her gaze fell on the valise she had placed neatly beside the chest of drawers and another thought struck her—if her father had meant to smuggle something, what were the odds that he had stowed it in the luggage he had packed for his journey to New York?

She'd taken his things out hastily and repacked it with her own clothes the other day She was fairly certain she hadn't seen anything of value among its contents—but what if there was something hidden in the valise itself?

Quickly, she laid it on top of the covers and began examining it. She was patting down its interior when a knock came at the door of her guest room. She went to answer it at once, wondering if María del Mar had any refurbishments to her travel wardrobe that required Aura's help.

It was Eduardo's face, however, that became bathed in lamplight when she opened the door. His errands had kept him out of the house until after dinner, and though she had heard his arrival a couple of minutes before, she had imagined that he would want time to himself to bathe and eat. Though he had shucked off his jacket and loosened his tie, as she was beginning to see was his habit immediately upon getting home, it appeared that he had come directly to Aura.

"I know it's the height of impropriety to intrude on your bedroom," he began.

"I think we might be beyond propriety at this point," she said, amusement swirling through her at his stricken look.

Then she realized that the expression was due to another matter entirely.

"Going somewhere?" he asked, nodding at the valise on the bed.

She shook her head. "It was my father's. I searched it when I was packing my things, but I was in a hurry and so flustered. I thought I might have missed something."

"Like what?"

She stepped back so that Eduardo could come inside. "I keep thinking maybe I'll find something—a secret compartment, a rip in the lining…"

"And have you?" Looking at the valise in fascination, Eduardo ran a hand over its empty interior, then shaped it into a fist to knock on its side.

Aura shook her head and regretfully closed the lid, trying not to show how disappointed she was. "Nothing. I think I should go back to the house and search again. There's got to be dozens of places I haven't looked yet—the pockets of his trousers, the lining of his jackets…"

"I'll go with you," Eduardo offered. "As soon as I can arrange for a guard to escort us. In the meantime, there's something I was hoping to discuss."

"Is something wrong?"

"Everything's wrong—starting with the fact that you haven't a proper wedding dress. Or rings to exchange tomorrow."

"Oh. Well, that's all right," Aura said, trying to look unconcerned. "There really was no time for much. And I do have the dress I wore to María's party."

"Well, I didn't think it was right that a woman should get married while wearing mourning clothes. So I went and got you something."

His frown melted into a smile, and he went to fetch the large box he had stowed just outside the open door. He placed it on the bed and lifted the lid for Aura to see yards and yards of pale fabric. Her pulse quickened as she lifted out the dress and laid it out on the bed. Against the crisp white of the bedsheets, it proved to be dark ivory in color, and so beautifully trimmed that her heart squeezed inside her chest.

"Eduardo, it's perfect," she exclaimed, examining the exquisite lace detailing on the bodice.

"I'm sure it's nowhere near as fine as anything you might have been able to make yourself. But it'll do, I think. Aren't you going to try it on to see if it fits?"

She glanced up to see his teasing smile. "Maybe I should." But the onrush of heat that followed that rejoinder was so strong that Aura sharply veered away. "I suppose I should be surprised that a man would think of such details."

Eduardo shrugged, as if to express nonchalance, but the small smile playing on his lips suggested that he was pleased with himself. "I have to make myself useful."

"Why is that?" Aura stepped closer to him, her gaze trained on his face with an intensity she usually reserved for her stitches. "Why do you always feel the need to prove your worth?"

He looked a little flummoxed. But all he said was, "I wasn't aware that I did. Is it such a terrible thing?"

"Only if you believe that other people should prove their worth to you in order to gain a place in your life."

He shrugged, grinning. "Before I count them as friends, I make all my acquaintances go through a trial period in which they prove their usefulness and loyalty. Oh, I almost forgot." He dug into his pocket and presented Aura with a small parcel wrapped in tissue paper. "In case you wanted them for tomorrow."

Left blinking at the abrupt change in subject, it took Aura a second to focus on the items Eduardo was holding out. The carved ivory combs and the gleaming strand of pearls looked more like family heirlooms than something he might have purchased at any of the stores in town, even the ones with the finest imported wares. Aura, who had been planning to adorn her mauve dress with a few flowers from the garden, felt herself unable to say a single word.

This was too much.

"They were my grandmother's. Of course, if you'd rather something new—"

"You have no idea how much I appreciate your thoughtfulness," she began, and hesitated as she deliberated over how best to word it.

"But you would have wanted to choose something for yourself?"

"No, I just…" She stroked the pad of her thumb over the necklace's oval-shaped clasp, which was inset with small, unobtrusive diamonds. "The combs and necklace are beautiful, but they're much too precious to wear to the registry office. And… I'm afraid I'm not used to so much luxury."

"You'll be a Martínez soon. Luxury comes with the territory. But I won't insist if it'll make you uncomfortable." Striding to the dresser, he dropped the bundle on its polished wooden surface. "I'll leave these here in case you change your mind, though. You can return them after the wedding if you like."

"I hope I didn't hurt your feelings," she said haltingly.

"I don't think I have any of those." Eduardo turned to grin at her, even as he rubbed a thumb over a nick in the wood. "I hadn't realized this room was so shabby—it'll have to be refurbished. The upstairs parlor, too. Would you like to take charge or would you rather I hire my friend Paulina?"

Shabby? Aura had thought this room was as luxurious as a palace.

"Won't your grandfather mind?"

"It's my house, not his. I inherited it from my mother's family. My grandparents raised me at their estate in Santo

Domingo, but they made a point of spending the summers here so that San Pedro also felt like home."

"How lovely of them."

"Well, there was a business advantage to having a pied-à-terre in San Pedro," Eduardo said wryly. "My grandfather might be wonderful in every way, but he isn't sentimental where business is concerned. I heard that when my father told him he was courting a girl from San Pedro, Abuelo's first thought was about how he could finally expand the company."

It was the first time Aura had heard Eduardo refer to his father. She would have wanted to ask more, but he seemed to realize his lapse and added quickly, "Of course, the house will be half yours after tomorrow."

Aura frowned, and Eduardo forestalled her with a raised finger. "That also means you share half the custody of María del Mar, so really, I'm the one who's coming out ahead. Though she and Gregorio offered to find other arrangements if we wanted our privacy."

"I wouldn't think of it," she said crisply.

Eduardo grinned. "Well, she's not here often enough to make too big a pest of herself, so I suppose that'll be all right. And I'm hoping that Celia will finally drag Gregorio to the altar now that he won't have me to worry about."

"What about the rest of your family? Will I get a chance to meet them?"

"Soon enough—they'll descend on us en masse as soon as they hear about the wedding."

The guest room was equipped with a table and chair where she'd been working on her rosettes as well as a small, cane-backed love seat. Aura had moved it in front of the window, where it was cooler. Perching on one end, a pile of ribbon on her lap, she waved Eduardo to the unoccupied spot.

"Can I ask an impertinent question?"

He dropped into the seat and stretched out his long legs. "You can ask twenty of them if you want," he said easily.

"Why is it that you haven't any romantic attachments?"

Setting aside the fact that Eduardo was handsome and genuinely kind, he was one of the heirs to a fortune so large it barely diminished when split with however many cousins he had. Surely, he had to be one of the most eligible bachelors in San Pedro.

Aura's gaze was on the rosette taking shape in her hands, but she saw his shrug out of the corner of her eye.

"I suppose because I'd never met a woman who charges after pickpockets or tries to fend off intruders with a watering can."

She bit her lip. Eduardo's reticence to speak openly about himself or his past gave her pause—but not enough to call off their plan. She couldn't expect him to bear his soul to someone he'd just met, after all. Once they were married and had time to grow accustomed to each other…everything would be different then.

Still, she couldn't help but probe gently one more time. "There aren't any tragic romances in your past?"

"Not a single one," he said cheerfully. Aura raised an eyebrow and he added, "Is that so difficult to believe? And here I was, so sure I didn't look like the kind of man who went howling around moors or kept wives in his attic. I don't even have an attic."

The references went right over Aura's head, but she supposed they had to do with all the books she had spied crowded into the bookcase in the upstairs parlor. A cursory glance at the titles on their spines had told her that the books were in a variety of languages, mostly Spanish, English and French. All three of the Martínezes she had met seemed to be extraordinarily well-read, though none of them seemed to care about showing off their vast knowledge. She didn't think that was what Eduardo was doing now—if anything, he was probably trying to distract her from probing too hard into his affairs. Which, to be fair, was his prerogative, irritating though she might find it.

Eduardo grinned at her. "Are you asking me because *you* have a tragic past romance that you're about to confess to?"

"Well, no," Aura said, striving to keep her tone brisk. "I haven't any romances at all, as a matter of fact. In my past or in my present."

"Now, how is that possible? You'd think every man in San Pedro would fall head over heels for someone of your beauty and charm."

The narrowness of the love seat meant that they were sitting very close together. Aura couldn't help but remember what he had said the day before, about how much kissing there would be if they married. All it would take was to lean forward and tilt her head up.

"You're a reckless flirt," she told him, narrowing her eyes.

"And unrepentant—I don't see anything reckless about flirting with one's intended."

"I do when it's midnight and you're in the lady's bedroom."

"Do you want me to leave?"

"Not just yet," she replied, a little faster than she'd meant to. She masked her eagerness by asking the one question she was sure he wouldn't want to evade. "María del Mar told me you like to invite your friends from abroad to spend winters here at the house. And there was an incident with a goat once?"

Eduardo relaxed, and tucked a green silk bolster pillow behind his head as he began talking animatedly about some of the romps he had presided over, each story wilder than the last. Apparently, he had grown accustomed to hosting parties at the house at least once a week, a practice she wondered would continue after they married.

"I don't expect it will," he said when she asked. "Most of my friends have grown boring and conventional within the past couple years."

"They married?" Aura guessed.

Letting out a laugh, Eduardo adjusted the pillow behind his head. "Unfortunately. How dare they be so inconsiderate?"

He'd clearly said it in jest—and yet, Aura thought she could see a hint of something that could have been sadness in the cast of his expression. There was every chance that it was a product of the lamplight and the play of shadows over his eyes. But she didn't think so.

"I thought you were the envy of all your married friends. The consummate bachelor, remember?"

He shrugged "Yes, well. Now they'll envy me for my beautiful wife."

His smile should have dazzled her. Instead, Aura felt something splinter inside her chest. "How old are you?"

"I'm sorry?"

"I'm twenty-five," she told him. "In order to get an annulment or a divorce without the consent of an older relative, one is required to be twenty-five or older."

"The wedding hasn't even happened and you're already trying to get out of it?" Eduardo asked teasingly.

"I just wanted to make sure that you had a way out if you ended up regretting it."

Eduardo took gentle hold of her chin and lifted it until she was looking directly into his eyes. The bruise over his eyebrow was so dark it looked like a shadow, one that followed his movement when he inclined his head toward hers. "I don't believe in regret. But I do believe I'll like being married to you."

Where the air between them had been friendly and companionable, now it was thick with tension. Aura's fingers tightened around the rosette she had stopped twisting, crumpling the ribbon as she reminded herself that they weren't married yet.

Perhaps seeing the conflict reflected in her expression and feeling that he had discomfited her, Eduardo stood. Aura longed to ask him to sit back down a little while longer, to keep her company and tell her more amusing stories while she continued to work. Although, the way her body was reacting, it was probably for the best if he did leave.

"I ought to let you get back to your..." He waved a hand at her sad excuse for a rosette clamped in her fist. "Good night, Aura. Don't get yourself into any tragic romances while I'm sleeping."

The first thing Eduardo had done upon waking the next morning had been to head down to the telegraph office to send his grandfather a message with the news, unwilling that the older man should find out about his grandson's marriage through someone else.

Then he returned home to fetch his bride.

The wedding party waited for him in the front terrace, Gregorio paging idly through a catalog and María del Mar making final adjustments to her ensemble. Eduardo's gaze skipped over his cousins and came to rest on Aura, who looked...

Stunning.

Dozens of small, overlapping petals had been sewn to the waist of the dress he'd brought her the previous evening, arranged so that they trailed down the skirt. The half-transparent fabric of the petals fluttered in the gentle breeze like real flowers would have.

She must have stayed up all night to do it, and the effect was breathtaking.

Eduardo was chiding himself for having remembered everything but a bouquet for her when Aura caught sight of him halfway up the steps and hurried over, holding something in her hand.

"I made something for you," she said, motioning for him to stay where he was.

Carefully, she pinned a flower to his lapel. It took Eduardo a moment to realize it wasn't a real flower at all, but one she had made from the same fabric as the ivory-colored petals adorning her dress.

"I thought the intruders had trampled all of these," he said, watching the entrancing curl that had escaped the braided arrangement at the nape of her neck and was bobbing lightly in the breeze.

"I managed to salvage some."

"They're…" Eduardo touched one of the fluttering petals. "You look beautiful."

She was too absorbed in the flower she was pinning to his lapel to take much notice of his less-than-eloquent compliment. Stepping back with a frown wrinkling the space between her eyebrows, she gave the flower a tweak and sighed.

"It'll have to do, I suppose. I didn't have the right materials for it, so I had to do some improvising."

"It's perfect," Eduardo reassured her, though he suspected that her fussing might have more to do with wedding nerves than with any true concern that the silk flower wasn't up to par.

He was proven right when the group arrived at the registry office. Gregorio and María del Mar had gone on ahead; they were already inside the building when Aura halted suddenly in the shadow of a stopped carriage.

"Is something wrong? Did you snag your skirt?"

There was something frantic in the way she shook her head. "Do you want children?"

Eduardo blinked. "I never stopped to think about it, but I suppose I do. Eventually, in the future. Do you?"

"I—yes. Eventually, in the future."

The faltering smile she gave him was so unlike her that he blinked again, before he realized that she was nervous.

"It'll be easy enough to take precautions so that it doesn't happen until we want it to," he said reassuringly.

She nodded, though she looked unconvinced. "This is ridiculous—we hardly know each other."

"I know you twice as well as some couples do," Eduardo said, shrugging.

"How do you know we're doing the right thing?"

"I don't." Eduardo held out his hand, palm up. After a moment's hesitation, Aura laid hers on it. "I have always been partial to the color green, but sometimes blue is just as appealing. I liked watching you eat pitayas more than I like the fruit itself. When I was little, I used to beg Gregorio to tell me the stories he read in books, because I never had the patience to read them myself. I have a scar, right here—" he gestured toward his collarbone with his free hand "—from when I tried to climb the mast of a ship and failed spectacularly."

He closed his fingers around hers. "And I'm twenty-six."

Aura frowned. "What—"

"That means I'm legally able to divorce without anyone's consent. It's as you said—if it does turn out that we made a mistake, it's one that can be easily righted with the help of an attorney and two signatures."

That was one of the things one learned early on when one came from a family as influential and prosperous as his—when one had access to lawyers and vast amounts of money, there were few mistakes that couldn't be put to rights.

"Eduardo, why don't you want to wait to marry someone you love?"

No other question could have lanced into his heart as that one did. Only Eduardo's rigid control over himself kept him from inhaling sharply. And only that control allowed him to take the sharp, bright pain and turn it into an unconcerned smile. "Because there's nothing easy or uncomplicated about love. Aura, we don't have to do this if you don't want to."

Her chest rose and fell with the strength of her breaths. And then she did it—she squared her shoulders and, almost imperceptibly, tilted up her chin. "We must be out of our minds," she said crisply, but she motioned to Eduardo to head inside.

At that moment, María del Mar popped out, asking impatiently, "What's the delay? Waiting for me to explain the facts of life?"

Eduardo met Aura's eyes and they both gave in to a burst of laughter that cleared some of the tension from the air as they followed María back inside the registry office.

With both his cousins acting as witnesses, Eduardo and Aura stood over a table as a clerk made record of their marriage. The entire affair was as unsentimental as it was brief, and over in mere minutes.

Eduardo waited until María del Mar was bounding toward the carriage, Gregorio walking at a more sedate pace behind her, before tapping Aura's shoulder and asking her to hang back for a moment.

"I have something for you."

He reached inside the breast pocket of his jacket, pushing down a slight, sudden and incomprehensible flutter of nerves. Withdrawing a red velvet box, he opened it to reveal a ring fastened to the creamy satin lining by the kind of impossibly narrow ribbon Aura had woven through her hair.

When the jeweler had taken out his ring trays for Eduardo to select among the ready-made pieces tacked to the dark velvet, Eduardo had glanced through every diamond and pearl, dissatisfied until he spotted three fiery stones that reminded him that he'd never seen Aura wearing bright colors.

He'd had to guess her ring size, but the three rubies, separated by slightly smaller aquamarines and set in a dainty band of white gold, looked just wide enough to span her finger.

"Don't worry, it's not a family heirloom. In fact, it's brand-new—the jeweler worked through the night to have it ready for this morning."

She didn't look any less hesitant. "It looks expensive."

"This worthless bauble?" he said cheerfully, motioning for her to hold out her hand. "My suit costs more than this ring does."

"That says more about your taste in tailoring than it does the price of the ring. You get your suits in London, don't you? Savile Row?"

"I can't get anything past you." He took Aura's hand, holding on to her fingers as if about to raise them to his lips. "Tell you what. Wear this for today and tomorrow I'll go back to the jeweler and tell him to make you a ring out of pewter or tin. Or would you prefer dried palm fronds braided together like the hats they make out in the country?"

Aura shook her head in exasperation, but she did let Eduardo slide the ring onto her fourth finger. "A plain silver band would have been sufficient, you know."

He winked at her. "But where's the fun in that?"

"Did you get a ring for yourself?"

Eduardo fished in his pocket for the plain band he had gotten for himself, prompting a head shake from his new wife. Smiling, he said, "Will you do the honors?"

She took his hand. And suddenly, even though they stood on the sidewalk in front of the registry office and the traffic of handcarts and carriages trickling down the street, the moment felt as private as if he and Aura were the only people left in their region of the world.

The ring was warm from hours in his pocket, almost as warm as Aura's fingers as she slid it into place.

"There we go," Eduardo said softly, turning his hand in her grasp so that he was the one holding hers. "It's official."

Not real, perhaps, not in the way he'd always thought his marriage would be, but official nonetheless.

The pronouncement made the moment feel so heavy, Eduardo couldn't resist lightening it up by extending an arm out with a flourish and marching her toward where Gregorio and María had tactfully waited in the carriage.

Aided by María, he kept up a steady stream of chatter on the way home. As they turned into their street, however, a line of carriages became visible and Aura idly asked if someone was having a party.

"We are," Eduardo said as the carriage came to a stop in front of the house. The front door, twice as tall as he was, had been thrown open, and through it he could see a great deal of people. "You don't mind, do you? It didn't seem right to let the occasion slip by without a small celebration."

"Small? There must be more than fifty people in there." He was relieved to see amusement in the curve of her lips. "I ought to have expected it, actually."

Eduardo leaped out. Before he could reach for Aura, she waved his hands away and descended gracefully on her own, not in the least hindered by her long skirts.

"So independent," he teased, almost breaking into laughter when she rolled her eyes in response and took the arm he was offering.

"I hope you don't expect me to be anything else," she said lightly.

On the other side of the carriage, Gregorio and María had already made their way down and were moving toward the house.

"I wouldn't expect you to be anything other than what you are."

She cast a glance at him from beneath her eyelashes. "And what is that?"

"Other than independent? Beautiful." He let his gaze rake over her. "Resourceful. The kind of person you want to have on your side in a fight."

It was Aura's turn to laugh. He paused, feeling again like a young man who was about to steal a kiss from a girl at a party. Which reminded him.

"What's wrong?" she asked.

"We haven't had our first kiss as husband and wife yet."

"We're in full view of the house," she protested, though Eduardo didn't fail to catch her tiny, interested pause. "And the street. What will everyone say?"

"That I am the luckiest man in San Pedro. But here." Lowering his arm so that he could grasp her hand instead, he tugged her around the side of the house, toward a corner shielded from both the street and from the eyes of his guests. "Better?"

She nodded and placed her hands on his chest, on either side of his slate blue tie.

They hadn't kissed since their embrace in the gardens. Afterward, Eduardo had found it easy to convince himself that while undeniably good, the kiss hadn't been as earth-shattering as he'd imagined it to be in the moment. Not nearly as dangerous. No kiss had ever been, in his experience—why should kissing Aura be any different? Why should kissing her rob him of all powers of speech and thought and reorient his world around the taste of her mouth?

It was only the excitement of having done something as wild and unexpected as getting married that was making his pulse gallop as fast as his friend Julián's racehorses.

That, and the sight of Aura's perfectly shaped lips smiling knowingly up at him.

"All right, then," he began, and got no further as she surged onto her tiptoes and claimed his mouth with her own.

They had barely moved, but it felt like they were crashing together.

It was a different kiss than the last one. Less hesitant and more…more. More intense. More tempestuous.

More unrestrained.

His arms were tight around her waist, and he told himself he was only supporting her so that she wouldn't tire of being on the tips of her toes. But her grip on his lapels was just as tight, crushing the silk flower pinned on one side, and her mouth was eager and warm and boldly adventurous.

"*Now* it's official," Aura said, breathless and a little smug as Eduardo's eyes widened at hearing the echo of his own words.

"Was that retribution for the ring?"

"A warning," she told him, and leaned closer to whisper in his ear. "That I can give as good as I get."

Eduardo stood as if stunned for a moment, and then he was crashing into her again, taking thorough possession of her mouth and feeling something inside him expand at the hot urgency of her response. Turning her around, he pressed her against the side of the house and dove into her neck, breathing in her cool water scent until he heard her breathing grow unsteady. That was his signal to return his mouth to her clamoring one.

He had no idea how much time had gone by when they finally parted again, gasping for air.

"We should stop," he said. "And go inside. Unless you had your heart set on having your wedding night under a laurel bush."

Heat leaped between them like a live flame as they both realized, seemingly at the same time, that their wedding night *was* fast approaching. That if it hadn't been for his brilliant idea to have a party to mark the occasion, they would have been upstairs by now, her clever fingers making quick work of his buttons.

Giving her a rueful smile, Eduardo pressed one last kiss to her open mouth before reluctantly stepping away.

"Is my hair in disarray?" she asked him, patting down a wayward curl and smoothing a hand over the fluttering petals on her bodice.

"It's perfect. As are you."

"Nobody's perfect, Eduardo," she said crisply. "But if my hair's all right, I'm ready to go inside."

Arm in arm, they went into the parlor and paused in the

middle of the crowd for a long, full moment of applause and well wishes. When his friends had quieted, Eduardo pulled Aura a fraction closer and said, "Amigos, may I present to you Aura Soriano de Martínez—my new wife."

Chapter Eight

Between the party and the flurry of María del Mar's departure, shortly after lunch had been served, it was very late in the afternoon when Aura finally went upstairs.

Eduardo's bedroom was more sizable than the guest room she'd been staying in, so she had agreed to have her things moved in there while she and Eduardo were at the registry office. It wasn't a surprise to turn the doorknob and find her hairbrush, comb and her bottles of hair oil and scent arranged neatly next to Eduardo's shaving implements, her spare pair of shoes alongside his and her lidded sewing basket on top of a small, glass-fronted bookcase. Both the hastily packed bags she had brought with her were on top of the wooden wardrobe.

Folded on the bed's crocheted coverlet was a nightdress. As soon as she saw it, anticipation began drumming a delicious tattoo on her ribs. Anticipation—and excitement.

Aura didn't have anything that came close to resembling a trousseau, but she had worked through most of the previous day to make herself a version of a Grecian inspired nightdress she had seen in a magazine. The three yards of seafoam green satin it had taken to make it had been a present from María del Mar, who'd convinced Aura that the color was better suited to her darker complexion. A long column of it fell from three pleats right between her breasts. The neckline was a thin webbing of handworked lace that covered the top of her breasts and her shoulders, and fastened at the back with a single satin ribbon, so thin it could fall open at the merest breath.

Aura undressed quickly, draping the dress she had been wearing over the back of one of the two armchairs by the window and sweeping a cool, damp washcloth over her body before slipping on the nightdress.

Catching up her curls into a matching length of satin, she tied it into a bow just as the door opened and Eduardo entered the bedroom.

He was still laughing, his necktie askew and his waistcoat hanging unbuttoned under his jacket. The laughter faded as he closed the door behind him and spotted Aura standing by the bookcase, replaced with a look of stunned appreciation.

Heat rushed over Aura, and she turned to the bookcase to conceal her expression from him.

"Who is this handsome gentleman?" she asked, seizing a tiny silver horse that had been lined up next to a porcelain bowl full of assorted buttons and a dog inexpertly carved out of pale wood.

Eduardo came up to stand behind her, leaving only a whisper of space between his warm body and hers. "His name is Sancho Panza," he said, reaching over Aura's shoulder to tap a miniature flank. "He traveled the world with me as a child and accompanied me to university in Madrid seven years ago." He let his hand rest on her shoulder. "Did you have a good time today? Was it everything you thought it would be?"

"So much more," she told him, striving for honesty even as she shied away from telling Eduardo she had found the unexpected party a little overwhelming, not wanting to sound ungrateful. She turned around to face him. "It really was a lovely day…so extravagant."

That was an understatement. While they were at the registry office, the house had been transformed into a bower. Garlands of greenery adorned doorways and the gold-framed paintings in the parlor, while vases of white roses and orchids and tall sprays of tiny yellow flowers with spotted petals crowded every available surface. Even the columns of the terrace were festooned with gleaming satin ribbons.

And then there was the food.

Tiny meatballs in pineapple sauce, *pastelitos* stuffed with shredded chicken and raisins and fried to a perfect crisp, quail eggs, ham croquettes, delicate tea sandwiches garnished with ingenious flowers carved out of radishes and grape-sized tomatoes, salmon mousses and batata soufflés that puffed proudly out of white porcelain ramekins, all carried by a seemingly never-ending procession of crisply uniformed waiters. Champagne had flowed even more abundantly than at María del Mar's party.

There was no lack of desserts, either. Tables covered in lace tablecloths had been arranged in the terrace and parlor, and all of them held a wide variety of sweets. Cut crystal coupes of enormous proportions were piled high with *polvorones*, round walnut cookies covered in a fine dusting of powdered sugar. Silver bowls filled with ice to protect the brightly colored dishes of sherbet from melting in the day's heat. Trays laid out with slices of layered cake filled with custard cream and decorated with thinly sliced oranges and all kinds of imported delicacies, like marzipan bonbons and squares of *turrón*.

All that abundance in addition to Aura's dress and the

rings made her almost dizzy as she contemplated all the trouble Eduardo had gone to for what was basically an impulsive, last-minute wedding. She had no idea when he had found the time to arrange it all. She couldn't even begin to imagine what Eduardo and his staff might have produced if they'd had the advantage of several months of planning. His household staff were used to entertaining great quantities of people, that was true, but everything about that day had been so excessive that she couldn't help but feel for the added amount of work it had made for everyone.

She had caught a handful of people murmuring to each other or looking at her from behind their fans, but for the most part his friends had been gracious, even welcoming. With the exception of one or two women, who Aura supposed had designs on Eduardo, most of the guests had appeared to be truly happy for him—and as for the women she had met at María del Mar's party, they had outright told Aura how pleased they were at the match. Amalia de Fuentes had even gone so far as saying that she intended to host a dinner party in honor of Aura and Eduardo as soon as Aura had gotten settled in her new home.

A slow, flirtatious smile flared to life on Eduardo's face. "Oh, I see."

Aura tilted her head. "What do you see?"

"You were disappointed that we didn't come up here right away," he replied teasingly. "You spent all day counting down the minutes until you could ravish me."

It was so close to the truth that her heart began pounding.

"I did no such thing," she said loftily, starting to turn.

Eduardo caught her by the hand and tugged her until she was pressed close against his chest. "You can't fool me. I can see how much you want me." He lowered his voice at the same time as his head dipped, so that his next words were delivered to the sensitive skin of her neck. "Only because I want you just as much."

Her pulse sped up and she broke into a smile that Eduardo, occupied with exploring the delicate tracery of lace covering her chest, didn't see.

"That's why you married me, isn't it?" Her hand drifted up to cup the back of his head.

"No," he replied, pulling back just enough so she could see the wicked glint in his eyes. "This is."

And then his lips were brushing hers softly, nudging them open and teasing them with gentle flickers of his tongue.

He tasted like champagne and brandy, and vaguely sweet, as if he had been eating *polvorones* before coming upstairs. Aura licked at his lower lip, relishing in the taste and in the sensation. The faint spiciness of cigar smoke clung to his clothes and hair, though Aura had noticed that he didn't smoke as the other men did.

He pulled away, murmuring huskily, "I did say there would be kissing."

"I can't say I wasn't warned," she replied.

Warm, mellow afternoon sunlight spilled into the room through the open shutters, painting stripes of light on the whitewashed walls, interrupted only by the shadows cast by the tree that grew just outside Eduardo's window.

"Ready to finish what you started under the laurel bush?"

A smolder came into Eduardo's gaze and Aura realized that he wasn't as intoxicated as she had thought, merely drunk on excitement. "You have no idea how ready I am."

His warm hands reached behind her neck, making her shiver as he grazed her sensitive skin. With one firm gesture, he pulled the ribbon that held her nightdress closed and it slid off her shoulders, the fabric pooling at her waist.

His hands spanned her ribs, his thumbs brushing the underside of her breasts as he took in the sight of her.

Aura watched him gaze at her, warmth stealing along her limbs and over her chest and tightening her nipples. Eduardo's thumbs moved up to stroke them. At the hitch in her breath, a devilish smile formed on his mouth and he lowered it to her stiffening nipples.

Her breath did more than hitch this time—it left her entirely.

And so did all the strength in her knees when he released her nipple and breathed on her exposed skin, overwhelming her with sensation.

"I've been wanting this from the moment we met," she murmured, leaning against him for balance.

"How very shocking," he said teasingly. "In a public park?"

"Well, maybe not the exact moment we met."

"Don't you take it back now," he said, laughing. "If I had known, I would have pressed you back against a tree trunk. Released you from that prim little shirtwaist and left you bare and exposed while I reached down to lift your skirt past your knees and—"

Wrenching a handful of his shirt, she pulled him down into a searing kiss. "Enough talking," she gasped. "Haven't you heard that a single action is worth a thousand words?"

"A picture is. But if it's action you want…" Eduardo pulled up her hem and gave her bottom an appreciative squeeze. "I'm only happy to oblige."

Eduardo felt his breath grow unsteady as Aura reached up and carefully undid his necktie. One by one, her quick, clever fingers worked each of his buttons free, until his shirt was open and she could slide her arms around his heated midsection.

Her breasts were pressed against the hard planes of his chest. She must have liked the way it felt, because she rubbed herself lightly on his skin, seeking friction. Holding her loosely by the waist, he watched her eyes flutter closed and a small line appear between her finely arched eyebrows.

Her nightdress was made from some cool, slippery fabric. He couldn't name the exact shade, but the rippling blues and greens reminded him of sweet river water. It struck him that, due to the current fashion for high-necked dresses, this was the first time he had seen her throat uncovered. The sleek, graceful line ended in a little hollow, like a pool he could sip from, her pulse on his lips.

He dragged his mouth lower, wanting to drown in the soft swell of her breasts. He could do it. He could dive in between them and never resurface.

He guided her backward until she was sitting on the edge of the bed, her hardened nipples pushed into prominence as she leaned back on her palms.

Eduardo sank to the floor in front of her, placing her foot on his shoulder so that he could kiss his way up her smooth brown calf. He raised her hem as he went, higher and higher until it skimmed her thighs and gave him a tantalizing glimpse of what lay between them.

He allowed himself one more kiss on the inside of her thigh, just above her knee, before he moved his head back and asked, "Is there anything you want? Or don't want?"

Frustration made her lowered eyelids spring open. "I don't know," she said, looking down at him. "I've never…"

"Then I suppose we'll have to find out together, won't we?"

With his tongue, he traced a wicked arc on her silky skin. In lieu of an answer, Aura let her head fall back.

"Are you—do you—"

Whatever she had been about to say was lost to a deep sigh as he slid both hands up her thighs and gently spread them apart. Her hand was a guiding pressure at the back of his head, stroking his hair even as she urged him closer.

Feeling devilish, Eduardo pulled away slightly. "Can I take that to mean you like it?"

She gave him another narrow-eyed look. "You can take that to mean that I might kick you if you stop again."

"I like a woman who knows what she likes," he murmured, grinning up at her.

He used his thumbs to part her heated flesh and explored her with his lips and tongue. With each of her breathless murmurs, he could feel himself straining harder and harder against the placket of his trousers, but he was too caught up in the ripples and eddies of her pleasure to pay much attention to his own need.

In any case, nothing would have given him more pleasure than to know that she was enjoying herself.

Muttering something that sounded like a curse, she fell back against the mattress. He took the opportunity to slide his hands underneath her and lift her hips up to his mouth.

She jerked against him, using her leg to pull him closer. After a moment, she reached down to twine her hands around his open shirt and urge him up onto the bed with her. He wanted to keep going until he could taste her climax, but he was nothing if not obliging—casting off his shirt and letting it fall to the floor, he joined her on the mattress and tangled their legs together.

"Had enough?" he asked innocently, laughing at her incredulous look.

"How can it ever be enough?"

She cupped her hands on either side of his face, studying his face as his lips quirked into a crooked smile.

"It's never enough," he told her, reaching for her hem. "That's why you do it over and over and over again..."

The nightdress rippled in the afternoon light as he pulled it off her body. He bent over her, scattering kisses on her skin, brushing them over her until she was pleading for him.

For all her inexperience, Aura knew exactly what she liked and she wasn't shy about communicating it. Eduardo moved at her command, matching her rhythm, feeling like he would never have enough of this. He would never have enough of *her*.

What a joy to know that this was merely the beginning. What an unutterable luxury.

Her long, bare legs wrapped around him and Eduardo let himself be carried along in the undulating currents of her desire until she was burying her cries in the crook of his neck.

He stroked the long line of her thigh while her quivers subsided, rocking slowly and gently inside her. They lay side by side, her body warm and relaxed against his. Her hand trailed down his chest, a questioning touch that made him breathe in sharply when it wormed its way between them and her slender fingers closed around his hard flesh. She stroked him as he continued to move in and out of her, his breath growing unsteady.

Eduardo didn't cry out when his climax threatened to overtake him, but he did pull out of her and bury his face in her hair, murmurs falling from his lips that he wasn't sure were lavish promises or desperate curses.

He didn't know how long he lay there, gathering control of his lungs and his heartbeat. His limbs were a hopeless cause, at least for the next few minutes. The only thing that seemed to be working was his mouth, which roamed gently over the curve of her ear as he asked how she was feeling.

"Good," she murmured, shifting into a more comfortable position. "To say the least. That was…"

"Yes."

"Is it always…"

"Not for me," he said, and let out a tired chuckle as she made a noise that was full of self-satisfaction.

Hours later, after he had roused himself long enough to clean her up and offer her a glass of water from the covered pitcher on his bedside table, Eduardo lay back in bed and watched as the cobalt blue of twilight claimed the sky.

Down the hallway, the clock chimed the hour. Eduardo tensed as the sound reverberated through the room, presaging the arrival of night. Aura stirred in his arms, and he relaxed.

She wasn't going anywhere.

Chapter Nine

Eduardo's bedroom was still dark when Aura drifted out of a deep, refreshing slumber, her back pressed against him and his arms encircling her. She'd believed she would find it difficult to sleep with someone else in the bed, no matter how comfortable she found it, but sleep had come with ease after their exertions.

"Are you asleep?" he whispered.

"I'd like to be," she said, but obligingly rolled over and nestled deeper into Eduardo's arms, too drowsy and hazy from their recent intimacy to keep her distance. "Is something troubling you?"

"Everything is right with the world," he said. "But it did just occur to me that I didn't ask whether there was anyone you would have wanted at the reception."

"Oh, I…" Aura shrugged, knowing that Eduardo would feel the gesture even if he couldn't see it in the dark. "I don't think they would have come. There was no time to ask, in any case. Two days wouldn't have been enough notice to make travel arrangements."

"I'm sorry to hear that." She could hear the sincerity in his voice. "You've been alone for a long time, haven't you? Even before your father died."

"I'm used to it." She felt her lips twisting up into a wry smile. "You'd think I'd have learned my lesson."

Aura had been eleven years old the first time she'd lost a friend because of her father.

They had just moved to Puerto Plata, and next to the small house they had rented lived a family with a girl her own age. The two of them became inseparable. About a month or so into their friendship, Aura had discovered that her new friend had been taught how to make various sweets by her grandmother.

They had been agonizing over two dainty pairs of girls' stockings in one of the stores that sold imported goods and quickly came up with the idea to sell sweets to their neighbors.

They started with *dulce de habichuelas*, a dessert made from milk and shucked beans. Making it was a labor-intensive process that required hours of ceaseless stirring while hunched over a blazing fire. By the end of the first day, they'd produced ten waxed paper-lined shoeboxes full of the delicately flavored dessert, which they'd sold for a tidy profit even after accounting for the two pounds of sugar and the expensive vanilla beans and cinnamon they'd had to purchase.

They'd run to Aura's house to count the money, and were sitting happily at the kitchen table with their pile of coins when her father came in. His eyes lit up at the sight and he immediately started working on convincing Aura and her friend to part ways with their hard-earned money.

"If you entrust it to me," he said, his eyes dancing, "I'll make sure that by the end of the week you have triple what you started out with. You'll be rich, without needing to put yourselves through any more work."

Aura's friend had been ambivalent, but Aura was always easily caught in her father's spell, her imagination ignited when he enthusiastically described all the things they could do with their newfound wealth.

In the end, both girls gave up their earnings. And of course, her father's scheme failed—the sacks of coffee he used their money to purchase were full of mold, with a thin layer of good beans on top to hide the quality of the product. The men who'd sold it to him disappeared, as did their associates who had approached her father separately to offer a fantastic price for a certain amount of coffee if he knew anyone who was selling.

The parents of Aura's friend were irate at their daughter's tearful account. It didn't really matter that Aura's father hadn't intended to deceive them and had been cheated himself—he shouldn't have taken the girls' money in the first place.

They'd been right, of course. That didn't make it all the less painful when they instructed their daughter to stay away from Aura. Aura and her family had moved to another town not long after that.

Eduardo dropped a kiss onto her bare shoulder. "You don't have to go through life on your own anymore. You have me—and my entire family."

Aura couldn't reply, at least not immediately. Her throat felt so tight that when she finally spoke, it was almost in a whisper. "I have a family of my own. I have siblings that I haven't seen in years—two younger sisters and a brother. And…and my mother."

"Oh?" Eduardo asked quietly.

"She divorced my father almost three years ago, and moved with my siblings to her sister's house in Santo Domingo. When she made the decision to leave, I didn't react as well as I should. I took my father's side and told her that she'd never had any faith in him and to avoid seeking us out when we did strike it rich." The heaviness in her chest made Aura ache to lay her forehead on his bare shoulder.

Instead, she moved away from him so that her head rested on her own pillow. "I haven't seen any of them since."

Even having moved away, she could feel his solid presence at her side. The heaviness in her chest didn't lift at saying the words out loud, but it did ease somewhat.

The mattress shifted as Eduardo rose up onto an elbow, facing her even though she doubted he could see much more than she could in the dim moonlight coming in through the open shutters. He didn't reach for her, but his unwavering attention gave her the encouragement to continue.

"I convinced myself that he was capable of great things and all he needed was someone to believe in him."

"That kind of loyalty is admirable, Aura."

"And foolish," she said. "Though I'm embarrassed to say it wasn't until several months went by and all his wild dreams failed to materialize that I began to realize that they never would. So I started working harder and harder, seeing for the first time all that my mother had done to make sure that we'd been fed and cared for. She'd kept chickens for the eggs, both for us to eat and to sell. She'd found bachelors without cooks and arranged to make their meals for them, and did their mending. I hadn't even noticed."

"It's not always easy to see what's right beneath our noses. Or give credit to those who deserve it most. I take it you didn't keep chickens or feed bachelors?"

"All I knew how to do was sew. My mother taught my sisters and me how to do fine work when we were very young, and we earned our own pocket money by making silk petals and rosettes for local milliners. Staying in one place for a couple of years meant that I could start building up a clientele and I took all the work that was offered. Last year, though, I fell ill—influenza. My father took excellent care of me, but fever made my eyes ache so badly that I couldn't sew for nearly a month. That's when I decided that I needed to open a store."

"I hope your father supported that dream as unflinchingly as you did his."

Aura shook her head. "Oh, it wasn't grand enough for him. He was disappointed that I had such provincial aspirations. I could give myself a squint sewing dresses for other women to wear, or I could hand over my savings for him to invest in this once-in-a-lifetime deal and in a month at most I'd be the one having silk gowns fitted at the finest Parisian couturier."

"What did he think was such a good investment it warranted spending all your savings?"

Aura scraped a hand over her face. "I can hardly remember now. It was always something or another—coffee beans that turned out to be moldy, refurbished sewing machines that broke within a day of use... I believe at one point he tried to peddle some horrible tonic that was supposed to cure baldness and ended up being nothing more than peanut oil. He believed in all of it, you know. And he'd scoff at me when I told him that gold and property were the only things worth investing in."

"Not silk stockings?" Eduardo asked. "Or champagne?"

"Stockings and champagne aren't investments—they're indulgences."

"Necessities," he said. "For the spirit, at least. A person can't live on gold and property alone."

"So impractical," she chided softly.

"Is it? I was raised to believe that beauty and comfort are as needed as water and air."

"Not when your tin roof leaks and you haven't eaten in two days and are hiding from the butcher and the fishmonger," Aura said automatically, then wished she hadn't.

She may have confided in Eduardo about the difficulties of living with her father, but she hadn't meant to expose the hardest parts of their poverty to someone who'd never experienced anything similar. Not because she thought it was beyond his understanding, but only because it felt disloyal to share how much they had actually struggled.

Lightly, she added, "We had our fill of champagne and chocolates when we could. And I did eventually convince him to buy the house. Though I'm not sure what will happen to it now that Rafael Marchena claims that my father gave him the deed in exchange for a loan."

"I'll look into it," Eduardo promised her. "In the meantime, my solid roof is yours." His head dipped low so that his breath trailed along the shell of her ear. "And I have all the exotic fruit you could want. Shall I tell you about the shipment of Anjou pears we're receiving sometime this week?"

His hand landed on her hip. Aura turned into the touch, angling herself so that her mouth met his when he lowered his head farther.

The second time was slower than their first urgent joining. Afterward, she lay awake for a long time, watching the room lighten around her.

Her father had been wrong. Contentment was only to be found in other people. That was the riches a person should aspire to—the comfort of companionship and friendship, and safety of having someone in one's corner when push came to shove. Not the money, and definitely not all the trappings of elegance he thought were so important.

If Eduardo did nothing else with his life, he was going to make damn sure that Aura had property and gold as well as silk stockings and champagne and all the exotic fruit in the world.

The welcome weight of her in the mattress beside him greeted him as he awoke the next morning. She was lying on her stomach, her head pillowed on one slim forearm, the ring he had placed on her finger glinting in the morning sunshine. She must have kicked at the blanket in her sleep, because her legs were bare and dark against the sun-bleached white of the bedsheets.

The slippery nightdress she had worn the night before was folded neatly at the foot of the bed, though Eduardo remembered leaving it pooled on the floor, next to the silky head wrap that had bound her thick curls. At some point during the night, she had retrieved that, too, and retied it.

Her eyelids began to flutter. Folding an arm behind his head, Eduardo shifted his gaze to the window behind her so that she wouldn't wake to the disconcerting sight of him staring.

Her murmured "Good morning" came a few seconds later. Eduardo replied in kind, rolling onto his side to place a kiss just below her ear, which she received with a lazy curl of her lips. She skimmed the scar on his collarbone with her fingertips, but instead of leaning in for another kiss, she let out a soft noise and headed for the adjoining lavatory.

Eduardo waited several minutes. When it became clear that she was getting ready for the day, he went into the bathroom to investigate.

She was at the sink, washing her face with something that smelled faintly of violets. Her nightdress was still at the foot of their bed—in the morning light coming in bars through the shutters, her bare brown skin looked gilded.

Eduardo stepped up behind her and pressed his body against her back, sliding his arms around her and dipping his face into the place where her shoulders met her neck. "Come back to bed. I don't like it there without you."

"It's almost seven," she said, scandalized.

Eduardo laughed at her shock. "It's the day after your wedding—after your wedding night. No one would blame you if you stayed in bed, say, until eight o'clock." He nipped at her neck. "Or even later."

Eduardo would have wagered his entire fortune that if her skin hadn't been as dark as his, she would have been blushing fiercely. She started to say something, reconsidered, started again and finally settled for saying, "Hand me a towel, please."

Now laughing in earnest, Eduardo stepped back to reach for the towels folded on the stool by the bathtub, noticing as he did that there was a small rectangular rug under his feet that hadn't been there before. It was made up of dozens of strips of fabric in muted greens and blues.

He toed the corner he had kicked up back into place. "That's new."

"To catch drips," Aura explained, reaching for her toothbrush.

"Did you make it?"

"I had help."

"Not María del Mar?" Eduardo asked doubtfully, unable to imagine his hellion of a cousin engaged in such a pursuit.

She shook her head, a small smile playing on her lips. "Gregorio. He wanted one for Celia and I told him it would be more meaningful if he made it himself. All I had to do was show him how to pull the strips of fabric through the backing and he turned into an instant expert."

Eduardo laughed as he sprinkled first her toothbrush and then his own with Colgate's Antiseptic Dental Powder, another product his family imported by the crates for their own use. "Sounds like him."

A few seconds of quiet followed as they brushed their

teeth in tandem, the quotidian routine rendered almost fun by the sheer novelty of doing it with someone else. Their eyes met in the mirror, and Aura raised a quizzical eyebrow.

Eduardo rinsed and slid his toothbrush into its holder. "I've never had company while brushing my teeth before. I can't believe I waited so long to get married."

"And I can't believe you maligned your friends for doing just that."

"Clearly, they're all much smarter than I am." He reached for her again, too fascinated with the suppleness of her nude body to bother practicing restraint. "And I didn't know what I was missing."

She leaned into his touch, as eager as he was, tilting up her head so that he could graze her lips with his own.

This was an interesting development and one he hadn't foreseen, even considering the passion inherent in the kisses they had shared. He'd have married Aura even if there hadn't been this urgent heat between them, for all the reasons he had given her—but the fact that their bodies seemed to crave each other's was a pleasant benefit.

It made things almost simpler, in a way. Not because he thought that physical desire would mask any sentimental stirrings either of them might feel, because he knew that Aura wished to avoid those as much as he did. If anything, this attraction between them might even help them remain strong on that point—after all, the more consuming the physical nature of their relationship, the less need there would be to complicate it with any romantic notions.

He waited until her mouth parted before sliding the tip of his tongue along the sinuous curve of her lower lip. Her arms crept around his neck, her breasts pressed against his chest, and Eduardo slid a hand slowly, luxuriously down from the small of her back, over the swell of her hips and over the length of her thigh—

A sudden knock at the door had her pelting back to the bed and diving under the covers.

Eduardo let out a bark of laughter. "It's just the breakfast tray I requested yesterday, as I thought you would want to sleep in this morning."

Her voice was muffled by the cotton sheets. "Sleeping in is for dissolute aristocrats and people with poor health."

He pulled on a pair of trousers before he went to accept the silver tray from the housemaid who had brought it upstairs.

"Gracias, and good morning," he said. "Is your mother any better?"

The young woman nodded. "She's improving, Don Eduardo, thanks to the tonic you sent her. She wants to make you some of her baked kibbeh to show her gratitude."

"Tell her I'm looking forward to it."

Closing the door, he laid the heavy tray at the foot of the bed, telling Aura, "You can come out now."

Cautiously, she lowered one end of the blanket. It came the rest of the way down when she saw the food.

Having noticed that Aura seemed to prefer a singular bowl of oatmeal in the mornings, he'd asked the cook to make sure to prepare her some with brown sugar, cinnamon and the apples that had come in his grandfather's latest shipment.

She dipped a sterling silver spoon into it, eyes widening when she tasted the finely chopped apples. "This is incredible. I don't think I've had this fruit before. What is it?"

"Apple. There's a whole barrel of them in the kitchen whenever you want more."

The tray also held a plate with the squares of fried cheese, pork sausages and hot, buttered triangles of toast that Eduardo favored, as well as two cups of coffee and the covered silver bowl filled with sugar. Eduardo started with the coffee, adding sugar and cream to his cup and handing Aura the other one when she shook her head.

This late in the morning, the sun was angled in such a way that the tree outside his window cast shadows shaped like leaves on the bed's white sheets and on the gleaming brown skin of her shoulders. She looked like she belonged on his bed. Like some kind of flower that had sprouted there overnight.

Spreading a thin piece of toast with some of the imported preserves that lined the shelves in the pantry, Eduardo offered it to her. "If you don't intend to lie in bed all day like dissolute aristocrats and people suffering from poor health, what were you hoping to do with your day?"

She nibbled at the edge of the toast and set it on one side of the tray before returning to her oatmeal. "Well, I have plenty of sewing to do. And… I believe I might take a bath."

"Aura, did you marry me for my bathroom?"

"How ever did you know?" she asked, her eyes bright with humor.

The modern lavatory was one of three that had been put in only a few years before, when they'd converted an unused bedroom and a large linen closet. This one had two doors so that it could be accessed both from Eduardo's room and from the hallway—that way, anyone who came in to clean it or to bring up the kettles of hot water required to fill the tub didn't have to go through his bedroom.

It was an exact match to the bathroom in the suite at the Paris Ritz where Eduardo and his grandfather had stayed the last time they had visited the city of lights. Everything, including the claw-foot tub, the enamel and brass sink, the sconces flanking the mirror, and even the pale blue tiles, had been shipped over from abroad at enormous cost to his grandfather. As a courtesy to his frequent houseguests, Eduardo kept all three bathrooms amply stocked with all kinds of fragrant soaps and bath oils.

"You wouldn't be the first woman to want to marry me for my bathroom," he told her, laughing. "Just the only one who succeeded."

The bedsheet she was wearing slipped down, exposing the upper curve of her breast, and Eduardo nudged it farther down so that he could stroke her satiny skin. She straightened subtly, and the sheet fell lower.

That was all it took for Eduardo to abandon his breakfast and dive into her, careful of the tray as he pressed her back into the pillows and rained kisses on her neck and shoulders.

"I thought you were hungry," she said, wriggling under him.

"Starving," he told her, and delicately bit her shoulder.

After finishing their breakfast, Eduardo got dressed and took the tray downstairs himself for the express purpose of arranging her bath. Half an hour later, he was leading an amused Aura to the bathroom.

Bars of sunlight filtered in through the half-closed shutters, but the room was dim enough to make the glow of the candles he had placed around the bathtub stand out. He'd sent a couple of housemaids to collect every single taper they could find around the house, in their respective candlesticks. Gleaming brass and polished silver reflected the flickering tongues of flame rising from each wick. The bathtub was full of gently steaming water, perfumed with lavender soap, bright curls of orange peel and the herbs he had clipped from the garden himself, grateful that he had paid attention to all the botanical lessons his grandfather had dispensed over the years.

"What do you think?" he asked Aura as she paused in the doorway to take in the sight.

He was looking, too, only it wasn't the candles and flowers that had captured his attention. It was the smile blooming on Aura's face, which for the first time since he had met her, spoke of nothing but bright, straightforward happiness.

And he'd been the one to make it happen.

"I think," Aura said, turning toward him and reaching for the buttons of his shirt, "that you had better join me."

Chapter Ten

The sounds of a party awoke Aura from a deep slumber.

She fumbled her way out of bed, wrapping a light cotton shawl around herself as she crept down the hallway. The music seemed to be coming from the upstairs parlor, and as she passed the grandfather clock, she saw that it was almost three in the morning.

Her first thought was that Eduardo, who had sent a messenger to tell her that he wouldn't be able to make it home in time for dinner, had forgotten that he was not still a bachelor and had brought a group of friends over for some late-night carousing.

But when she followed the music to the upstairs parlor, she found it empty save for her husband and a phonograph. His head was pillowed on ledgers and letters and a precariously balanced inkpot, and he was fast asleep.

Until the sound of the record skipping jolted him awake and he sat bolt upright.

Aura placed a hand on his shoulder, unable to resist giving him a soothing caress through the fine material of his shirt. "Shh. It's just me."

He rubbed a hand over his face, then reached over and switched off the phonograph. "I'm sorry if I woke you— Gregorio's so used to the noise, I forgot you wouldn't also be able to sleep through it."

"I thought you were having a party."

He shook his head. "I can't concentrate when it's too quiet and I still had a great deal of work to finish. But don't worry, if the music bothers you, I won't turn it back on."

"It doesn't bother me." Aura threaded her fingers through his hair, half-guiltily telling herself that she meant nothing more than to arrange his disordered curls. "I could bring my sewing in here and keep you company."

"Are you making another one of those fetching nightdresses for yourself?" he asked as a gleam of interest replaced the sleepiness in his eyes. One of his hands began to roam over the thin, half-translucent cotton of the nightdress she was wearing. It was nothing like the one she had made for their wedding night, but it was pretty enough, decorated with ribbons threaded through eyelet lace.

"A shirtwaist," she said absently as Eduardo nuzzled her stomach. She placed a hand on top of his head and glanced at the documents illuminated by the spill of lamplight on the table. "What are you working on?"

"A new project." Eduardo looked up at her. "When Lucía and her husband, Leo, stayed at Abuelo's house in Santo Domingo, he and I came up with a venture that I think will become extremely profitable in time. Leo is part owner of a sugar mill, you see. He'd been looking to purchase a ship to export the sugar they produced, but he knew very little about the business and had no experience with ships."

"And you do."

Eduardo hummed his assent into her side. "The partnership made sense. And it's been working out so far."

"Is there a reason why you're doing it on your own instead of through Martínez & Hijos? With the way sugar prices continue to rise, it seems like a sound investment."

"Have you any idea how delightful it is that you know

about sugar prices?" Eduardo demanded, planting a kiss on her rib cage before releasing her and sitting back in his chair with his hands twined behind his head. "My grandfather has always believed it's less of a risk if all the company does is transport merchandise for other people. He has no interest in the speculation involved in purchasing stock to export or import—beyond the delicacies he brings back for the family's various households."

"And you think you could convince him to expand operations if your venture proves to be profitable?"

Eduardo picked up his gold-and-black pen again and began fiddling with it. "I had hoped to take this venture on myself. But since I'm close to the limit of my personal finances—"

"Because you gave all your money away to young pickpockets and impecunious dressmakers?" she asked tartly.

"Because my grandfather still controls the bulk of the Martínez fortune as well as my inheritance from my maternal grandparents," he explained, before breaking out into a rueful smile. "Because he knows that I'd give most of it away to young pickpockets and impecunious dressmakers if left to my own devices. In any case, it makes financial sense to solicit capital from my grandfather instead of a bank. The only problem is that Gregorio and I have spent the past couple of years making a case for how reliable we can be—I can't ruin our hard work by running off and taking risks with the company's funds."

"You wouldn't consider another investor?"

"If the right person came long, I might. With Leo moving to Vienna soon, though, I need to get our affairs in order. Aura, how would you feel about paying a visit to Leo and Lucía in a few months, once they've gotten settled and the business is running smoothly? We'd stop in Madrid and

Paris as well, of course—this time next year, you could be selecting stock for your store in person, from the best European manufacturers. I know we never talked about a honeymoon, but you'd like that, wouldn't you?"

Eduardo's family owned an entire fleet of ships. Even if Aura hadn't known that, the casual way Eduardo had spoken about travel would have alerted her to the fact that he found it as easy as a visit to the corner store. She just hadn't realized that it now included her.

And she hadn't realized that he would be interested in something so traditionally…romantic. Could he possibly have changed his mind about the nature of their arrangement?

The possibility sent a rush of electricity up her spine. She didn't—she wasn't—

She couldn't think clearly this close to him.

"I…" Aura bit her lip briefly. "I think I'm distracting you when you should be working. Let me go get my sewing basket—I'll be right back."

She quickly returned to their bedroom and, carefully draping a pinned-up bodice over one arm, she took a deep, steadying breath. Of course Eduardo hadn't changed his mind. And neither had she, regardless of the way her body responded to his touch. Or his proximity. Or the mere sight of him in his shirtsleeves and tousled curls.

Lifting her sewing basket from where she had stowed it in the wardrobe, she returned to the upstairs parlor.

He glanced up at her entry. Something came over his expression—an appreciation, or perhaps it was simple gratitude. Aura didn't know why he should feel that way about such a small thing, except… Eduardo didn't seem to like being alone.

Aura had always been a light sleeper, and in the three

nights they had spent together, she had noticed Eduardo's tendency to startle awake, his body rigid with tension, until she made some subtle noise or movement that reminded him she was lying next to him. It had happened again the night before, and Aura had been hesitant to mention it.

But as she came through the open doorway, she remembered what he'd told her on that first night in the garden—that he spent most nights at drinking establishments or friends' houses.

Was that why? Because he hated being alone?

Was that the real reason why he'd married her?

As she passed by his chair, Aura nodded at the phonograph. "Do you need the music to stay awake? I don't mind it, if you're sure it wouldn't disturb anyone else."

Eduardo shook his head. "Gregorio could sleep through a hurricane, and the staff bedrooms are too far away. But I don't need the music if you're here."

"So it's the lack of company you dislike, not the quiet?"

Aura couldn't miss how quickly his shoulders grew rigid with tension.

"You can leave your sewing things here, you know," he said, utterly ignoring her question as he frowned down at his expensive pen. He opened an ink bottle, then seemed to think better of it and set it aside. "Heaven knows Gregorio and María del Mar leave all manner of things strewn around."

Aura, who was in the act of moving a catalog aside so that she could sit, raised an eyebrow and said, "I noticed."

The truth was, she found the cheerful chaos of the family room much more appealing than the elegance of the public rooms. The amateur landscapes and the humorous portraits María del Mar had drawn of her relatives and pasted onto the whitewashed wall above the bookcase might not have been as elegant as the opulently framed oil paintings downstairs, but they made the room all the homier. The rattan chairs with their flowered cushions, the multitude of plants and books and musical instruments…it looked like she'd always believed a home should.

Lifting her gaze from the work on her lap, Aura examined him through the veil of her lashes. He was humming under his breath as he scratched out figures on a scrap of paper, looking much more awake. It hardly seemed possible that someone could be so handsome in shirtsleeves and ink-stained fingers. Or that the mere sight of someone could lift her spirits so high.

Eduardo glanced over at her and caught her staring. "Enjoying the sight?"

"Just wondering if you have any mending for me to do," she said loftily.

His smile broadened, his teeth a bright flash in the dim room. "Not on anything that I'm currently wearing. Would you like to check?"

"Of course not, I'm terribly busy," she told him, her gaze firmly on the shirtwaist. "And so are you."

But it was impossible to hide how much she liked his teasing, or how it forged small moments of closeness between them. She loved those moments—craved them, even, as much as she craved the intoxicating thrill of Eduardo's hands on her.

Closeness wasn't love, but it was satisfying in its own way—and not nearly as risky. And knowing each other better could only help them be better partners to each other.

Aura pulled a threaded needle from its pincushion. "Have you always had trouble sleeping?"

"I don't have trouble sleeping," Eduardo replied swiftly. The abruptness with which he abandoned his teasing tone and returned his gaze to the papers in front of him made Aura blink. "But I do have a great deal of work to get through tonight, if you'll excuse me."

He hadn't spoken harshly, but the finality in his tone put miles of distance between them.

Eduardo was no stranger to pushing himself beyond his limits, but when he caught Aura stifling one yawn after another, he decided he might as well stop working, if only because it was almost five in the morning and Aura tended to start her day as the sun started its climb over the horizon.

Daylight usually found her dressed and hard at work, hands moving deftly as she twisted ribbons into rosettes and mended their pillowcases and plied endless stitches into pieces of fabric that turned into garments under her hands.

Eduardo had already asked Gregorio to order her a sewing machine from one of his catalogs.

Covering a yawn of his own, Eduardo tidied up his papers and cleaned the ink off his pen nib with a little wiper Aura had made for him the day before. He switched off all the lamps but one, then went to her chair and held out a hand.

She slid her needle through a fold of fabric and tried to set her sewing aside before returning the mass of fabric back to her lap with a jerk.

"What's wrong?" he asked.

A drowsy frown appeared between her dark brows. "I think I sewed the shirtwaist to my nightdress."

She lifted it in illustration, and they both blinked as the filmy white fabric of her nightdress rose with it.

"Then we'll just have to leave the nightdress, won't we?"

He waited for her to snip the thread and spear her needle through a felt pincushion before pulling her to her feet.

Reaching for her hem, he dragged the light fabric up with his fingertips, making her shiver as he brushed the gentle swell below her navel and the sides of her breasts. Her nightgown was a flirty thing, made out of dreams and whispers, and it floated to the floor and into a patch of moonlight.

"What are you doing?" she murmured sleepily as he scooped her into his arms.

"Taking you to bed."

"I'm too old to be carried."

Her attempt at indignation was interrupted by a yawn that gusted into Eduardo's neck, just above his loosened collar.

"Don't worry," he said. "I'll let you carry me next time."

"You might be trying to be funny, but I'd wager anything I can do it."

"Aura," Eduardo murmured, "I have no doubt you can do anything at all."

"Look at you," she said dreamily. "The consummate bachelor. The envy of all your married friends."

"Was that what I said? It might have been the other way around."

She was asleep by the time he laid her on their bed and covered her with a thin, cotton blanket.

Eduardo couldn't count the number of evenings he had spent at restaurants and at friends' homes, lingering long after the last guest had left, just to avoid returning to a dark and quiet house. He had fallen asleep at concert halls as symphonic music filled the air around him. He had napped through operas and the liveliest theatrical performances. But he had never slept so well or so deeply as when he lay in bed next to Aura, her soft breath in his ears and her arm flung around his chest.

He still awoke in the middle of the night. But when he

did, all he had to do was turn to see Aura with her head nestled on her pillow, her profile bathed in moonlight, and then he would fall asleep again as easily as if his dreams had never been chased with nightmares.

She had noticed—of course she had. Aura was nothing if not perceptive. And Eduardo knew that she hadn't meant anything by asking. Under different circumstances, he wouldn't have minded confiding in her about the nights he had spent locked alone in the cabin of a ship on his way back from New York, his own ragged breaths loud in the silent darkness.

He'd been twelve years old and it had been bad enough that his parents had found their life there too important to accompany him back to the island, hiring instead a distant cousin to take him.

Merely thinking about it seemed to cast him right back to that cabin—talking about it felt close to impossible. Slamming the door shut on the whole business was the only way he'd found to avoid being caught in the grip of terror.

He'd explain that to her, too, if he could. He would have done anything for Aura.

Everything, save put himself back in that cabin.

Chapter Eleven

$\mathcal{The}$ next day, a crate of fruit arrived at the house.

Eduardo had opted to arrive late at the office in favor of spending an extra couple of hours in bed, catching up on sleep after his and Aura's late night. So it wasn't until he went into the kitchen to beg the housekeeper for a second cup of coffee that he saw it, perched innocuously on the table next to a brace of plantain.

His heart leaped at the sight—mostly with joy, but there was some apprehension at the fact that he hadn't been able to make any more progress in finding answers regarding the smuggling scheme. Granted, it had only been a few days—but he had to admit to himself that the reason he'd failed to even try to unearth more information was entirely because he'd been too wrapped up in Aura.

Still, he probably had time to—

The rumble of a carriage on the drive cut that particular thought short.

"I should have known he'd come," Eduardo muttered.

"Can you blame him?"

At the sound of his cousin's exasperated voice, Eduardo turned to see Gregorio—who should have long since left for the office—standing in the doorway. They hadn't really had a chance to speak in private since the day before Eduardo's and Aura's wedding—something that Eduardo had done on purpose after Gregorio had tried to voice his objections the night Eduardo and Aura had announced that they really were getting married.

"You got married on a whim and communicated the news via a telegram," Gregorio continued. "Of course he was going to rush to San Pedro to see what possessed you. I've been wondering the same thing myself. Eduardo, you didn't get married out of some misguided notion of arranging it so that I could marry Celia, did you?"

"Do you really think I'd do something so boneheaded as getting married just so you could?" Eduardo scoffed, then reached out to ruffle his cousin's tight curls.

Gregorio dodged him in one practiced move, the frown still between his brows. "Maybe not entirely. But, Eduardo, you've known Aura for less than two weeks. I know you have a penchant for rescuing anyone you perceive to be in distress, but—"

Eduardo interrupted his cousin before he could begin to ask any more uncomfortable questions. "I didn't rescue anyone. Aura is twenty-five years old. She knows her own mind as well as I know mine, and we both entered this marriage with full awareness of what we were about to do."

"I'm not trying to be difficult, or to imply that you made a mistake." Biting his lip, Gregorio took off his spectacles to polish them with the handkerchief he pulled out of his pocket. "I just—"

"You're just trying to be protective. I know that and I'm grateful, but there's no need for it, not this time. Now, come on. Let's not make Abuelo wait."

Without waiting for Gregorio to reply, Eduardo headed toward the front of the house. His grandfather had been helped out of the carriage and was now striding into the house with the aid of a handsome wooden cane.

There was a new frailness to the old man that made Eduardo's heart race inside his chest. Less than a month had passed since Eduardo had seen him—when had his silvery hair grown so white?

"I got your telegram," his grandfather announced after he had greeted both Eduardo and Gregorio, who had followed Eduardo to the front of the house, with hearty parts on the back. "What's this about a wedding? You couldn't have waited for me, little boy?"

He didn't seem angry or hurt, just perplexed. Eduardo stuck his hands in his pockets and shrugged, feeling a little guilty for dissembling as he said, "When the heart speaks, all you can do is listen, Abuelo."

"And yours told you to rush into marriage without so much as introducing your betrothed to your family?" Leaning on his cane, he gave Eduardo a scrutinizing look. "It's not like you to be reckless, or even impulsive. What's wrong? She's not in trouble, is she?"

Eduardo barely had time for a quick and mostly sincere denial—the only trouble involved in his and Aura's marriage was the not-so-small matter of smuggling that he couldn't reveal to his grandfather—before the old man's gaze shifted to the staircase behind Eduardo.

Aura had chosen that moment to run lightly downstairs. Dressed in white and black, her waist cinched with a black leather belt, her hair pulled back in a simple arrangement at the nape of her neck…there was nothing in her appearance to make the three of them pause and stare.

But her eyes brightened with genuine interest when she saw the visitor, and her smile caught the light, and she seemed to be opening up like a flower unfurling its petals to the sun.

Eduardo snuck a quick look at his grandfather, amused

that the old man was as transfixed as Eduardo had been a moment before. He could only hope that his *abuelo* would find Aura's demeanor as captivating as her looks—and that if he disapproved of the marriage, he wouldn't disapprove of Eduardo's wife.

Holding out his hand to Aura, he helped her down the last couple of steps. "Abuelo, I'd like you to meet Aureliana Soriano. Aura, my grandfather, Amable Martínez."

"Don Amable, it's such a pleasure to meet you," Aura said warmly, extending her hand. "I'd been looking forward to getting to know the man who put together such a lovely garden."

Her stark white shirtwaist was softened with a collar embroidered with minute violet flowers, and Eduardo didn't miss the way his grandfather took in this marker of mourning. "Not nearly as much as I have looked forward to meeting you, my dear," his grandfather said, taking Aura's hand and holding it for a long moment.

Eduardo needn't have worried.

Aura's natural reserve seemed to melt away under his grandfather's gallantry. Eduardo couldn't have said who'd charmed who. All he knew was that by the end of the day, both Aura and his *abuelo* appeared to be as fond of each other as if they had been acquainted for years.

Dessert finished, Aura excused herself to head upstairs to bed—mostly, Eduardo thought, as a tactful way to give him and his grandfather a little time to speak privately.

Feeling pleasantly hazy after post-dinner liqueurs, Eduardo sat sprawled across from his grandfather at the wrought iron table in the private garden. Gregorio had dined with his fiancée and her family that night and still hadn't returned, so it was just Eduardo and his grandfather now that Aura had gone upstairs.

"It's about time you found happiness," the old man said with a heavy sigh, setting his Fernet aside. "I've worried about you, you know—I know how difficult things have been for you ever since your parents—"

"Abuelo," Eduardo began, and stopped. He didn't want to discuss his parents.

"Gregorio has made his own life. I had begun to wonder if something was holding you back. I'm pleased to see that's not the case."

Eduardo didn't often find himself at a loss for words. He had never lied to his grandfather, not even by omission. And he didn't think he was lying now when he said, "Aura is everything I could have hoped for."

His grandfather nodded. "She certainly seems like a good match for you. Would it have been wiser to wait until you were both better acquainted? Or at least long enough for your aunts to help her plan a proper wedding."

"I know it was unseemly to rush. But Aura has no family, and no one to protect her. I didn't want to waste any time."

The old man nodded along to his explanation, though something in his gaze made Eduardo suspect that the old man knew there was something more to the whole affair.

He didn't demand any explanations, though. And that, more than anything, confirmed to Eduardo that maybe his grandfather did trust his judgment. But if that trust was based on deception rather than honestly earned…did Eduardo really want it?

Leaving Eduardo to share one last glass of aperitif with his grandfather in the garden, Aura went upstairs to ready herself for bed.

She'd never had the opportunity to meet her own grandparents. Her mother's parents had died long before Aura had been born, and her father's parents had disowned him after one of his schemes had brought scandal and disgrace to their doorstep.

The hours she had spent with Eduardo's grandfather had made her wistful for what she'd never had. Not that she hadn't liked Don Amable for himself—he was intelligent and interesting and generous when it came to sharing his knowledge. His easy grace had reminded her of Eduardo, in fact. It was easy to see from whom he had gotten his way with people.

She had bathed and slipped on her nightdress and was sitting in bed, wrapping her hair, when Eduardo came into their bedroom.

"My grandfather has informed me that there's to be a ball," he said, dropping onto the edge of the mattress.

He started to reach for his tie, and Aura interceded before he could pull it, scooting forward in the bed and swiftly undoing the knot. "What's the occasion?" she asked as she pulled the tie free and rolled up neatly.

"To celebrate our marriage, he says. Though knowing him, it's also to show society that there was nothing unseemly about our scandalously hasty wedding."

Eduardo said it with his usual humor, but Aura sensed the worry behind his tone.

"Do you wish we had waited?" she asked softly, drawing up her knees and pleating a fold of the blanket between her fingers.

"Because of a little gossip?" Eduardo scoffed. "I have faced fiercer and more brutal foes than a handful of debutantes whispering behind their fans."

He fell sideways into her, making her laugh breathlessly as she tried to wriggle out from underneath his heavy weight. With a resounding kiss on the side of her neck,

Eduardo let her up after a few moments and stood to continue undressing.

"I hope it's all right with you that I said yes to the ball. I can't bear to disappoint the old man. He's done so much for me...he raised me alone, you know, after my grandmother died. My aunts and uncles helped, but he was the one who took on most of the work. Speaking of whom, it seems that Abuelo telegraphed the rest of the family with instructions that they should stay away until the ball, so as not to overwhelm you. So it looks like you'll have a reprieve."

He went over to the door to the lavatory and paused her, gazing back at her speculatively. "I'm going to take a bath. You wouldn't want to join me, would you?"

"I'm in my nightdress," she protested.

But she slid out from under the covers and went to join him. When she reached the doorway where Eduardo still stood, he clasped her loosely by the waist. Even though he hadn't said anything, Aura could tell that something was bothering him.

She bit her lip, debating over whether to ask. He had made it more than clear that he didn't appreciate her prying into private matters. She wanted to respect his wishes, but after sharing so much of her own past and fears and hopes for the future, knowing so little about him felt...uneven.

Cautiously, she asked, "I thought the day went well. Did your grandfather have any complaints?"

He squeezed her gently before letting go of her waist and going the rest of the way into the bathroom, where the tub had already been filled by one of the industrious housemaids.

"Not a single one. My grandfather loved you—he spent the past quarter of an hour making plans for when you visit his Santo Domingo estate." Without giving her a chance to answer, he went on. "Abuelo will return in a couple of weeks. He'll need a hand with the preparations for the ball, if you have any time to spare and are so inclined. I told him I could handle the preparations, but he said something extremely uncomplimentary about my party-planning skills."

"I'd be happy to do anything I can." Aura shifted a stack of clean towels to the sink and perched on the low stool where they'd rested.

Lifting the kettle, Eduardo poured its contents into the cool water already in the tub and stepped inside. As he submerged himself, Aura dipped a washcloth into the water and rubbed it briskly with soap before passing it to him.

She wanted Eduardo with a voraciousness that scared her. She wanted to step into the warmth of the tub and find her place in his arms where she could lean back against his chest and let him trail the washcloth over her arms and breasts. She ached to pull him out and lead him, dripping, into their bed, and she wanted to stay there for hours and ignore the world outside their bedroom door and forget that she'd ever had any troubles.

And that was exactly why she couldn't.

Lazily extending a hand, he dribbled warm water onto her knee. "Are you sure I can't tempt you?"

The droplets sank into the fine white fabric, rendering it transparent where it clung to her skin. It must have distracted her, because she spoke without thinking. "You tempt me all day long. Even when you're not here."

Eduardo's gaze heated. "That's only fair, seeing as my mind is always filled with thoughts of you."

"How productive," she remarked lightly. "It's a wonder Gregorio hasn't thrown you out of the office yet."

"Well, he almost did today." Seeming to understand her unspoken desire to reroute the conversation from its current path, Eduardo launched into a story about something that had happened that afternoon, in the handful of hours during which he and his grandfather had gone to the office.

Aura listened to him, smiling and commenting in all the right places even though she was silently reminding herself that she hadn't been swept away. That she hadn't gotten too attached to Eduardo and his family. That she was still in control of herself.

But she was all too aware that her self-control was beginning to fray. With every day spent around Eduardo and the other Martínezes, she was falling more and more in love with the idea of belonging among them. She would have rather come by them honestly, but after spending the day with Don Amable she was just happy to have them.

For most of her life, she had been filled with the yearning that came from always being on the outside, looking in. That had only grown stronger after her mother and siblings had left.

And now it was as though Eduardo had taken her by the hand and pulled her into the light and laughter. She had always expected to make her own way in the world. More than that—she wanted to. She wanted to live a life where she relied only on herself, because that meant that she would never be disappointed. But Eduardo wasn't just making himself useful. He was making himself indispensable. In less than two weeks, Aura had become so used to the weight of him on the mattress beside her that she felt disoriented when she turned over to find him gone.

Far from making her feel secure, she just felt all the more vulnerable.

Chapter Twelve

Lingering over breakfast at home for the sole purpose of watching Aura smile sleepily into a cup of hot chocolate had put Eduardo slightly behind schedule, so it wasn't until almost ten in the morning that he reached Martínez & Hijos.

Exchanging greetings and lighthearted remarks with the clerks, he strode into the office he shared with Gregorio and riffled impatiently through the correspondence that had been placed there earlier. Most of it was business, but there were a few personal letters that had made their way to the office instead of his home—including one envelope with foreign stamps that made his stomach clench.

Another letter from his parents that he didn't intend to open. Part of him wanted to toss it out the window, but he made do with flipping the envelope into an open drawer instead.

Jerking the drawer shut with his foot, Eduardo started when he noticed someone in the doorway.

"I hope I'm not interrupting," Aura said.

At the first sight of her dark brown eyes, Eduardo felt his spirits rising. He was aware that he was beginning to feel insatiable about her—the more time he spent with her, the more he craved to be around her. It was making it damn hard to carry out his usual duties—but he was quick to reassure himself that it was only physical desire, nothing more.

"Not in the slightest," he told her, rising from his seat as he beckoned her into the room. Whereas his cousin's desk was neatly arranged, with everything at right angles, Eduardo's side of the office could only be described as cheerful chaos. He'd have to clear off a spot for her to sit. "What happened? I thought Gregorio was letting you take the carriage to call on Lucía."

"I am," she said. "I was."

"But you stopped by because the urge to see me again overpowered all rational thought?"

Sliding a hand into her pocket, Aura produced a short stub of wood with a broken point. "Actually, I was hoping to borrow a pencil for taking measurements."

"That's a good excuse," he said approvingly. "I'll definitely be taking notes from you."

"Then I hope your pencils are in a better state than mine."

Eduardo reached for a can full of pencils of varying lengths and held them out to Aura with a flourish. "A bouquet for madame."

Looking amused, she picked out a pencil. Eduardo dropped the rest back into the can and held out his hand for it, gesturing to the metal sharpener fixed to a corner of his desk. As he inserted the tip and began turning the crank, Aura leaned forward to peer at the corkboard on the wall behind his desk.

Crammed to near overflowing, the wide board had started out as a place to pin anything that needed his immediate attention. Over time, it had become a repository of maps and notes and telegrams and even a photograph or two.

"I hadn't realized that Martínez & Hijos had offices in Puerto Plata," she remarked.

She was standing so close that the smell of ink, paper and seawater that filled the office was replaced with her fresh, green scent. The aroma was so intoxicating that Eduardo was finding it hard to come up with a reason why he shouldn't fling the pencil aside and pull her even closer.

Until she was within kissing distance.

He handed Aura the sharpened pencil. "Puerto Plata is the most strategically important port in the island, being in the North. Most of the imports from the United States arrive there first and are taken to landlocked cities like Santiago by the new railroad. Two of my uncles run the offices there, though one of them has been making noises about taking over San Pedro now that it's growing in importance."

Surprise flickered over her face. Sliding the pencil into the small handbag hanging from her wrist, Aura said, "Really? That seems unfair, after all the work you and Gregorio have put in."

He leaned against the side of his desk and shrugged. "Oh, we're not really the kind of family who shove each other out of the way just to climb the ranks of the company. We're all very protective of each other, and my grandfather has expanded his business concerns over the years so that everyone who wants to work can easily find their place. My uncle just wants to do what he can to keep Gregorio and me from overextending ourselves—or endangering the business in any way."

A week before, he'd been ready to hand over the reins if it meant not being home alone. Now, thanks to Aura, he didn't have to give up all he'd worked so hard for.

"Is there any danger of that?" Aura asked.

"Not at the moment," Eduardo said firmly. "But you have no idea what it took Gregorio and me to convince Abuelo to let us take the reins of the San Pedro branch of the business—things have been a great deal more compli-cated since the Americans took over Customs in 1907."

Aura nodded knowledgeably. "Hmm, yes, there's been a lot about it in the press over the past couple of years. So many changes to import duties."

"New guidelines, too. Gregorio and I were only allowed to take over the management on the condition that we work together, and then only on a trial basis. Abuelo still visits every quarter to make sure we haven't messed things up too badly." Eduardo grinned. "Of course, he used to come once a week. I like to think that Gregorio and I are finally proving ourselves trustworthy enough to be left to our own devices."

Aura cast a pointed glance at the collection of empty rum bottles lining his windowsill, which was all that remained of the last wild evening he had shared with his clerks—Gregorio tended to rumble at any after-hours carousing, but Eduardo had found that letting the young men have a frolic every now and then made them more conscientious than harsh discipline could.

"I can see why," she said dryly.

He grinned. "We're very good at our jobs. I can't say we're all that concerned with being good in other aspects of our lives."

A voice came from the half-open doorway. "Speak for yourself, you miscreant," Gregorio said. "I'm a soon-to-be-married man—I have no choice but to be the very picture of virtuosity."

"Don't remind me," Eduardo muttered.

Gregorio ignored him. "My apologies, Aura, but will you excuse us? I need Eduardo on an urgent matter."

Aura clasped her hands together. "I'm the one who should be sorry—I shouldn't be intruding when you're working."

"Nonsense," Eduardo said firmly. "You're not intruding. Will you wait for me?"

She answered him with one of those smiles that had the power to make his heartbeat flare to life. "Yes, of course. I'll wait for you."

The *Leonor* was a ship, not a person. And given the photograph Aura had just seen pinned to Eduardo's corkboard, there was no possible way that he didn't know that. Which begged the question—was he planning on enlightening Aura? Or was the fact that Rafael Marchena being somehow connected to Martínez & Hijos meant that he intended to look into the matter on his own?

There was also the matter of her crates. Eduardo seemed to be no closer to finding out what circumstances had led to their contents being replaced with rocks. Now that she knew about Rafael Marchena and the smuggling, Aura could guess.

She waited a handful of moments after Eduardo left the office before venturing out herself. She received several curious looks from the clerks striding to and fro in the corridor—it was evident that Eduardo never received female visitors at the office—and she met them all with bland, polite smiles as she walked out of the building and toward one of the several wooden warehouses bearing the company's name.

Lacking any other leads, the ship was as good a place as any to start searching for answers.

San Pedro being the busy shipping port it was, there were plenty of people around. Aura attracted more curious glances, but the combination of her gender and respectable clothing allowed her to continued passing through without being questioned or otherwise stopped.

It was one of the reasons her father had employed so

much time and effort in trying to convince her to abandon what he called her interminable drudgery in favor of his occupation. Women, particularly pretty young women who were fastidiously dressed in modish frocks, not only alerted less suspicion, they made most men practically fall over themselves trying to provide assistance.

Which was exactly what he would insist Aura do when she finally found the *Leonor*. Instead, she snuck aboard.

Well, that might have been overstating it, as there really was no need for subterfuge. All she did was step onto the wooden gangplank she had just seen used by a young man bearing cleaning supplies, and walk aboard with enough purpose that anyone who might be tempted to object would think twice about doing so.

Aura's hopes and dreams had always been too rooted in practicality for her to feel comfortable indulging in wild fantasies. Just for a moment, though, she allowed herself to imagine that she was boarding the ship in preparation for some voyage.

After her father died, the prospect of a blank slate had been tempting. She'd considered saving up just enough to book passage in a steamer that would take her to Cuba or Puerto Rico or even farther, to Venezuela or Colombia.

But that was what her father did—when things got too hard somewhere, or when he was being pursued by too many creditors, he left and started fresh somewhere else. That was how they had come to San Pedro. The thriving cattle industry and the rise in sugar exports had made it a prosperous place, full of exciting new opportunities. But not for her father, who had tried in vain to find success among all the new arrivals from Cuba and Scotland and the United States.

The last time he had begun speaking about moving on

to a new city, Aura had resolutely put her foot down, telling him that she had undergone enough upheavals and the thought of trying to make a home someplace new made her want to sob.

So instead, he had resorted to smuggling?

Masts rose to soaring heights, sails tightly furled around them. Bypassing the neatly stacked deck chairs in the shadow of an overhang, Aura opened the first door she came to and stepped through it quickly, pulling it firmly closed behind her. A gasp flew out of her mouth.

The *Leonor* was a floating mansion.

Though it was twice its size, the high-ceilinged main cabin felt like an extension of the Martínez home. Whoever had furnished the latter clearly had a hand in selecting the shapely yet sturdy armchairs and ornately carved tables in the space, and the needlepoint pillows on the love seat directly opposite the door reminded her of ones she had seen in the Martínezes' parlor.

And like Eduardo's home, this ship had clearly been designed for entertaining. Countless doors interrupted the wainscoting running down the length of the cabin—most were closed, but through a couple that were open, Aura glimpsed beautifully decorated bedrooms, all flooded with the light streaming in from the windows.

At the end of the main cabin, a grand staircase led to what appeared to be the social spaces. There was a library with books locked away behind leaded glass doors, a sitting room with love seats upholstered in silk damask and table lamps made out of stained glass in dazzling shades.

Aura wandered through a pair of double doors and into a dining room with two long rectangular tables that could have seated two dozen people comfortably. A carved wooden bar took up the length of one wall, stocked with bottles of liquor secured in cubbyholes. Aura picked up what looked like a restaurant menu from the pile folded on one end of the bar. The printed text inside detailed a ten-course meal so lavish that Aura wondered if the family employed a French chef exclusively for the ship.

The Martínezes must have been even wealthier than she'd thought.

Even after seeing the exterior of the ship, Aura hadn't quite realized how enormous it was on the inside. Conducting a thorough search of it would be impossible even if she were more familiar with the way its cabins were laid out and all the hundreds of hiding places among all the wardrobes and cabinets. Had she really thought it would be so easy?

A brief movement reflected on the etched glass that decorated the back of the bar had Aura whirling in panic—too late.

A large rough hand closed around her upper arm and a man's voice growled, "What the devil are you doing here?"

She'd been caught.

Eduardo ended his conference with Gregorio and Ruiz as soon as he could. When he returned to his office, though, it was empty—Aura must have taken the pencil she'd come in to borrow and left for her appointment with Lucía.

It was just as well. He still had a great deal of work to do and he'd see her that afternoon when he returned home anyway.

Still, disappointment flooded through him.

Feeling suddenly restless, he roamed out into the hallway where he ran into one of the detectives who had been employed by the company since his father and grandfather had founded the San Pedro branch. He'd asked one of the clerks that morning to have him summoned, and Aura's visit had driven it entirely out of his mind.

Ushering the man into his office, Eduardo asked him a few careful questions, the answers to which confirmed one of his suspicions: Rafael Marchena worked as an intervenor for the customs house, which was ostensibly how he had managed to get into Aura's crates without causing a ruckus. With all the new procedures put in place by the Americans after they had taken over customs operations, Eduardo's warehouse supervisor would have thought nothing of giving an official access to merchandise if he'd demanded it, much less to someone whose job was to inspect all the goods being imported.

Now all Eduardo needed was to decide what the devil to do with the information. As satisfying as it would have been to send a couple toughs to Marchena's home to scare him as much as his ruffians had scared Aura, the situation warranted more discretion than that. And he didn't yet have any proof that the men had been sent by Marchena—they could very well be rivals in his search.

Eduardo's grandfather had already assigned day and night guards to the ship, after an attempt at a break-in a couple of years before. Eduardo was confident that no one would be able to gain access to the ship without the guards knowing…but whether or not the guards were able to be bribed was another question.

A quiet word with the detective was all it took to arrange for the *Leonor* to be placed under constant surveillance. No one would so much as breathe near it without Eduardo finding out about it.

He walked with the man back to the front room. "Report back to me if—"

"Don Eduardo." The rough voice of the *Leonor*'s purser,

coming from the main entrance where he was backlit by the morning sunshine, made most of the clerks look up with avid curiosity. "I caught this woman aboard the *Leonor*. She says she knows you."

The clatter of the typewriters slowed—and so did Eduardo's heart when the purser finished stepping into the room, his fingers clamped tightly around a woman's arm.

Aura.

Something in Eduardo snapped at the sight of the purser's strong fingers gripping Aura with bruising force, and he charged forward without further thought, snapping furiously at the purser, "Release her right now."

He hadn't raised his voice, but even in his angry haze he was aware of the clerks' heads jerking up, and of their eyes following his process across the office.

Aura's lips were pressed tightly together and she wasn't even attempting to struggle, but Eduardo recognized the annoyance flashing in her eyes. Annoyance, he discovered when her gaze transferred to him, that was directed as much to Eduardo himself as to the purser who held her.

So she'd figured it out, hadn't she. She must have seen the ship's name in one of the photographs hanging behind his desk, or one of the many documents littering his office. He couldn't blame her for having gone to investigate on her own.

"Are you all right?" he asked her as she stepped away from the purser.

"Perfectly fine," she replied, a trifle coolly.

Eduardo turned to the purser. "What's the meaning of this?"

"Like I said before, Don Eduardo, I caught her poking around your family's ship. I thought you'd want her apprehended."

It was not an unreasonable assumption to make, and ordinarily Eduardo would have been inclined to take the man at his word and thank him for being so vigilant. But Eduardo had always relied on his instincts, and something in the man's demeanor—not to mention his rough treatment of Aura—raised his guard.

"She wasn't poking around," Eduardo told the purser with what little calm he had left. He couldn't do anything about the way he had reacted a moment before, but he could do what he could to control his temper now. "She was on the ship because I asked her to wait for me there."

A smirk flitted over his face. "Ah, I see."

The smug expression and the notion that someone could have mistaken Aura for something she wasn't renewed Eduardo's fury. He managed to restrain himself, but barely.

"What exactly," he asked with quiet dislike, "do you see?"

The purser's gaze flitted uncertainly from Eduardo to Aura, and he wisely chose not to answer. He stared straight ahead, as if he couldn't notice the clerks' terrible attempts to conceal their avid curiosity.

Eduardo swallowed back a swear. The attention of the entire office was focused on them—so much for discretion.

There was only one way to salvage the situation. Eduardo reached for Aura's hand, half expecting her to refuse and more than a little surprised when she let him take it.

"This," Eduardo said, projecting his voice just enough for the clerks to hear along with the purser, "is my wife."

Chapter Thirteen

What with all the clerks crowding in close to offer their congratulations, Aura and Eduardo didn't get a moment on their own to discuss what had transpired until they had returned home.

The house had an unusually large staff—Eduardo seemed to have no qualms about offering employment or even just temporary housing to anyone who came to him with the merest mention of a personal difficulty. At that hour, with most of them occupied either in the preparation of the midday meal or in consuming their own, there was no one to see Aura and Eduardo as they crossed the patterned tiles on the front porch and went into the formal parlor.

Aura took a seat on one of the cane-back armchairs, but Eduardo began pacing restlessly in front of the tall doors that led out to the balcony.

"I don't know what the devil he was thinking," Eduardo fumed, "manhandling you like that. I should—"

"This partnership won't work if we don't trust each other."

He halted suddenly. "I could say the same to you. In fact, I think I will say the same thing to you." He raised a finger and wagged it in teasing admonition. "Aura, this partnership doesn't work if we don't trust each other."

But she was in no mood to be teased. "You recognized the name Leonor and didn't say anything to me about it."

Eduardo shrugged. "I wished to look into the matter before risking alerting anyone to whatever's going on. And there's the matter of safeguarding the company's reputation to keep our clients from losing confidence in our ability to keep their goods from being stolen or tampered with." He strode the length of the terrace and turned back, sliding his fingers through the knot in his tie and pulling at it to loosen it. "Tell me, did you find anything on board?"

She shook her head. "There were no hidden caches of smuggled goods, if that's what you mean. To be honest, I didn't know what I hoped to find." She didn't feel defeated, not quite yet, but she was beginning to get a sense of how much deeper this nonsense ran. "What if we were to pay a call on Rafael Marchena, now that we know he's behind everything? After all, who better to enlighten us as to what's going on? Discretion doesn't seem to be getting us anywhere and I really just want to get to the bottom of things."

Eduardo's stride didn't falter as he shook his head. "We have no proof that he's the one behind the smuggling—not yet. What do you know of his partnership with your father?"

"Beyond Marchena's claim that he loaned my father a large sum that was never repaid, not much." Aura spread her hands. "I disapproved of my father's schemes, so I took care to limit my knowledge of them."

He yanked impatiently at his tie again, digging his fingers into the knot.

Aura sighed. "You'll ruin your collar *and* your shirt if you keep pulling at your tie like that."

Her skirts rustled around her ankles as she abandoned her seat and met Eduardo by one of the polished side tables.

Doing something with her hands had always helped Aura think. Undoing his tie, however, was nothing like shaping flower petals out of organdy. For one, she was close enough that she could smell the sharp notes of his eau de toilette. She could see each fleck of light brown in his dark eyes. And she couldn't ignore the way he continued to look at her like he wanted to kiss her until she forgot she was annoyed with him.

Avoiding his gaze, Aura deftly tugged the silk tie out of its knot and undid the button that fastened his starched collar to his shirt because otherwise he'd start tugging at it and she'd had enough of popped buttons. Not to mention, someone had gone to plenty of trouble starching the thing and it would be a shame to let it crumple.

Eduardo was still looking at her. "Gregorio set a date for the wedding. That was what he wanted to tell me earlier."

"I know," Aura replied. "That was why he was late arriving to the office—he wanted to stop by Celia's first. Eduardo…why was it so important that you marry before he did?"

Her desire to know the reason Eduardo had proposed their marriage was eclipsed by her desire to know if he would actually answer her question.

"A family curse," Eduardo said promptly. "It's all to do with our great-great-grandfather, who stole a goat from—"

"*Eduardo*," Aura said, hearing the reproach in her own voice.

Her husband held up his hands. "It would take me months to untangle those particular threads, to use a metaphor you might appreciate, and we've an appointment at the bank after lunch. Which I believe will be served soon," he added, waving at the clock. "We ought to go wash our hands."

He held out a hand and Aura took it, though she didn't move from where she stood.

"If you're trying to distract me, it won't work."

"Will this?"

With one swift motion, he lifted her hand high above her head and twirled her around as if they had been dancing. She fetched up against his chest, opening her mouth to tell him she couldn't be dissuaded that easily.

One look at Eduardo's eyes, however, and she was stepping back into his arms, driving him backward until his back hit the damask wallpaper, surging onto her tiptoes to reach the heat of his mouth with a low, urgent noise.

The slimmest ribbon of reason kept her from wrenching his lapels inside her wrists. Eduardo seemed to be having the same problem. His hands roamed lightly over her as if he didn't know where to touch her if he wanted to avoid mussing her hair or disturbing the ironed flounces on her shirtwaist. He settled for tangling their fingers together, their grip tight on each other as their mouths engaged in silent conversation.

Their hands and lips were their only point of contact, and it was simultaneously enough and not enough. Pleasure curled through her—hot, molten tendrils of it, moving from where their hands touched to fill the rest of her body. And still, she craved more. She *needed* more.

Taking a deep breath, she disentangled her hands from his and stepped back, casting a quick glance at the doorway to make sure no one had seen them. "You're impossible."

"But you like it, don't you?"

There was something a little anxious in the way he looked at her that made her want to reassure him. "I like *you*," she said. "But—"

One of the housemaids appeared in the doorway that had

been vacant a mere couple of seconds before. She glanced from Aura to Eduardo and said apologetically, "So sorry to disturb you, but your lunch is on the table."

Against her better judgment, Aura dropped the subject and followed Eduardo to the dining table. The arrangement of ferns and birds of paradise that usually adorned its center had been moved to the sideboard to make room for four serving platters. Aura was so busy eyeing the crispy fried fritters on one of the platters that she didn't see the narrow box on her plate until she had sat down.

"What is this?" she asked.

Eduardo grinned at her from his seat. "Something I thought you would need for our appointment at the bank this afternoon."

Feeling apprehension well inside her, Aura undid the bow and lifted the lid. To her relief, the object inside the box wasn't a bracelet—it was a pen. When she took it out to inspect it, however, and saw the gold nib and the clip on the cap, she realized that it might as well have been a bracelet for how expensive it was.

She set the pen down next to her empty plate, her appetite gone. "Eduardo, you don't have to get me something every single day."

"I know I don't have to," he said, reaching for the rice bowl. "I want to."

"It's not necessary," she said firmly.

"We'll have to agree to disagree on that point. Here, have some *arepitas*."

She stifled a sigh and held out her plate so Eduardo could drop two fritters onto it. She'd have a serious talk with him soon. Until then...

"Hand me the beefsteak, please?"

Chapter Fourteen

As well as some underthings and six shirtwaists for Lucía's journey to Europe, Aura was making the heiress a traveling suit cut out of a sleek charcoal-colored gabardine with minutely pleated trim. Lucía had impressed upon Aura her need for clothes that allowed her ease of movement, saying impishly that she climbed every trellis she came across, so Aura had added two kick pleats to the skirt and a line of decorative cloth-covered buttons from the edge of each pleat to the high waistband. It would take a great deal of work to have everything ready before the steamer sailed, but it was work she enjoyed.

Making use of the large table the laundresses used for folding the family's clean clothes, she had already made the patterns and cut all the pieces. All that remained was to schedule a fitting in order to make any last-minute adjustments before doing all the finishing work.

Filled with the calm satisfaction that only came from a productive day, Aura took her sewing basket to the family parlor and settled into an armchair to finish pleating the trim for the traveling suit.

With María del Mar gone and both Gregorio and Eduardo at work, a deep quiet had descended over the house. Aura would have stayed out back with the laundresses if she thought she'd be welcome—but she was all too aware that she didn't have Eduardo's easy grace with people and her position as the lady of the house meant that everyone felt like they had to be at rigid attention around her. They'd get used to her soon enough.

And in the meantime, maybe Eduardo would teach her how to play records on the phonograph. Then again, asking him ran the risk of him deciding that what she really needed was for him to hire a violinist to follow her around the house, making constant music.

"What in the world can be making you frown like that?"

"Eduardo." Aura lowered her needle and twisted around to look at him lope into the room, automatically tilting up her face to receive the kisses he brushed first on her cheek and then over her lips. "What are you doing here this early?"

Eduardo was in the habit of coming home for the midday meal, but that was still a good hour away.

"I was trying to think of an excuse to come see you and then I realized that as your husband, I probably don't need one."

"Probably not," she agreed, amused. "Though I have always been partial to a good excuse."

"All right, then, how's this—I was desperate to show you something and I couldn't wait one more minute."

Dropping a set of rolled-up papers on the table, he beckoned her closer and began to spread them over the table, using books and pots of ink as paperweights.

"What are those?" she asked curiously as she approached him.

"Plans," he told her. "For your new store. When Abuelo was here, he reminded me that we own an empty lot near Calle Duarte that would do very nicely. So I met with an architect and asked him to design something suitable."

Aura looked over the unfurled plans, distress growing inside her chest.

"The first story would be your shop," Eduardo said animatedly, before turning to the next page. "The second, an atelier. And the third I imagine would be used for storage, though I think it would probably be better to have a set of rooms at the back for additional stock, to avoid having your shopgirls scurrying up and down all day."

Shopgirls? She'd considered hiring an assistant, and maybe an errand boy, but not until the store was well established, which she knew could take years.

"A friend told me about a department store in London called Selfridges that opened last year that has restaurants and reception rooms and even a writing and reading room."

"A department store?" Aura murmured.

"I'll arrange a meeting between you and the architect, of course," Eduardo went on eagerly. "As soon as can be managed. I know you must have a great deal of questions you'll want to ask him."

It was too excessive.

Just that morning, Aura had awoken to find that while Eduardo had already left for the office, he had left a long, cardboard box in his place. Untying the ribbon that held it together had revealed half a dozen silk stockings, as light as a whisper and dismayingly expensive.

The day before, it had been a marquetry dressing table, complete with a monogrammed hairbrush and a silver-backed hand mirror.

Aura understood that people like Eduardo and the rest of his family were accustomed to a degree of luxury in their daily lives, and she certainly didn't want him to renounce it all just because it made her uncomfortable.

A few years before, her father had become obsessed with

a merchant from Santiago called José Manuel Glas, who just before dying had spent over fifteen thousand pesos on importing a fine marble mausoleum from Italy. He'd also commissioned a sculpture of himself from a French sculptor, at great expense.

And Aura herself had sewn for women who thought nothing of trimming an evening gown with real freshwater pearls or spending a small fortune on a costly fabric only to decide, after the dress was half-made, that the color didn't suit them, after all.

But the only times in Aura's life that she had access to that kind of luxury was when one of her father's schemes paid out and he became almost feverish in his desire to spend all his newly acquired money on everything he felt he and his family had gone without. All too soon, the money would be gone and Aura dispatched to beg scraps from the butcher.

"It looks like you went to a lot of trouble to have all this put together," she said, laying a hand on his arm. "I hope you know how much I appreciate it."

"I just want you to have the best." He gestured at the plans on the table. "That's only the beginning of all the things I'd like to do for you."

He looked so earnest and so pleased with himself that she could hardly bring herself to disappoint him. But a large, flashy store was nothing like she'd had in mind—the cost of the building itself aside, it would take an absolute fortune to stock it and to light it. This wouldn't give her independence and a secure, steady income. It would become nothing more than a headache.

It had made her stomach curl tightly with fear and unhappiness—after all she'd told Eduardo about her father, why didn't he think anything of acting the same way? Of acting like her humble aspirations were too provincial for words.

"The best for me would be something much smaller," she said carefully. "I wouldn't want to risk overextending myself."

Eduardo shrugged. "I'll be there to help you, whatever happens. I'll do anything in my power to make things easier for you."

The problem was, life had never been easy for her. Eduardo, she knew, had lived a much different kind of life. But was it so different that he couldn't understand the source of her anxiety?

Far from noticing her dismay, Eduardo looked like he was trying to contain himself, but his sheepish expression gave him away.

Aura wrapped her fingers around the back of a chair, feeling cold despite the sultriness of the ocean breeze coming through the open balcony doors. "You bought something else, didn't you?"

"I ordered a sewing machine for you a couple of days after the wedding. I noticed you didn't have one and—"

"I do have one, Eduardo," she said. "At home."

Eduardo shrugged again. "Oh, well. This way you'll have a spare—or the beginnings of an atelier, should you wish to hire someone to do your sewing for you."

"I don't want an atelier, and I can do my own sewing. You'll have to send a telegram and cancel your order."

She knew she sounded upset, and she knew that he probably thought she was being unreasonable, but she was unable to help the note of anxiety that had crept into her voice. She knew the dangers that came when a person's ambitions far outweighed their means.

And most importantly, she knew the dangers of trusting anyone else with her dreams.

"You've been too generous already," she said, softening her tone to make up for her outburst. "And you've given me too much. I'd have no way of paying you back."

"Pay me back? Dole out payments as if I were some kind of bank? I'd never ask for that."

"I know you wouldn't, Eduardo," Aura said, desperate for him to understand her. "But I can't be in anybody's debt."

"But I'm your—"

"Not even yours."

Eduardo didn't answer right away. There was a tightness in his jaw that she didn't know how to decipher. Did he think her ungrateful, or believe she was overreacting? Or was he trying to conceal some other emotion?

She opened her mouth to ask, but before she could say anything, she saw a charming, practiced smile flash over his mouth. And she knew that whatever came from his lips next would be the kind of soothing things her father used to say when he wanted to avoid being berated for yet another scheme gone wrong.

Before that could happen, she choked out an apology and rushed out of the room.

This was exactly the kind of thing her father had always done—generous, lavish gestures that looked considerate from the outside, but that failed to take into account what the person on the receiving end actually wanted. Like the time when he took her mother out for a drive and stopped in front of a large, expensive house, gleefully announcing that he had rented it and not understanding why her mother had been so dismayed.

And then he would be hurt that his gifts weren't met with more enthusiasm, and he'd wave away any attempts at reasoning or explanation. Aura could feel her stomach clenching just remembering some of the arguments that had preceded her parents' divorce.

This wasn't what she wanted—or what she needed. And it most certainly wasn't what she'd thought she was getting into. She hadn't married Eduardo under some kind of romantic delusion of undying love. She'd done the sober, practical thing and entered into a partnership she had believed was based on mutual respect. She would never have done that if she'd known that Eduardo was the kind of man who did things with no regard for his wife's real needs.

She would have never married him if she had known that he was just like her father.

Aura had already awoken when Eduardo opened his eyes the next day. She was curled up in one of the armchairs by the window. The tree that grew just outside was laden with dark leaves and gracefully twisted branches, and it provided the perfect backdrop for her as she wove careful stitches into a pinned-together garment made from some dark fabric.

She could have been a painting—or something out of his wildest dreams. Morning light streamed into the bedroom, golden and warm and filtered through the leaves, making her needle glint.

He had felt her moving around just after daybreak. For the past two or three days, she had been getting out of bed at dawn in order to work on some of the blasted clothes she was making for Lucía.

Aura was more industrious than a bee, buzzing with intense concentration between one project and the next, full of determination and ambition. He had seen the drive in her from the day they'd met, and he admired her for it. And he could certainly respect her desire to achieve success on her own. All he'd wanted to do was give her a boost.

Instead, what he'd done was overstep. Worse than that, he'd overlooked Aura's desires in order to satisfy his own. At first, when she greeted each of his gifts politely but with a marked lack of enthusiasm, he'd told himself that she was just having trouble adjusting to her changed circumstances. After years of enduring the financial strain she had described, it would be no wonder if his costly gifts made her nervous.

He couldn't help wondering if his friends had found marriage easier. Sebastián Linares was a leader among men. He'd given up his claim on a profitable sugar mill to turn it into a cooperative so that the people who labored in it could profit as well and was content with smaller endeavors that allowed him more time at home with his wife, Paulina, and their numerous little ones. Julián Fuentes was a daredevil who raised racehorses while his wife oversaw her family's considerable fortune. Leo Díaz had a head for business that put J.P. Morgan to shame, and he had given up most of his endeavors of that nature to accompany his wife to Vienna, where she intended to continue studying the violin.

Eduardo had aspired to nothing more than to put all the things life had given him to the service of others. To be useful to his friends, family and business acquaintances. And his wife.

He was under no illusion that independent, self-contained Aura was relying on him out of anything but necessity. After a brief discussion with her, he had hired a man to keep guard over her house and prevent Marchena's men—if that was who they were—from accessing her father's things. Another two men patrolled the Martínez house, sleeping on opposite edges of the property, so that no one got any bright ideas about accosting Aura at home. That seemed to be all that she would allow from him, however.

After yesterday, she was more aloof than ever. And yet, she never left the room while he was still sleeping. When he stayed up late, slogging through correspondence at the table in the upstairs parlor, she quietly brought her sewing basket into the room and kept him company. And when he was especially restless in the middle of the night, she never hesitated to lay a hand on his arm or his shoulder in a silent reminder that he wasn't alone.

Through the branches, he could see that the sky was a perfect, unmarred blue. And even though the sun was beginning to climb, the breeze still held a hint of coolness. Down the hallway, the clock struck the hour.

Aura glanced up at the sound, setting down her sewing so she could bring a hand up to hide her yawn. Noticing that his eyes were open, she lowered her hand and offered him a tentative smile. "Good morning."

"Good morning yourself," he replied easily, raising himself up just enough to shove her pillow on top of his. "I'll be up in a few minutes. Are you coming down to breakfast or would you like a tray sent up?"

"I'll come," she said quickly. "Eduardo, about yesterday— I wanted to explain…"

What was there to explain? She'd grown visibly upset and Eduardo had reacted the way he always did, with heart-pounding panic that he had tried to mask by being the unrepentant charmer everyone seemed to love. Except for Aura.

It had been the wrong way to approach her, and he would have realized that in time if it hadn't been for the fog of panic obscuring his thoughts. Abruptly excusing herself, she had fled the room and he hadn't seen her again until they were sitting across from each other at the dinner table in silence, which he tried to make less awkward by pretending everything was fine.

Talking about it would only bring the panic back to the surface and Eduardo needed his wits sharp.

Touching was always easier than talking about something difficult. If he was sure his advances wouldn't be rebuffed, he would take her by the waist and brush his lips over hers and ask her forgiveness that way.

Instead, Eduardo waved an insouciant hand in the air. "There's no need. I'm glad you told me how you felt—I promise I'll stop besieging you with presents." He paused, then added, "But I really should get to the office as early as possible because there's a shipment or two that I really should cancel."

Aura hesitated, then she bit her lip and nodded.

Eduardo pushed the blanket away and got out of bed. When he reached the door to the lavatory, he paused and glanced back at her. She seemed to have reached the end of her thread—beginning what seemed to him like a complicated procedure, she knotted the end of the thread and snipped it with a miniature pair of scissors. An adorable wrinkle appeared at the corner of her eyes as she squinted in order to insert a fresh length of thread into the needle.

On the eve of their wedding, Eduardo had promised himself that he would do whatever it took to make her happy. He'd convinced himself that it could be accomplished without having to reopen old wounds. That he could just use his wealth to provide the things she'd lacked.

He hadn't counted on the fact that it wouldn't be enough.

The problem was, if she didn't want silk stockings or silver hairbrushes or even sewing machines, what could he offer her to make up for the fact that he couldn't give her his heart?

Chapter Fifteen

The size and capability of Eduardo's staff meant that there was little for Aura to do around the house. If it hadn't been for her sewing and the few things she'd done to help Don Amable prepare for the ball he was hosting the following month, Aura would've had no means of occupying her time.

She was taking a much-needed respite from hemming the last of Lucía's shirtwaists when Eduardo came into the upstairs parlor.

Aura tensed, but no gifts were forthcoming. Instead, he said, without preamble, "I have news. Not good ones, I'm afraid."

She set aside the bowl of apple slices she'd been enjoying and looked up at him.

"I had one of my clerks look into the matter of your house. The deed is indeed registered to Rafael Marchena—it was transferred late last February."

"Just before my father died at the beginning of March," Aura said, crestfallen. "He must have sold the house then, as Marchena said, in exchange for a loan."

"Or as collateral for whatever he was meant to be smuggling."

Aura nodded slowly. "It was something costly, then—or dangerous." And the promised payment must have been a sum large enough to dazzle her easily misled father after he had *promised* her that there would be no more schemes. And after he'd already asked for most of her savings. She held back a sigh. "There's no chance of the document being wrong?"

"I went to look at it myself and saw that it was stamped and signed by a public notary, so there's no question of the legality of the transfer. I'm sorry, Aura. I'd hoped to give you better news."

She forced herself to smile. "It was just a house. Maybe Marchena will be willing to sell it back to me."

"You think so?"

"I think it's worth a try." She let out a frustrated noise. "Although if he had wanted his loan repaid, he would have approached you as soon as he got wind of our marriage. I wouldn't blame him for assuming that was why I had married you."

"Why *did* you marry me?" Eduardo asked with a flirtatious raise of his eyebrow.

It wasn't so much that he was trying to get back into her good graces, but that he wished to diffuse some of the tension between them—without actually discussing it. Aura didn't think it was right to let him clear the air without at least an attempt at talking out what had upset her, but it was a relief to relax after being excruciatingly careful around each other since their argument the day before.

"For the fruit, of course," she said lightly, gesturing at the bowl on the side table.

"And here I thought it was my winning personality."

She felt a smile tugging at the corner of her lips. "No, sorry, that had nothing to do with it. If Marchena isn't receptive to the idea of having his loan repaid, I wonder if I could persuade him to make an exchange—you know, for what he's looking for."

"Does the house really mean that much to you?"

Didn't it? Until that moment, Aura hadn't really thought she had any emotional attachment to it. She and her father hadn't lived in it long and there weren't any treasured memories attached to it. In time, she would most likely find another place that was just as ideal for her store. It wasn't like her to be sentimental or inflexible.

But if she wasn't willing to let Eduardo's generosity compromise her vision, why should she let Marchena?

Aura folded her arms across her chest. "Well, what else would you suggest?"

"There is one thing." Eduardo reached for the bowl of fruit and helped himself to an apple slice. "We need proof that Marchena is indeed a smuggler—we need to find out what he's smuggling and why. And we can't approach him directly. I had a private detective collect information about Marchena. He wasn't able to find anything out of the ordinary. But then, he had no way of gaining access to his house for a closer look."

"I do." As a matter of fact, María del Mar had inadvertently given her the perfect excuse to pay a visit to Perla de Marchena by asking Aura to return the dress she had borrowed.

It was almost eleven, which meant that if Aura changed her clothes quickly enough, they could time their visit so that it wouldn't coincide with the Marchenas' midday meal, and so avoid running into Rafael.

Aura went to change while Eduardo waited in the terrace with a cup of coffee. To soften the severity of her plain black skirt, she had selected the most delicate shirtwaist she owned, made of half-transparent lawn with lace inserts and cloth-covered buttons. The neckline was trimmed with the slimmest black ribbon, and she had tied a black bow to her straw hat. She had no other adornment—aside from her wedding ring, that was, and it was extravagant enough that she didn't need anything else.

Suitably attired for paying a visit, she and Eduardo set out on foot.

According to the directions María del Mar had scribbled on a scrap of paper and pinned to the borrowed dress, the Marchenas lived fairly close by. They reached the house within minutes. It was small and neat, painted white and ringed with a wrought iron fence. Philodendrons had been planted on either side of the short front walk, and more flowers grew in terracotta pots on the steps leading up to the porch and the front door.

If Eduardo hadn't thought that Marchena looked like a smuggler, Aura thought that the house was too pretty to be a smuggler's residence. There were no ruffians in sight, burly or otherwise—the only person visible, in fact, was the gangly young man pruning a tree in the side yard.

Even so, Aura felt apprehensive as she and Eduardo climbed the steps. Particularly when he paused halfway through and lowered his head to whisper directly into her ear even though there was no one around to overhear. "If I say or do anything that sounds out of place, will you go along with it?"

She nodded her agreement and went to ring the doorbell.

They were greeted at the door by a housemaid in a starched apron, who led them to a stylish, light-filled sitting room with open floor-to-ceiling shutters that looked out into a narrow side garden. A moment later, Perla de Marchena bustled in.

Aura had only met her two or three times. The vague impression she'd had of a bright, ebullient woman some ten or fifteen years older than her was confirmed as Perla leaned in to kiss them both on the cheek, chattering away.

"It's so lovely to see you again, Aura. And may I offer congratulations on your wedding? Your rascal of a cousin never told me about it," she added, batting playfully at Eduardo's arm.

If she wondered why he was accompanying Aura and not at work, she didn't let on. Aura had argued against it under the reasoning that Marchena might find a threat implied in it if he happened to come home, but Eduardo wouldn't hear of her paying a visit to the Marchenas' house on her own.

"Oh, you *can't* have come all this way for a simple frock?" Perla set the proffered dress aside. "I would have sent someone for it, you know I would have. Sit, sit—and don't you dare tell me you haven't time for some light refreshment because I already asked my cook to make up a tray."

Eduardo looked as dazed as Aura felt. They both allowed themselves to be ushered into a love seat, while Perla took the rocking chair opposite, still talking.

With some difficulty, Aura regained control of the conversation. "It really is no trouble to bring you the dress. In fact, I told María del Mar that I welcomed the chance to ask about it. The construction is exquisite—and the detailing!"

"All the work of my wonderful, clever dressmaker. I'll introduce you if you like. Oh, but you sew yourself, don't you? I—"

"I do," Aura interrupted calmly, "which is one of the reasons I was so intrigued by those lovely buttons down the back." Aura had considered sewing the mislaid button back on, but in the end she had decided against it, telling Eduardo to keep it safe in case they needed it for evidence later. "Would you happen to know where your dressmaker found them? I haven't seen anything similar in any of the stores in town."

"That's because they were a gift from my husband."

Aura fought the urge to glance at Eduardo. "Oh?"

"It was meant to be a surprise," Perla said confidingly, leaning toward Aura and tapping her on the arm. "Nothing gets past me, though!"

She burst into a peal of laughter, and both Aura and Eduardo joined in politely.

"If you ask me, it was horribly silly of him to think he could keep an entire crate full of the loveliest ribbons and buttons and threads a secret. Not in my household! Of course, he was so upset that I had stumbled across it before he had a chance to properly present it to me. Men can be so silly sometimes, don't you think?"

"On the subject of gifts?" Aura said, resolutely not looking at Eduardo. "Definitely."

Perla, on the other hand, had no compunction about giving him a wicked smile. "But it's so amusing when they grow flustered."

"We enjoy it," he replied, all smiles and smooth charm. "Being flustered, I mean, though gift-giving is of course just as pleasurable. Or it is when the recipient is appreciative of what is offered."

Aura drew in a careful breath before remembering what he had whispered to her outside. "Some of us don't *appreciate* being besieged by useless things purchased without our consent or opinion," she said sharply, before turning to address Perla. "I'm sure *your* husband doesn't spring all kind of unwelcome surprises on you."

Their hostess was watching them both with wide eyes. "Well, my Rafa is the picture of generosity."

"Buttons are one thing," Aura said with a dismissive gesture, knowing she was being unpardonably rude. "I'm sure you haven't had to deal with gaudy jewelry and ugly furniture. All painfully expensive, of course."

"Forgive me for wanting my wife to have the best," Eduardo shot back with such a good impression of someone whose pride had been injured beyond repair that Aura had to wonder how much of it was an act.

Perla laughed nervously, her gaze darting between them as she probably wondered what had possessed Aura to turn a simple visit into an opportunity to air out her grievances against her new husband. "I'm sure you have nothing but the best intentions."

"I think," Aura said softly, looking directly at Eduardo, "that what you really want is to feel like you're rescuing me."

His eyes widened, true shock peeking out through his facade.

"Aura," he began, but she'd had enough of this game.

She didn't know if it was what Eduardo had intended, but she clasped her hand to her mouth as if to stifle a sob and fled the parlor as she had fled the Martínezes' parlor the day before. Her distress wasn't entirely feigned—there had been more than a grain of truth in what she'd said, though obviously she would have chosen a different way of saying it, and she suspected that Eduardo had also been honest about his feelings.

If that was true, it would be the first time since she had met him that he hadn't hidden his true thoughts behind that charming facade.

A couple of genuine tears squeezed out of the corners of her eyes, which came in handy when she ran into an aproned housemaid just outside the parlor and asked frantically where the nearest lavatory was located.

Pointed upstairs, Aura charged up without hesitation. She didn't really think that Marchena would keep smuggled or otherwise illicit goods around the house, not without risking alerting his wife and his staff of his activities, but surely there must be something to at least connect Marchena with the ruffians who'd barged into her home...

The interior of the house looked no more like a smuggler's den than the exterior had—in fact, there was really nothing in it save Aura's buttons to indicate that Marchena received anything more than a government salary, or even that they were living beyond their means.

The house wasn't large, but searching it would be even more futile than attempting to search the *Leonor*. Not only was the house full of people, Aura had very little time to pretend to be discomposed. She'd have to be strategic— she'd need to find an office, or a desk.

Urgency drove her into a bedroom that seemed to be the only one in use. Under the window was a narrow secretary, its lid open and littered with a mess of shopping lists and letters and invitations and bits of ribbon and lace. Not Marchena's, then.

She cast a glance at the brass pulls on the secretary's drawers, but made no move to touch them. It was bad enough that she had intruded into the Marchenas' bedroom—she had no stomach for rooting through someone else's drawers. Maybe this had been a mistake.

Aura was about to turn away when she caught sight of a familiar name scrawled at the edge of a grocery list. She picked it up, and realized that the scrap of paper had actually been an envelope. The corner with the stamp had been ripped out, but the sender's address still remained. The English words were unfamiliar to Aura, but she recognized the line on the bottom—*New York City*.

What had caught her attention, however, was on the center of the envelope. The recipient's had been scribbled over with loops of black ink, but part of it was still visible and Aura recognized enough of it to make out what it had said.

Alfredo Soriano.

Why had her father been receiving letters from New York and why did Marchena have them?

Sliding the torn envelope into her pocket, Aura quickly wiped her face clean of tears and went downstairs at a much more sedate pace than the one that had carried her upstairs.

When she reached the parlor, Eduardo was saying, "I'm so sorry for the disturbance. I would have liked to meet your husband—Aura has spoken highly of him—but my wife and I should continue this discussion at home."

Perla pouted. "It's a shame that you can't stay. Rafael is always so busy, off working at all hours of the day or night. I'm sure he would have liked to see you too."

She had no idea that her husband was a smuggler. Another woman in the dark about the havoc the men in their lives were wreaking. Aura's chest felt tight at the thought that this bright-eyed woman might find herself coming to the same realization Aura had. She wished she could warn her—but not without solid proof.

"He was very kind to my father—and to myself. I hope he knows that I appreciate everything he's done for us," Aura managed to say, extending her hand to Perla, who gave it a sympathetic squeeze.

"I'm sure he does, my dear. And if you ever need to talk, please feel free to pay me a visit."

Aura murmured something polite in response, hardly able to meet Perla's gaze. Not just because she'd made a spectacle of herself, or because she'd abused the woman's confidence in order to snoop around her house—but because she was certain that her smoldering anger at Rafael Marchena would show in her eyes.

By tacit agreement, she and Eduardo refrained from speaking about what had just happened.

Instead, as they descended the steps to the sidewalk, Aura asked, "Back to the house for lunch? Unless you're in a hurry to return to the office."

"Ordinarily, I'd rush back and have one of the messengers ask someone at the house to make me a basket. But today, I believe I'd like to take my new bride out to a restaurant."

She smoothed a hand over her skirt. "I'm not sure I'm dressed—"

"You are, as always, flawless. And I'm famished. You wouldn't let your husband starve, would you?" He held out his arm, smiling winningly at her.

For all she was still irritated with him, the sight of his smile stirred things inside her that were better left dormant. Trying not to show it, Aura gave him a nod and took his arm.

Chapter Sixteen

The restaurant he took her to was part of one of the new hotels built in the center of town. Jaunty striped awnings, velvet drapes, crisp white tablecloths laid with gleaming silver...

Aura had been here before, with her father. He loved frequenting places like this even when he hadn't the money to order more than two coffees. Dressed in her finest frock, she would sit across the table from him and listen as he spun wild tales about taking all their meals in places like that when he struck it rich. Always when, never *if*.

A chorus of greetings directed at Eduardo rose at their arrival. Glancing around, she realized that he seemed to know almost everyone in the elegant dining salon. Her hand still gripping the crook of his elbow, she found herself being led from table to table to be introduced to Eduardo's acquaintances or to exchange brief conversation with some of the people she had met at their wedding.

As they went around the elegantly appointed room, Aura couldn't help but wonder...was it her? Was Eduardo's reluctance to open up something to do with her, specifically? He seemed to have so many friends—close ones. Surely, he must confide in at least a few of them. Surely, he didn't hold them all at arm's length like he did Aura.

It took close to half an hour for Eduardo to finally finish making the rounds. As soon as he helped her back into her seat, a uniformed waiter appeared and offered them both a leather-bound menu.

She bit her lip, trying not to let on how scandalized she was by the prices. He wanted to please her, and it wasn't his fault that spending money made her heart pound in a way that left her feeling dizzy. She had seen the way he had lit up when they'd arrived to find so many of his friends in attendance. This was what he would have been doing if it hadn't been for her, and she had no intention of holding him back.

She ordered a soup, saying that she wasn't too hungry, and didn't protest when Eduardo reviewed the *carta de vinos* and chose a bottle of something French. Aura knew what her father would have said if she'd made any remark about having an entire bottle of wine at lunchtime—that she shouldn't be so tediously provincial.

She refrained from saying anything as the waiter finished filling their glasses with iced water from a silver pitcher.

Eduardo leaned forward as soon as the waiter left, setting his hand on the tablecloth so close to Aura's that for a second, she thought he meant to hold it. "I apologize for my choice of subject back there."

Expectation made her straighten in her seat. Finally, an opportunity to talk about what she'd said in the Marchenas' sitting room.

But nothing further came from Eduardo, at least not on that subject.

She lifted her chin, trying not to show how much it bothered her. "What happened when I left?"

"I received a great deal of earnest advice about how

to make my wife happy," Eduardo said wryly. "Which I suppose I deserved. Nothing more that shed any light on Marchena's extracurriculars, though. Did you find anything?"

Aura withdrew the torn envelope from the waistband of her skirt and slid it across the tablecloth to him. "I think Marchena has been intercepting my father's mail."

He took it with curiosity, a flicker passing over his expression as he read the information on the back.

"Before you ask, I don't know who my father knew in New York. I don't know what the letter is about, or if there are more, or if this is at all related to the journey he was supposed to be going on." She sighed heavily. "I could fill a suitcase with all the things I don't know."

Frown lines gathered between Eduardo's brows. "The return address is mostly complete. Why don't we try writing? I'm sure that whoever was corresponding with your father will have some answers."

She nodded. "That's something, at least. A place to start. Though it feels like I'm ending the day with more questions than when we started."

The waiter who had taken their order returned with the wine, and Aura waited in silence while he poured a stream for Eduardo to taste.

He signaled his approval with a nod, waiting until his wineglass had been filled and the waiter had stepped away before speaking again. "These things take time. We may never learn the full truth of what your father was planning to do, but I *will* keep you safe. I *will* keep Marchena away from you."

She wasn't reassured, and he must have seen it because he kept up a steady stream of flirtatious banter all throughout their meal, his cheerful onslaught so relentless that Aura relaxed by degrees as she let it wash over her.

By the time their empty plates were taken away, she'd had enough wine that a pleasant lightheadedness had replaced the buzz of anxiety. Doubtless that was why her brain didn't mount an objection when she touched the tip of her index finger to the hand Eduardo had casually laid on the crisp tablecloth and asked, "Eduardo, what is it that you really want?"

"What do you mean?"

"I know you have all kinds of aspirations when it comes to your work, but what do you want out of life? What did you envision for your future? Surely you wanted more for yourself than parties and houseguests."

There was a moment in which Aura thought that this time, Eduardo would answer her seriously. He held her gaze for the space of a heartbeat, then another, something moving behind his eyes. Her heartbeat quickened, and she was distantly aware of her lips parting with the anticipation of hearing what he had to say.

And just when Aura thought that he would finally open up to her, he opened his mouth instead and said, "Dessert— that's all I want in my immediate and distant future. The ones here are especially good. The restaurant employs a pastry chef who trained in France."

Aura was starting to get acquainted with the shades of meaning in each of his smiles. The one he flashed at her from across the small table made her stomach sink. All froth and no chocolate, as her mother used to say whenever she encountered something of little substance.

Eduardo's froth was so appealing, but all she wanted was chocolate. She wanted to know the man beneath the charm and the practiced smiles and the funny anecdotes she had come to realize he used as a diversion whenever the conversation came too close to his feelings.

And most of all, she wanted to stop feeling like this partnership of theirs was entirely one-sided.

He signaled the waiter, who approached the table bearing a pair of dessert menus set into black leather holders. Eduardo opened his right away and swept his gaze over it, saying something about ordering one of everything so that Aura could try it all.

She placed her hand on the menu.

"You give too much of yourself," she said firmly. "Someone has to put a stop to all that reckless generosity. If you really want dessert, there's somewhere I want to take you."

Eduardo hadn't really realized that the market stayed open past the early hours in the morning when it was frequented by the housewives and housemaids who hurried there in preparation of their household's daily meals. He'd seen them often enough, their baskets hanging from the crook of their elbows, as he returned home after one frolic or another. But it turned out that quite a few of the stalls sold goods other than cooking ingredients, like pots and pans and brooms.

And *dulces*.

The sweet aroma announced itself before Aura bypassed a group of barrows and pushcarts laden with papayas, guavas and pineapples and halted in front of a stall. Inside the slim wooden supports, a young woman labored over a steaming cauldron while someone who looked like her grandmother deftly wrapped pieces of hard candy in twists of oiled paper. Aura offered her hand to the older woman, who clasped it between her two gnarled ones.

"What do you like?" Aura asked Eduardo, already examining the sweets on display with her usual brisk efficiency.

"Everything," Eduardo confessed.

With a flourish, the older woman whipped off the fraying towel she'd been using to cover one of the trays on the table in front of her. Stacked on the tin surface were half a dozen bricks of dulce de leche.

"Starting with one of those," Eduardo said, winking at the older woman.

Aura gave him a censorious look. "We don't need the whole brick. Two pieces will do."

"Gregorio would never forgive me if I didn't get some for him. And my clerks are all sugar hounds. There are the messenger boys, too... Come to think of it, a single brick won't be enough."

Before so much as two minutes had passed, Eduardo had persuaded the man on the adjoining stall to part with one of his baskets and the *dulce* seller had filled it to the brim with peanut brittle wrapped in paper, coconut shells that had been scooped out and dried in order to be used as containers for sweet pastes made out of oranges and guavas, as well as the dulce de leche that had caught his eye.

"I truly don't know how you do it," Aura sighed as Eduardo placed a couple of banknotes in the older woman's hands and slid the rest of his money back into the silver clip that held all the bills together.

"Do what?" he asked.

"Manage to spend so much money on things that would cost another person mere cents."

"It's my one talent," he said, taking the basket in one hand and putting his other arm around her.

They said goodbye to the *dulce* sellers. As they strolled

through the market, Eduardo was filled with the oddest sense that his life was finally falling into place.

Never mind that the business with Rafael Marchena was still unresolved. That he hadn't quite worked out if he was guilty or what exactly was Aura's father's role in the smuggling business. That he had yet to prove to his grandfather and his uncle that he and Gregorio were equal to the task of keeping things running smoothly in San Pedro while they were occupied elsewhere.

All those things—and his and Aura's recent argument—aside, Eduardo was filled with contentment.

They still hadn't reached the large gate at the entrance to the market when someone brushed up behind Eduardo. The fingers that slipped into the pocket of his trousers were subtle, but not subtle enough—reaching behind him, Eduardo clasped his hand around a skinny wrist and turned around to find a familiar face.

"Were you trying to pick my pocket again?" he asked the boy who had attempted just such a thing at the park a couple of weeks before.

"Pick your pocket, *señor*?" the boy said, so smoothly that Eduardo was forced to revise his estimation of the boy's age. His scrawny frame and short stature had led Eduardo to assume the boy to be around seven or eight years old but he had to be twelve at least. "I wouldn't do that."

Eduardo released the boy's hand and reached into his own jacket for the bundle of bills he had tucked into its inner pocket. "If you had, you wouldn't have found anything there anyway."

The boy's watchful gaze followed Eduardo's movements as he pulled out two banknotes, ignoring Aura's exasperated sigh.

"I hope this is enough to make you reconsider helping

yourself to the contents of other people's pockets," Eduardo told him. "I also have a job for you, if you want it."

The boy's gaze turned wary. "A job? What kind?"

"First, I'd like to know your name."

"Why?"

"Because that's how gentlemen conduct business."

"It's Juanci—" The boy drew himself up to his full height, his thin shoulders straightening in a way that reminded Eduardo of Aura. "Juan Laureano Pardo."

"It's a pleasure to meet you, Juan," Eduardo said, biting back a smile to preserve the boy's dignity, as Juan had intended by cutting off the diminutive nickname and offering his full name instead. "I'm Eduardo Martínez and this is my wife. I work at one of the shipping offices down by the docks and we're always looking for fast, trustworthy boys to act as messengers."

"That's all I'd have to do? Carry messages?" His expression was eloquent in its skepticism.

"And run the occasional errand. Meals are provided three times a day. Those who wish to improve their schooling are trained to become clerks or bookkeepers, and those who wish to enter into a trade are found positions as apprentices. Everyone decides for himself what to do with his future—but everyone does have to make a decision."

That had been Gregorio's insistence—not all of the boys took them up on the offer, but quite a few of the older ones had found better positions for themselves within the past couple of years.

"I might make time for that." The boy affected nonchalance, but the light that had come into his eyes when Eduardo had mentioned schooling was bright enough to illuminate the square at midnight.

"Tell you what. Stop by Martínez & Hijos tomorrow and

have a talk with the other messengers, see for yourself if the work appeals to you."

With a curt nod, Juan took the proffered bills and sauntered away.

"That was kind," Aura observed.

Eduardo shrugged and shifted the basket dangling from the crook of his elbow. "I wouldn't have met you if it hadn't been for him," he said, letting his lips curl into a careless smile that he hoped concealed some of the emotion behind his words. "I'm not being nearly as generous as I'd like to be. Come on, I'll walk you home."

Aura reached for the silver watch hanging from his waistcoat pocket and made a face when she saw the time. "We'll have to hurry—I'm late to meet Lucía. She told me she would be stopping by after lunch to try on some of the things I'm making for her. And when I'm finished with her, I mean to go see her sister, who needs some dresses for her daughter. Oh, and I wanted to pay a visit to a couple of my old clients in case they require my services—they won't know where to find me with the house closed up."

Aura was already sewing far into the night. Eduardo felt a frown establishing itself between his brows. "Was the amount we settled on for the bank loan not enough? I can have your line of credit extended or—"

"It was more than enough," Aura said. "But I can't turn down work when it's offered. You can understand that, don't you?"

"Of course, but you're working so hard already." Eduardo drew in a careful breath, anxious to keep from repeating the argument from the previous day. "I know that you're used to fending for yourself. But you're not alone anymore, remember? You're my wife now, and I will do everything in my power to make sure that you have everything you could ever want."

"I know you mean that," Aura said, and bit her lip.

"I do. But it feels like you expect me to let you down. Like it's only a matter of time until I do. If you gave me a chance to prove—"

"I can't depend on *anybody*." Her voice was quiet enough that it wouldn't carry to any of the nearby pedestrians, but it was no less intense for all that.

Eduardo's heart was pounding in earnest. "I know, but… I just don't understand why you agreed to marry me if you didn't intend to let me do things for you. Or are you only willing to accept my help when there are ruffians ransacking your house?"

"You don't have to save me, Eduardo. Not from my own life." She pressed her palm to her chest, just below her collarbone, as if her heart was also racing. "I placed my faith in the wrong person and he let me down. I'm not willing to let that happen again."

"I'm not your father, Aura."

"No." She met his gaze and held it, and what he saw in her eyes made his stomach sink. "But you act just like him sometimes."

Given everything he knew about her complicated feelings toward her father, Eduardo didn't think she could have said anything that made him feel more wretched.

No, not wretched—raw.

"Do you really believe that?"

Her gaze skipped away from him.

"Maybe we should talk more about this at home." He forced himself to keep his expression even. "Later, after you've attended to your duties."

"It's no use talking about it, Eduardo. People never

change," Aura said tiredly. "And trying to solve everybody else's problems won't give you whatever it is you're lacking in your life."

She turned around and walked through the doors of the market, and Eduardo had no breath left to call her back.

Chapter Seventeen

No one seemed surprised when a boy turned up at the offices of Martínez & Hijos and declared that Don Eduardo had offered him a job. Eduardo had been in the front room at the time. He'd cast a glance at Juan's thin, well-scrubbed face, and told his new employee to begin his workday by having buttered rolls and hot chocolate with the other messenger boys.

Gregorio, familiar with his cousin's ways and resigned to them, merely shook his head and instructed his secretary to procure a new pair of shoes and a cap for the boy.

It was business as usual for the rest of the day—as far as anyone could see. Adopting his usual demeanor didn't come easily, but Eduardo didn't let a word or even the merest flicker in his expression betray his inner turmoil. He did keep himself even busier than usual, though, all the better to avoid brooding about his argument with Aura.

For the past week, she had been working late into the night, curled up on her chair as she made tiny stitches by lamplight. Eduardo had grown used to the sight, but he still craved her warmth on the mattress beside him.

He couldn't stand the way his chest roiled when someone was angry at him. It made him feel like he was twelve years old again and being sent away by his own parents.

Taking an armload of folders that were destined for Gregorio's desk, Eduardo waved away the clerk tasked with organizing them and took them into the office himself. His cousin had already left to eat with his fiancée and her family, so Eduardo dropped the pile onto his own desk, eager for something to occupy his mind.

He was in the midst of sorting through receipts and approving payments when someone stopped at the open door. It wasn't uncommon for multiple people to seek out Eduardo over the course of the day—he had made a name for himself as always being available to anyone who needed his assistance or guidance or even just his company. The man at the doorway, though, was someone he hadn't seen in weeks.

"Felipe, my friend," he exclaimed, dropping the files and pushing back from his chair to greet the other man with a vigorous handshake. "Truly a pleasure to see you."

Tact prevented him from adding what he really wanted to say—Felipe looked well, with none of the deep lines bisecting his forehead that had been present the last time Eduardo had seen him.

"I hope everything has been resolved," Eduardo said, gesturing to one of the pair of chairs in front of his desk.

"All is well—very well, actually," Felipe said warmly as he sat. "Thanks to you."

Three or four months before, Felipe had come into the office wild-eyed, with a chest full of antique coins, asking frantically if Eduardo could buy them from him.

The only son of a family that took a great deal of pride on their long lineage, Felipe had taken over the management of his father's company upon the latter's death. And although he'd tried his best, inexperience had gotten the best of him and he'd driven both the business and his personal finances to the ground. That would have been bad enough, but he'd attempted to get out of it by borrowing increasingly larger amounts of money that he had no way of repaying and his creditors were not the kind of men who were willing to forgive a debt.

Eduardo hadn't hesitated in accepting his friend's proposition—and he had also taken pains to discreetly inquire over the extent of Felipe's debts in order to quietly relieve him of them. He'd refused all offers of repayment, knowing that Felipe needed everything he had to support his ailing mother.

And go after his wife, who had fled to her parents' home in Caracas, distraught at the potential scandal.

"I intended to write, but words on paper could not convey the depths of my gratitude. You saved me from ruin, my friend," Felipe said. His lips twisted wryly. "And divorce."

Standing, Eduardo reached for two glasses and the decanter of brandy he kept on the credenza. He was simultaneously glad to see that his friend was doing better than when he'd left, and that he had provided Eduardo with a good distraction from his thoughts. "How is your wife?"

"Much happier with me than she was three months ago," Felipe said, accepting the glass Eduardo handed him. "She's the only one who knows just how close I came to disgracing the entire family."

"All that is behind you now." Raising his glass in a toast, Eduardo sat back down. "Have you returned to San Pedro for good?"

His friend shook his head. "Only for a visit—and to try and convince my mother to move to Venezuela with us. We want to start fresh, you see, in a place without so many difficult memories. The past months have changed us a great deal, and it feels like San Pedro will always remain the same."

A knock at the door interrupted Eduardo's reply. Giving Felipe an apologetic look, he called for the knocker to come in and was surprised to see Juan poke his head inside.

The boy cast a glance at Felipe, then turned to Eduardo. "I'm sorry, sir. I didn't know you had company. I'll come back later."

"It's all right," Felipe said, setting his glass down and rising. "I won't take more of your time. I do, however, hope to see you again before we leave. Stop by for dinner sometime this week? You know my wife has a soft spot for bachelors."

"Actually," Eduardo said, clearing his throat. "I'm no longer one of those. I got married almost three weeks ago."

Felipe's eyebrows rose. "Maybe San Pedro has changed more than I thought. We'll have a dinner in honor of your new bride, then."

Leaning in to shake Eduardo's hand, Felipe returned his hat to his head and tipped it at Juan as he strode out of the office.

Eduardo set his brandy aside and glanced toward the boy. The reports he'd received from others in his staff had all indicated that Juan had been settling in well among the other messenger boys. He was quick and had a good memory for the errands he had been dispatched on—and even better, he was curious about all aspects of the shipping process and had undertaken to learn all he could.

The few times Eduardo had glimpsed him, Juan had been going about his duties with an energy that did him credit. Eduardo had made it his business to find out whether he and his sister had a decent place to live and had asked Gregorio to rectify the situation when he found out they didn't.

"What's the matter, Juan? The other boys aren't troubling you, are they?"

The boy shook his head decisively. "Not them."

Curious, Eduardo gestured to the seat Felipe had just vacated, but Juan shook his head and remained on his feet, though he did enter the room and close the door behind him.

Eduardo waited, giving Juan the space to gather his thoughts.

"I don't tell tales," the boy said finally, after Eduardo had sipped almost half his remaining brandy. "I wouldn't have said anything, only you gave me a job and I don't like to be in anybody's debt."

"Neither does my wife," Eduardo muttered. "Go on."

Apparently, the other boys had been talking about a man who had been coming around the loading docks with questions and hints that they could make a great deal of money by entering his employ. That wasn't uncommon—the docks were rife with unscrupulous men who didn't think twice about making grand promises to easily impressionable boys in order to gain their assistance for some criminal endeavor or another. This man, though, was telling the messengers that he knew someone who would pay them to take a voyage on a luxury steamer.

Earlier that day, he had approached Juan to ask the same thing.

"No one's taken him up on it so far, I don't think." Messenger boys were too shrewd not to notice when an offer was too good to be true, and so apparently was Juan. "I'd have said no flat out, but I thought you would want to know more about it. So I went with him."

Eduardo's eyebrows rose. "That was brave of you."

"I can take care of myself," Juan said, and shrugged. "The man took me to an empty warehouse. We were met there by another man. He told me he was looking for a strong boy to accompany his wife on a voyage, and that all I'd need to do was look after her trunks and such."

"Sounds like a fine position," Eduardo remarked.

"Yes," Juan said slowly, "but they were too nervous. It didn't feel right."

"I can respect a man who trusts his intuition. His gut," Eduardo added at Juan's blank look. His own gut was leading him toward a conclusion and he wasn't sure he liked it. "Can I count on you to let me know if he comes around again? I want to know who he is and who he works for."

"I thought you might, so I picked his pocket." Juan held out a folded piece of paper. "I didn't take no money, just this."

Eduardo unfolded it, his curiosity growing as he looked at what appeared to be a telegram—addressed to Rafael Marchena.

He swore, then forced himself to give the boy an encouraging smile. He'd spent much of the past week attending every event he'd been invited to—and several he hadn't—on the merest chance that he'd be able to unearth more information about Marchena. And there was the man, haunting his own warehouses.

"I think I'm the one in your debt now. Thank you for telling me, Juan."

He went home after that, and found Aura alone in the dining room. The table had been laid for one and she had already begun to eat, probably because he'd sent word that he wasn't going to be coming home. She looked about as tired as he felt as she spooned stewed red beans over the white rice on her plate, and Eduardo would have given up his share of the Martínez fortune just to take her to bed.

For a proper rest, of course, though he wouldn't be averse

to more. He *missed* her. He missed the rapport that had built between them and the way she burrowed under the covers and pressed her cold toes against his calf.

But she was back to being as self-contained as when they'd first met.

How was it that half the people in town felt comfortable coming to Eduardo with their troubles while his own wife continued to cling fiercely to the belief that she could only depend on herself?

She glanced up at him. "I didn't know you were coming home. Want me to fetch you a plate?"

He dropped into the seat opposite hers. "Don't worry, I already asked one of the girls." Shooting a look toward the open doorway, he lowered his voice. "Aura, Marchena has been coming around the Martínez & Hijos warehouses."

She released the ladle so quickly, stewed beans splattered onto the tablecloth. Muttering a curse under her breath, Aura dipped the edge of her napkin into her water and tried to scrub out the reddish flecks. "Do you think his wife said something about us being at their house?"

"If she did, I doubt it had anything to do with what I learned today." Quickly, he filled her in on what Juan had said. "I was thinking about it on the way home. He's searching for someone to smuggle the goods in and out of the country without running the risk of being implicated. It's possible he wanted to use your father as courier, only he died before he was able to carry out their plan."

Aura nodded thoughtfully, winding a fold of napkin around her index finger. "That would explain the steamer ticket to New York. And it would mean that whatever he was meant to smuggle for them was still in his possession— hence Marchena's men thinking I had it."

"Of course, it's all conjecture at this point. But I do believe that we're finally on the path to finding out what really happened."

"Maybe it's time to approach him directly, Eduardo. Ask him what he wants and try to negotiate a deal. All this subterfuge is…frustrating."

"You're right. But before we do, I want to impress upon him that you are not to be trifled with. I think it'd be a good idea if he saw for himself how well acquainted we are with the customs inspector and the docks administrator. Not to mention the governor, who's a personal friend of my grandfather's."

"How would we do that?"

"A party of course—how else?" Eduardo forced himself to grin, though all he wanted was to sink to his knees in front of Aura's chair and bury his face in her lap and ask—no, beg—her to come to bed with him. "We'll invite everyone associated with the shipping industry, as well as Marchena, and make a show of strength."

And lay a trap. But he'd share that part with Aura once he had worked out the details.

"How else, indeed," Aura murmured. "I suppose you'll want to hold it in the garden. Your grandfather left instructions for a dais to be built for the orchestra he hired for the dance. If you like, I can ask that it be built ahead of time so that it can be used for your party, too."

"Oh, I don't believe it'll be here."

"Where, then?"

He smiled. "On board the *Leonor*."

Over the course of the week following their argument, Eduardo had made a point of accepting every invitation that came his way. Aura couldn't blame him if he missed his old amusements. She certainly wasn't much fun—after the last fitting, she had devoted all her time to putting the finishing touches on Lucía's things, meaning to have them laundered and pressed by the end of the week at the latest so that she could move on to the half a dozen frocks Amalia de Fuentes wanted for her baby daughter.

Aura had more than enough to keep her busy—and that included making half a dozen drafts of the letter she meant to send to her father's acquaintance in New York. She had gone through an alarming quantity of paper before she'd been satisfied with what she'd written, and both Eduardo and Gregorio had helped her make an English translation to include as well as her original, just in case.

Using the pen, ink and creamy stationery Eduardo had told her she could borrow, Aura made fair copies of both versions of the letter. She slid them into a fresh envelope and carefully copied out the unfamiliar words in the address, checking several times to make sure she had it right. When she was finished, she cleaned the pen nib thoroughly and put the cap back on the pot of ink.

And opened it almost immediately after. Pulling a fresh piece of paper toward her, she hesitated only for a second before writing in looping script, *Querida Mamá...*

She wrote to her mother. And to each of her sisters and even her brother, even though he had been a boy of twelve the last time she had seen him, obsessed with marbles and horses and little else. She didn't know what kind of young man he'd grown up to be. But it was time she found out.

By the time she finished, she had used up all the spare paper Eduardo had left out for her. She blew on the letters to her family to make the ink dry faster, then folded them in half and worked them into envelopes. It was late afternoon, and almost time to get dressed for the party aboard the *Leonor*. After taking so long to draft the letters, it shouldn't have mattered if they went out on that day's post or not, but suddenly Aura was filled with urgency.

After sealing all the envelopes, she hunted around his inkpots and pens for stamps. There didn't seem to be any—he must have forgotten to set them out for her.

Aura went over to the sideboard where she had seen Eduardo keep his writing things. The first drawer held nothing but paper and a couple of pencil stubs, and the second was crammed with colored pencils with broken points and dozens of drawings that had to be the work of the youngest Martínezes.

The bottom drawer appeared to be stuck. Planting her shoes on the tiled floor, Aura pulled with all her strength on the brass ring set into the center of the drawer—and almost fell backward as it flew open and envelopes flew out like birds in flight, scattering all around her.

Breathing hard, Aura knelt and began to pick them up into a neat stack, realizing after a moment that they weren't unused envelopes. They were letters. They were postmarked New York, just like her father's had been, only these were addressed to Eduardo. There were dozens of them, some creased, some pristine—and all unopened.

After the discovery that her father had been corresponding with someone in that city, this felt like too much of a coincidence.

Feeling terrible for trespassing Eduardo's privacy, Aura looked at the names on the upper left corner. Some were marked Ramón Martínez, others Mercedes de Martínez. Cousins, perhaps? An aunt or uncle?

"Aura?" Gregorio asked, striding into the room. "Is your letter ready? I was hoping to go to the post office, but I'll have to run if I want to get back in time to dress for the party and—"

He came to an abrupt stop, staring at Aura as she crouched on the floor with a stack of envelopes in her hand.

"The drawer was stuck," she offered. "I was looking for stamps—I hadn't realized Eduardo kept his correspondence here."

"Just the letters from his parents," Gregorio said. "I gave the staff instructions to toss them in there whenever one arrives, to keep from upsetting Eduardo."

"When they arrive?" Aura's mouth opened and shut. "I was under the impression that his parents had…"

She allowed the end of her sentence to trail away, unsure about how to phrase the question of whether someone's relation was alive or not.

Gregorio clearly had no such qualms. "That they'd died?" he said bluntly. "Eduardo acts like it, sometimes. But my aunt and uncle are very much alive. My uncle heads our New York division—they moved there when Eduardo was around twelve or so. He doesn't like to talk about it, but I thought he'd have told you by now, given that…"

It was his turn to trail away delicately.

"Given that we're married," she said.

An apologetic wariness crept into his gruff tone. "I think you had better talk about this with him. Only…be careful. Eduardo is unreasonably touchy when it comes to his parents."

She nodded, and tried to smile. "Thank you, Gregorio. For the advice and for your honesty."

"I'm not sure you'll be thanking me once you do have that conversation with Eduardo," he said heavily. "In any case, I should get going to the post office. I forgot—did you have anything you wanted mailed?"

"Oh!" Aura picked up the letter destined for New York, ignoring the ones she had written to her family. She didn't even know where to send them. "It needs stamps. Do you have any?"

"I'll take care of it."

Thanking Gregorio again, she waited until he had left the room before stepping out into the balcony. Below her, Don Amable's garden stretched in a patchwork quilt in shades of green and brown, punctuated here and there by the colorful bursts of the flowers that grew in well-tended beds. The aroma of the roses growing outside the terrace mingled with the scent of the citrus trees by the dining room and the faint tanginess of the sea carried along in the warm breeze.

She could see the Caribbean Sea far beyond the garden, a glittering strip of blue against the steadiness of the horizon. The letter she had written to her father's acquaintance or associate would be on its way soon enough, in search of some of the answers she sought.

The only trouble was, the questions she'd had the week before had more than doubled.

The truth was inescapable. She had married someone she barely knew—and who didn't know her. And that was why she'd been right to keep her heart at a distance.

Hands spread on the sun-warmed railing, Aura took a deep breath and tried not to give in to the suspicion that she hadn't been altogether successful.

Chapter Eighteen

Without enough time to make herself a new frock for the occasion, Aura had decided to wear the ivory dress she had worn to her own wedding. After painstakingly removing the petals, she had tried to keep the dress from looking too plain by adding a black sash decorated with a single black rosette and edging the sleeves with black ribbons tied into bows just above her elbows.

It was undeniably a daytime dress, though, and Aura knew she would look out of place among the women in evening gowns. Over the years, her limited social calendar had made it easy for her to embellish her ensembles with ribbons or the greenery she grew in her window boxes, but even she had to admit that the party called for silks and décolletage.

She'd just finished getting ready when Lucía arrived to pick up her shirtwaists in a flurry of apologies for being late. The heiress had taken one look at Aura before graciously suggesting—and then insisting—that Aura borrow one of her many gowns.

Lucía was reed-thin, with narrow hips and a small bosom, and Aura didn't have a single prayer for fitting into her clothes. Her sister's friend Paulina, however, had a figure that more closely resembled Aura's and a wardrobe to rival Lucía's.

In what seemed like no time at all, Aura was outfitted in a gown that reminded her of a clouded sky, the blue-gray chiffon edged with silver braid and crowded with a constellation of silver and translucent glass beads. A fan, a beaded handbag, a bandeau for her hair and a pair of slippers completed the ensemble.

Aura drew the line at the jewelry. In their enthusiasm over dressing her, Lucía and Paulina offered Aura their costliest pieces, necklaces and earrings and bracelets so heavy with precious stones that the mere thought of wearing them made her feel faint.

Returned to the Martínez house by Lucía's coachman, she waited on the terrace with a glass of ice water while Eduardo finished getting ready upstairs. Gregorio had already left, according to the housemaid who had opened the door for Aura, and she remembered that he had said something about picking up Celia.

His absence was going to make her ride alone with Eduardo either more awkward or less, and Aura couldn't decide which of the two it would be.

His eyes widened when he saw her. He himself looked perfectly splendid in a dinner jacket and a low-cut waistcoat, his white shirt starched to perfection and his thick curls sleek with pomade.

The truth was, Eduardo was outrageously handsome, and would have looked splendid even without the benefit of formal wear.

Aura could have cursed out loud at the rush of desire that threatened to cloud her judgment so that she almost forgot herself and stepped right into his arms.

To keep from doing just that, she reminded herself that the man standing in front of her was little more than a stranger. One that knew exactly how to coax gasps and moans out of her, it was true, but one who hadn't thought to share information as basic as his parents' deaths or lack thereof.

The more she thought about it, the more irritation seemed to build inside her. He'd listened to her talk about her own father, and grieve over him, and she'd been so hesitant to ask about his in case she was probing a sore spot.

Rising to her feet, she smoothed a hand over her borrowed gown. And then she blurted out, "Is it true your parents are alive?"

Eduardo's easy, open expression shuttered. "Did Gregorio tell you? It wasn't his place to say anything."

"He didn't—only confirmed it when I asked."

"I was under the impression that we wanted the same things out of this arrangement," he said stiffly. "And it did not include you prying into my affairs."

"I was looking for stamps," Aura protested. "I hardly call that prying into your affairs. I've told you everything about me, Eduardo. And you haven't felt the need to tell me whether your parents are alive or not? Why would you lead me to believe otherwise?"

"I didn't lead you to believe anything," he said. "In fact, I'm reasonably sure that I haven't said a word about my parents to you. Or to them."

"Eduardo—"

"They moved to New York when I was eleven years old and they sent me away less than a year later. I was having a hard time being in a different environment and speaking a different language and they found it easier to discard their only son than to give up their evenings at the Metropolitan Opera. Is that what you wanted to know?"

Aura laid a hand on his arm. "Maybe they sent you away

because they knew it would have been selfish to keep you there."

"I think," he said carefully, "there was a time when I would have liked to believe that."

"Have you seen them since?"

"They came for a visit five years ago and there was a Sunday luncheon at Abuelo's estate with most of the family. Abuelo asked me to attend and I did for his sake, but… it didn't end well."

"I'm sorry," Aura murmured. She should have left the matter there, but the sheer amount of letters that had been in that drawer made her press on—her mother hadn't tried writing to her even once since the divorce. If anyone had been discarded, it was Aura. "And I understand it's none of my business. But, Eduardo, I know what it's like to let grief and pride keep you from people you love. And judging from all the letters in that drawer, it doesn't seem like they discarded you. Maybe if you wrote back—"

"Aura, my parents didn't even bother to bring me back themselves. They hired someone to escort me back home—a second cousin twice removed, or something like that. He took a fancy to another passenger and left me alone in the cabin most nights while he went courting. One night there was a storm, a bad one. I tried to get out, but he had locked me in so that I wouldn't go wandering the ship."

"Oh, Eduardo."

"To keep me safe, you see," Eduardo said grimly. "I didn't dare light the oil lamp—all the rocking, you see—so I huddled alone in the dark until morning." His lips twitched into a mirthless smile. "It's a wonder I'm not afraid of the dark."

But he *was* afraid of being alone—or, if not afraid, then he found it difficult to bear it. She didn't have to ask to know that was the reason he couldn't sleep when it was too quiet. Or why none of the doors in the house had locks.

And why he tried so, so hard to make himself indispensable, as if worried that otherwise, he'd be sent away again.

The memory of what she'd said to him at the market made her blood run cold. She reached for him, and he caught her fingers, but only to politely move them away.

"I don't wish to dwell on it," he said. For the first time since Aura had met him, his smile didn't reach his eyes. "It all happened a very long time ago, and I'm no longer that scared, lonely little boy."

"Aren't you?" she asked quietly, earning herself a raised eyebrow from Eduardo. "Why else are you so unwilling to discuss anything that's the least bit upsetting?"

"Because there's no point in it. Because I won't stand for feeling like I'm trapped in that cabin again. Because…" His eyes squeezed shut and when he opened them again, Aura could see that they were full of shadows. "Because I just don't want to."

"But I do. Does what I want matter at all?"

Eduardo didn't answer. He didn't even look at her. All he did was adjust his cuffs and say, "We should go. We'll be late to the party."

She stared at his retreating back, frustration and hurt swirling inside her. Had she really been so naive to believe that a lack of love or strong feelings for each other would make their marriage less complicated?

Her parents had loved each other deeply, at least at the start. It hadn't been enough. And maybe a partnership wasn't enough, either. Maybe marriage was always a miserable experience for all concerned.

In Aura's case, marriage might just have been the worst mistake of her life. She hadn't just married a man she didn't know—she'd married one who didn't want her to know him. Who kept the truest parts of him buried beneath a glossy veneer of charm and affability. Who actively made the decision to conceal things from her.

Who'd promised her nothing but kisses, it was true. Aura hadn't known then that marriage had to be based on more than that.

All the presents in the world couldn't make up for what he refused to give her.

Aura's miserable mood contrasted sharply with the festive atmosphere aboard the *Leonor*. The ship's polished deck was crowded with tables spread with pristine tablecloths. The cut crystals of the weighted vases on each table caught and reflected the afternoon's rosy glow as the sun descended slowly toward the horizon.

Invitations had been issued to—and accepted by—W.E. Pulliam, the customs general receiver, and his deputy, J.H. Edwards. Eduardo's guest list also included almost everyone who worked in any field related to shipping, as well as several prominent politicians. It hadn't surprised her that Eduardo counted so many important people among his friends and acquaintances—not just because of his family's own prominence, but because it was easy to tell, just from looking at him, that he had been raised to hold his own among such people.

He wasn't just well-read and informed on current events; he was well-versed in such a wide variety of subjects that he seemed to find no trouble in engaging anyone in conversation, whether that someone was a clerk or the customs inspector himself.

Unless that someone was his wife, of course.

Aura tried her best to keep her foul mood from showing

as she covertly scanned the crowd for Rafael Marchena. He didn't appear to have arrived yet, though it was difficult to tell in the sea of men dressed in crisp black and white.

Anxiety fluttered inside her chest, making her fiddle with her borrowed fan. It was a work of art, made out of charcoal silk embroidered in shades of saffron and rose, the only point of color in her ensemble. As Eduardo conversed with his guests, she fiddled with it, folding and unfolding it and running her fingers through the oversize tassel dangling from its end.

She wasn't just nervous about confronting Marchena, she realized. Her argument with Eduardo had rattled her more than she'd wanted to admit. And though he was outwardly unruffled, his demeanor welcoming and expansive as he chatted with his guests, Aura could tell that he was troubled, too.

"She's a relic from another era," Eduardo was saying fondly, in response to a remark someone had made about the *Leonor*. "Would you like a tour?"

Before the man could formulate a reply, she seized Eduardo's arm. "Would you excuse us?"

Bypassing the elegantly appointed drawing room where quite a few guests had congregated, Aura led him to one of the staterooms she had seen. He looked baffled and more than a little annoyed as she closed the door behind him and leaned against it.

"Aura," he said with uncharacteristic irritability, "this is neither the time nor place—"

"I know. And I'm sorry, Eduardo. But I won't be able to go through this evening without getting something off my chest."

She half expected him to take advantage of her words to make a joke about her chest, or say something to diffuse the tension, but all he did was look at her. And she looked back, momentarily rendered speechless by the sight of him.

In front of the lace curtains that covered the stateroom's only window, bathed in late afternoon light, Eduardo looked like one of the illustrations in the books crowded inside the bookcase in the Martínezes's private parlor. Like a prince, or a knight, his stiff posture making him look like he should be dressed in armor.

"What is it, Aura?" he asked, and the spell was broken.

"We can't leave things the way we did at the house."

"Don't you think I've given you enough, Aura? What more can you possibly want from me?"

"I want to know why you're so scared," she exclaimed.

His lips twisted into a mirthless smile. "I thought I already told you—of being locked alone in dark cabins while—"

"Why you're so scared to talk to me," Aura said. "Why you go to such lengths to avoid confiding in me. I've told you everything about my life, Eduardo."

"I didn't ask you to."

"And yet I did anyway," she said. "Because it wouldn't have been fair to enter into a marriage—or an agreement or a partnership or anything you want to call it—without telling you who I am and where I come from."

"You live in my house. You've met my family. Why isn't that enough?"

"Because I—"

Because she was in love with him. Because she wanted more than just a partnership—she wanted a real marriage.

She couldn't bring herself to say it. But something must have shown in her face anyway, because at the sight of it, panic flashed over Eduardo's face.

"We ought to get back out there," he said stiffly, glancing away from her. "No need to give our guests the wrong idea about what we're doing in here."

This time, she left first. Striding into the reception room, she accepted a coupe of champagne from a passing waiter and tried to smile graciously as she was introduced to the newly arrived Mr. Pulliam. Her attempt at a conversation went marginally better as she channeled her anger with Eduardo into sparring playfully with the American on the exportation of tortoiseshells, which had recently been outlawed.

"You must call me William," he said in his accented Spanish, eyes twinkling as he glanced from Aura to Eduardo and back again. "And you must call on me at home sometime."

Aura lifted her chin—Marchena's position as an interventor meant that he worked directly under Mr. Pulliam. As she murmured a reply to the American, she grew aware that someone was trying to capture her attention.

Perla? she mouthed.

The other woman was gesturing at Aura, too visibly upset to be discreet. Aura cast a glance at Eduardo, who had waved the governor over and was drawing him into conversation with Mr. Pulliam. Quietly, Aura went to Perla's side.

"What's the matter?"

"It's terrible," Perla all but sobbed. She was dressed in a pale blue gown overlaid with charmeuse in a darker shade, with sleeves that fell nearly to her elbow. Appliquéd flowers ran up the length of the skirt and crept over the bodice. "It's my husband, I—I think—"

The wail she gave was almost loud enough to be heard over the music. Glancing behind her shoulder, Aura put her arm around the other woman and guided her to a private spot near the gangplank, which still hadn't been raised in preparation for the ship's departure.

"He's not hurt, is he?"

"Hurt?" Perla said blankly before her face folded into furious lines. "He's a scoundrel. And a—"

She cast a glance at the throng around them and clamped her lips together. Aura could more than understand her reluctance to talk about her husband's exploits in front of his superiors.

"Perla, why don't we talk about it privately?" she suggested gently. "We could go into one of the staterooms—"

"I refuse to be trapped aboard a ship with that man while he lies to everyone we know. Please, Aura, you've got to come with me. I can't bear to be alone—and I can't bear for anyone else to know."

Aura nodded, glancing around for Eduardo, who had moved from the spot where she had last seen him. "I'll just let—"

Perla let out a loud sniff and began scrabbling in her handbag until she unearthed a handkerchief that could have found a second life as a bedsheet. One of the men glanced curiously toward them and said something to the man at his side, who had been introduced to Aura as the docks' administrator.

If Marchena was already on board, it was probably better to get his wife off the ship. Aura glanced around for Eduardo again, but he was lost in a sea of men in black suits.

She'd find a way to get word back to him.

"All right. Let's go. Quickly," she added as she saw two members of the crew prepare to detach the gleaming wooden staircase that had replaced the gangplank for the guests' convenience while boarding.

They descended swiftly, and Perla led her directly to an

open carriage stationed partly behind a pile of barrels and crates. "We'll be able to talk privately in here," she said.

The pile of crates obscured the interior of the carriage, so it wasn't until Aura had rounded the obstruction and was about to step up that she saw the man sitting inside.

Rafael Marchena.

Perla didn't betray any surprise at the sight of her husband. In fact…

"Finally," Marchena said irritably as his wife gave Aura a shove from behind that forced her to scramble up into the carriage. Perla hoisted herself in quickly after her and settled next to her husband, perfectly dry-eyed.

The coachman at the front snapped the reins and set off immediately, not giving Aura a chance to get out of the carriage.

Correctly reading the shock in Aura's expression, Marchena said, "My wife and I are partners in all aspects of life. Did you really think she wouldn't tell me that you went snooping in our home? Or that she wouldn't recognize your ham-fisted attempts to extract information from her?"

Aura narrowed her eyes. "It seemed only fair that I do my share of snooping, given how you instructed your henchmen to search my home."

The docks were rolling swiftly past them as the driver urged the horse pulling the carriage into a gallop. Darkness was beginning to fall, making the lights on the *Leonor* all the more noticeable. Marchena followed her gaze.

"I'm flattered, Señora de Martínez. All that, just for me?" He shook his head, looking mildly amused. "There was no need to go to so much trouble. All I wanted was for you to give me what's rightfully mine."

"Not this again," Aura said, letting her frustration show. "My father left me nothing."

Perla leaned forward. "You have it. You may not know you have it, but you do."

Irritation rolled over Aura. "I'd be able to tell you for certain if *someone* filled me in on what it is I'm supposed to have."

The Marchenas exchanged a look that was filled with exasperation. It was Perla who spoke. "I don't understand why you're so adamant in having us believe that your father never told you about the gold."

Shock sliced through her. Gold and property—that was what Aura had told her father to invest in. He'd bought the house. And then he'd asked to borrow her life savings.

"The gold that he stole from us," Perla clarified, watching Aura's expression through narrowed eyes.

"My father may have had a lot of faults, but he wasn't a thief," Aura protested.

"But he *was* desperate. He owed money to someone in New York, and he threatened to have my husband fired if he didn't help him smuggle the gold out of the country."

Aura didn't want to believe it. But hadn't that been her problem for years? She'd refused to believe what everyone else said about her father, including her own mother. And just look at how misplaced her faith had been.

Her father had been deeply hurt when her mother had left, taking their other three children with her. No one could have failed to notice the way he had renewed his efforts into making a fortune as quickly as possible, desperate to prove his wife wrong. Who was to say he hadn't resorted to theft as well as smuggling?

Aura looked at the Marchenas, finally recognizing the urgency in their eyes for what it was. Desperation.

"All right," Aura said, and licked her lips. "I'll help you find the gold. And then you'll leave me alone."

Chapter Nineteen

Caught in a whirl of anxiety, it was all Eduardo could do to hold himself together as he played the expansive host. This was why he hated talking about what had happened on his journey back from New York. Every time he talked about it—every time he so much as thought about it—he found himself back in that dark cabin, alone and scared as the world rocked wildly around him.

The experience hadn't given him a terror of ships, though that was probably because he'd spent most of his childhood in one or another. And spending time with his family meant being in the *Leonor*. The boards of its deck were as familiar as the tile floor of his own parlor, and it was steady under his feet.

Eduardo drew in a deep breath and returned his attention back to William Pulliam and Governor Santos. Aura was no longer next to him—he must not have heard her excuse herself. The ringing in his ears was so loud, he didn't think he'd heard much of anything in the past hour.

He looked around for her and found Gregorio instead, on the other side of the room. He didn't blame his cousin for having told Aura about his parents. He hadn't thought twice about tumbling pleasantly into an easy happiness with Aura because their arrangement meant there was no danger of being accosted with uncomfortable questions about things he'd rather not think about. He'd been wrong.

The worst part was, he had wanted to tell her. He wanted to tell her things he'd never told anyone. If only talking didn't make him feel so damn wretched.

He headed toward Gregorio, but was waylaid by a friend who'd been away on business for much of the past month. A practiced smile settled on Eduardo's lips as he exchanged pleasantries with the man, his mind drifting until a remark made him crash to attention.

"Was that Alfredo Soriano's daughter?"

"You knew Aura's father?"

"Of course," his friend said. "I met him at Martínez & Hijos a few months ago. You don't remember?"

Alfredo Soriano. Eduardo vaguely remembered the man who had talked his way into a private audience with Eduardo and Gregorio, going on about a once-in-a-lifetime business opportunity. Recognizing every sign that he was being sold a tall tale, Eduardo had listened politely to the harebrained scheme before giving the man a noncommittal answer and politely walking him outside.

That had been Aura's father?

Eduardo hadn't taken much notice of his features, save for the waxed mustache that commanded the lower half of his face, but he did recall the man's animated gestures and the way he'd leaned forward as he talked, punctuating his words with little taps against the surface of Gregorio's desk. Aura's father had been as smooth as Aura was prickly.

He hadn't given the man's request a second thought—people soliciting meetings with him and making wild claims in order to get him to invest in their various schemes happened with appalling frequency and he knew better than to indulge them.

If Eduardo hadn't turned him down, would he have resorted to allying himself with Rafael Marchena? There was no way of knowing—but that didn't keep Eduardo from feeling a pang of guilt at the thought of all his refusal had cost Aura.

Recalling that he was holding a glass of whiskey, Eduardo swallowed back a mouthful.

A memory followed hard on the heels of that thought. His meeting with Soriano hadn't ended with the refusal. Aura's father had been waiting just outside Eduardo's office when a distraught Felipe had charged past him, clutching a chest full of antique coins. Soriano, who must have overheard Felipe pleading Eduardo to buy the chest from him, had offered to take it off his hands.

Eduardo had agreed, especially since Soriano had a bundle of banknotes in his pockets and Eduardo wanted to settle Felipe's debts as quickly as possible—and without asking his grandfather for the money to do so.

The money Soriano had offered him had been Aura's.

Aura. He had to tell her what Marchena was after.

Thrusting the glass at his friend with an abrupt apology, Eduardo went searching for Aura. The last time he remembered seeing her, they had been standing just outside the ship's library with William Pulliam. Eduardo retraced his steps, flashing polite but discouraging smiles at anyone who tried to approach him.

Her gleaming gray-and-silver dress had made her glitter like a scatter of stars against the midnight sky. Like a river in moonlight. She should have been easy to spot. Unless she'd gone into one of the staterooms to freshen up?

Eduardo ran lightly up the staircase, nodding at friends and acquaintances as he passed them. A couple of minutes later and he was incapable of even that much.

"Are you looking for your wife?"

Eduardo's head snapped up as he saw the *Leonor*'s purser approaching him.

"She sent me to find you," the purser said. "Said to tell you that she found something. And…does the name Marchena mean anything to you?"

"Where is she?" Eduardo demanded. "Show me, quickly."

To his credit, the man didn't hesitate. He led Eduardo to one of the staterooms at the end of the hallway. Eduardo thundered after him, swearing under his breath. He shouldn't have left her alone.

"Through here," the man said, wrenching open a door.

Eduardo was through it and in the darkened room before his mind registered that it was also empty. He whirled immediately, mouth opening to furiously demand what the purser intended—and instead, he found himself shoved back inside and the door slammed shut in his face.

He flung himself against it, but he was too late. The key turned in the lock.

Every scrap of reason Eduardo possessed took leave of him in an instant, replaced by sheer wild panic. He rattled the doorknob so hard it should have broken off in his hands, pounding on the door with his fist as if he meant to knock it down. All to no avail.

He was trapped.

It wasn't until the Marchenas' coach reached Aura's house and she alighted awkwardly, trying not to get her shoes caught on the hem of her dress, that she realized their coachman was the ruffian who had intruded into her house.

Dealing with the Marchenas was one thing—this ruffian lent an air of danger to the proceeding that sent fear jangling through Aura's nerves.

And this time Eduardo was on the *Leonor*, which had probably set sail by now. This time, there was no one to help her if things got rough.

The man jumped down from the carriage and joined their party, giving Aura a smile that looked more like a grimace.

She tilted her head up. "I'm afraid we haven't been introduced."

"You can call me Caimán," he said, his features amused under the brim of his cap.

"That's not a name, that's an animal," Aura informed him, but was forced to cease her questioning as they neared the house and someone stepped out of the shadows and in front of the door. She tensed, then realized the burly man must have been one of the guards Eduardo had assigned to keep watch over the house.

"Aura," Perla said warningly, taking care to keep the smile on her lips.

"It's all right," Aura called to the man. She forced herself to keep a pleasant expression on her face. "I'm Aura de Martínez. Did my husband not send word that my friends and I were on our way?"

"No, *señora*," the guard replied, scrutinizing first her and then the others.

"That's odd. Well, we'll only be here for a few minutes. My friends are here to help me find something I mislaid."

The guard still looked unconvinced, but Aura swept past him and the Marchenas followed.

Dusk had come and gone in the time it took them to get from the docks to the house, and Aura found and lit an oil lamp by feel.

"We'll start upstairs," she announced, and it made her feel better to take command of the situation.

It made her feel better to come up with a plan of escape, too, in case it should prove necessary. She had done it plenty of times in her life—sneaking out of one place in order to avoid danger. Of course, that danger had usually come in the form of creditors. How foolish of her to think that she'd never have to do it again.

She had gone through most of her life without feeling a sense of permanence. That was what she'd been hoping to gain with the store. Permanence and security. Instead, she'd found it with Eduardo and his family. Aura didn't know when the Martínezes had become her family, too, but it was thoughts of them and of Eduardo that kept her steady as she searched her father's bedroom.

She should have done this weeks ago, she knew. Maybe she would have, if she hadn't gotten sidetracked with Eduardo. Or maybe she'd been too heartsick over everything she'd learned about her father to have wanted to reopen old wounds by going through his things.

The fine mahogany furniture her father had purchased for himself had long since been repossessed, and most of his belongings were tucked away in wooden crates and a pine dresser whose missing leg made it tilt hopelessly to one side. Aura went through every one of its drawers, going so far as to remove them entirely in case he had pasted anything to the underside.

The Marchenas didn't help. They stood blocking the entrance, overseeing her efforts as they conducted a conversation entirely in furious whispers.

They were speaking too low for her to be able to make out much. She didn't need to hear, however, to gather that Caimán made them as nervous as he made Aura. She realized that he wasn't there to guard them as much as make sure they didn't escape.

"How much do you owe him?" Aura asked as she struggled to lift one end of the mattress.

Perla scowled at her. "You don't know what you're talking about."

"I think I do, actually." Carefully, Aura examined the mattress, checking the stitching for rips and pressing her palms along its length in case anything was concealed inside it. "I know a creditor when I see one."

The only question was, why were they in his debt? As Aura had noted inside their home, the Marchenas didn't seem to lead an extravagant lifestyle.

"Is it gambling?" she asked, so caught up in her curiosity that she didn't realize it was an excellent way to provoke her captors until she saw the annoyance mounting in their faces. "A sudden illness? An investment gone bad?" She hauled the mattress back into place and placed her hands on her hips. "Did either of you happen to purchase two dozen sacks of coffee beans that turned out to be moldy?"

If Aura had learned anything in her twenty-five years of life, it was the many ways in which money could evaporate from a person's pocket.

A suspicion crept into her mind. "Are you being blackmailed?"

If Marchena, in his official capacity as an intervenor, was trying to make a business out of turning a blind eye to smugglers or even helping them evade duties…and if he'd approached the wrong person…

Perla exploded from the doorway like she had been fired out of a pistol, hissing, "Whatever you're trying to do, it won't work. Keep searching."

"Why are you so sure the gold is here?" Aura asked, sure now that she had hit upon the answer. Caimán had seemed to know her father. Had he been the one to suggest seeking out Marchena? "Isn't there a chance that my father got rid of it before he died?"

"I saw him that day—just before. He still had it," Rafael said flatly.

She sagged back against the bedpost, all her cockiness ebbing away. She'd been sewing in the front room when her father had hurried inside, upset about something he didn't want to talk about. Upset herself about the fact that he hadn't bothered to show up in time for lunch when she'd been forced to put her work on pause in order to labor over the stove, Aura had ignored him until she'd heard the thump that had sent her running upstairs.

"What did you say to him?" she murmured.

"Exactly what we're about to tell you now." Perla stalked forward. "You'll find the gold for us. And then you'll take it to its intended destination, as your father ought to have done. As your father *agreed* to. As the wife of Eduardo Martínez, you will have no trouble getting through Customs here or in New York."

"I'm not going to go to New York," Aura told her calmly. "I'm not going to go anywhere. I'm going to find your gold and then you're going to let me leave. It's only a matter of time before my husband finds me. And when he does, you—"

The Marchenas exchanged an amused glance that made her blood run cold.

"What did you do to him?" she asked sharply.

"Do to him? Why, nothing whatsoever," Perla said in a parody of innocence that made her husband laugh. Aura failed to see what was so amusing about it. "Our associate on the ship, on the other hand…"

Rafael continued, "He was left with instructions to lock the interfering bastard in an empty stateroom."

Locked up. Aura's heart ached for Eduardo. The March-enas couldn't have known the torture they were inflicting on him.

"Do you really think locking him up will stop him?" Aura snapped. "The ship is full of men who count Eduardo among their dearest friends. Someone will let him out."

"The hold of the *Leonor* is full of explosives," Rafael said briskly. "And it will have sailed by now. Our friend down-stairs arranged it all. One word from him, and your husband and all his guests will be met with an unfortunate accident."

Aura had seen a ship burn. It had happened the year be-fore, right in the docks where the *Leonor* spent most of her time. She and her father had been living close enough that their rented rooms had filled with the garish orange glow and the strong whiff of smoke. They had rushed out to see the *Caridad* engulfed in flames. The rumor that crates of rum were being stored in her hold seemed to have been confirmed by the sheer intensity of the fire.

If there were explosives aboard the *Leonor*...

Aura's heart squeezed inside her chest. "Won't your as-sociate be in danger of getting caught in the explosion? He'd have to be on the ship in order to blow it up."

Marchena shrugged. "Our friends are knowledgeable in those matters—we're not. All we know is that they were eager to provide you with enough incentive to keep from wasting our time."

Forget searching. She had to get Eduardo—and every-one else—off that ship.

"I don't think the gold is in here," she said, twining her damp palms in the fabric of her skirt. "Shall we move on to the next room?"

She wasn't surprised when Marchena grabbed her by the arm as she approached the doorway, his surprisingly strong fingers clamping around her with bruising force. It reminded her of how the *Leonor*'s purser had grabbed her when he'd caught her in it, and anger surged up inside her. She'd been hauled around enough.

Driving her elbow into Marchena's side, she grabbed two handfuls of her skirts and ran to the nearest window that looked out into the front of the house, shouting for Eduardo's guard. The Marchenas rushed up behind her but she managed to evade them, feinting to one side and dodging around them as she pelted for the stairs.

Caimán caught her before she could get very far.

She twisted out of his grasp, but after the last time, he knew what she was capable of. Seizing both her arms from behind, he held her at arm's length and called to someone standing just outside. Aura peered into the darkness, her eyes adjusting slowly, and saw that Eduardo's guard had been knocked unconscious. Standing over him with a length of rope was another man, one who evidently answered to the ruffian.

"Tell him to go ahead."

The other man nodded and melted into the darkness. Straining, Aura was able to see the ladder leaning against the house across the street. In a moment, a signal fire flared from a flat section on the roof.

Sometime between a moment and an eternity later, an answering glow could be seen in the darkened sky. Aura stood so tense that her muscles began to ache. It was just a ploy to scare her. Of course, these men wouldn't blow up a ship with dozens of people in it just to—

An explosion sounded in the distance.

Chapter Twenty

Only Caimán's firm hold on her prevented Aura from sliding to the floor as her legs went suddenly boneless. Probably sensing that the fight had gone out of her, he pulled her out of the doorway and released her, closing and locking the door behind him.

She was finding it hard to breathe. She struggled for one breath, and then another as the memory of Eduardo's murmured promise echoed in her ears. She wished she had insisted that they didn't wait until they were home to talk. She wished she hadn't involved him in any of this. He'd still be safe if he hadn't met her.

"Get back to searching," Caimán told Aura, nudging her with his boot. "Or it'll be you next."

The Marchenas were rummaging around the front room, as if the explosion had been meant as an incentive for them as well.

Aura couldn't move for the pressure in her chest. She couldn't move, and she couldn't think. All she could do was hold on to the wooden crate on the floor next to where she huddled. The cracked clay figurines nestled in hay and crumpled newspaper gazed blankly up at her from eyes that were little more than indentations on their reddish-brown faces.

Her hand closed around one of them and before she quite

realized what she was doing, she was lobbing it at Caimán with all her might.

She missed, her aim no better than when she'd thrown the vase at Eduardo thinking he was an intruder. The figurine smashed against the wall behind him, spraying Marchena and his wife with shards. Aura seized another one and prepared to try again—

A dull gleam caught her attention and her gaze fell on the broken pieces of the small figurine, which were interspersed with something that gleamed in the lamplight.

The gold.

Gold coins, to be exact. Aura looked at the figurine in her hand and dashed it against the edge of her worktable, covering her eyes as the clay broke into pieces. There were coins in there, too.

The Marchenas and Caimán fell on the crate with avid enthusiasm and Aura took the opportunity to scramble to her feet. She wrenched open the door and burst out of the house, sobs exploding out of her and tears making her vision blur.

She went as far as the sidewalk before she ran into someone whose arms closed reflexively around her. It wasn't until she breathed in the citrus scent of limes and mandarin oranges that she looked up and saw Eduardo.

He was alive.

He was alive and safe and Aura was so flooded with relief that she burst into sobs again. He clasped her to him, stroking the back of her head and alternating between murmuring soothing things into her ear and kissing its curve and the hollow just beneath it.

"You're safe," he told her, over and over again. "You're safe."

She calmed by degrees, as her heart caught up to the fact

that Eduardo was here and solid and unharmed. After several minutes, Aura found the strength to look up again. There were men rushing all around her, guardsmen from their uniforms, though here and there she caught a glimpse of men in evening wear. Behind her, she could hear the Marchenas and Caimán being questioned over their role in what had just happened.

Aura didn't care. She had no eyes for anyone other than Eduardo. He reminded her of a palm tree—strong, yet flexible enough to withstand the fiercest of gales.

"You're safe," he told her again, and Aura responded with a tremulous smile.

"No, you are. I thought—the Marchenas said they had someone lock you up and when I saw the explosion, I thought—"

Eduardo frowned and cast a glance toward the smoke in the distance. "We heard the sirens, but there was no time to stop. It sounds like it came from the docks."

"They said they were going to blow up the *Leonor* if—"

"The *Leonor*?" Eduardo's body grew suddenly rigid. "I have to get back. Gregorio's still on board."

The next quarter of an hour was among the worst in Eduardo's life.

Aura led him directly to an empty carriage down the street from the swarming crowd of guardsmen and customs officials. She jumped into the coachman's seat and Eduardo leaped next to her, grabbing tight hold of the frame that held up the canopy as she urged the horse into first a trot, then a gallop.

It was a good thing that Aura had taken the reins, because Eduardo would have wreaked havoc on the streets of San Pedro in his haste to get back to the docks.

If anything had happened to Gregorio…

A knot formed in his throat, growing bigger and tighter as the plumes of smoke rose higher into the dark sky. It had been thanks to Gregorio's catalog-ordered gadgets that Eduardo had managed to get out of the locked stateroom, once he had gained enough control of his surging panic to realize that Aura needed him. With grim determination he had employed the otherwise useless tool into a lever that allowed him to take the door off its hinges.

The purser hadn't been there when he'd burst out, angry as hell. He'd found the governor and William Pulliam, instead, as well as his friend Felipe, who had met his terse assertions that his wife was in danger by following him to the deck and onto a lifeboat that Eduardo had rowed to shore with furious energy.

Reaching the docks returned Eduardo's thoughts to the present. Aura drove the carriage directly to the place where the *Leonor* usually docked. Eduardo jumped out the second it started to slow. A moment later, he heard the clatter of Aura's heels as she rushed after him.

The docks were thronging with the usual mix of sailors and stevedores, but Eduardo caught the glitter of beaded dresses and jewels among them. That meant—

He looked wildly toward the water. The *Leonor* was much closer to shore than when he'd left it. Flames and smoked issued from the starboard side, but they were already beginning to subside, likely due to the efforts of the coast guard.

Eduardo held out his hand for Aura, to make sure he didn't lose her in the crowd, and charged forward. To his relief, he saw his cousin almost right away.

"Gregorio!" he called through the lump in his throat.

His cousin turned. "Everyone got out safely," he reported,

wiping his forehead on his rolled-up shirtsleeve and then gingerly removing his spectacles to clean those as well. "The explosion was a small one, and we managed to contain it until the coast guard and the fire brigade arrived."

"We'll need to make sure everyone is accounted for," Aura said urgently.

The wild roar of his panic was beginning to subside. Eduardo nodded.

A familiar face rushed by, and Eduardo stopped Ruiz, the clerk, with a gesture. "Here are the keys to the office," Eduardo said, reaching into his pocket. "Get a copy of the guest list and make sure you track down everyone on it. I want to make sure they're all uninjured."

The young man nodded and rushed off.

"Is that Juan?" Aura said suddenly, calling to the former pickpocket as his scrawny face appeared among the thronging crowd, smudged with soot.

"That," Gregorio said, "is the man who saved us all."

He waved over the boy, who explained how he had seen Aura being taken.

"I followed them to a house," Juan said. "I peeked in and heard what the men were planning, with the explosives and all, so I ran back."

Gregorio slung an arm over the boy's chest. "He borrowed a rowboat and rushed to tell us. It was an act of bravery like nothing I'd ever seen."

"It was nothing, sir," Juan said, but Eduardo could see the way his chest swelled with pride.

He pounded the boy's back, grinning widely. "I wouldn't call that nothing, Juan. You saved the lives of dozens of people. That's the kind of thing people are given medals for."

"What would I need medals for?" the boy said practically. "Cakes, though…"

Gregorio laughed. "I'll make sure you have all the cakes you can eat. When we're done here, I'll take you to meet my future wife. *Her* cakes are the best in San Pedro."

Joy transformed Juan's skinny face, and for the first time that day, Eduardo saw his wife smile. She exchanged a few quiet words with the boy and Gregorio took the opportunity to draw Eduardo aside.

"Any idea who set it off?" his cousin asked.

"Must have been the purser who locked me into your stateroom." Like Marchena, he had clearly been abusing his position. "He was working with one of the customs intervenors, who I suspect is a smuggler."

"The—" Gregorio shook his head. "You can tell me about it tomorrow."

"And the ship? What's the damage?"

"It's not beyond repair," Gregorio said carefully. "Though I do wonder if it's worth it."

"What do you mean?"

"She served us well, but it's time to retire the old relic," Gregorio said. "And time to stop clinging to the past. I know Abuelo would agree. Do you?"

Eduardo looked at his cousin. His spectacles were askew and his shirt was grimy and he was dripping with perspiration.

"Yes," Eduardo said. For all that he'd claimed he had no wish to dwell on the past, he had been clinging to it, and to his hurt and fear, for so long that it had become second nature. It was past time that he let it all go, if only to keep his hands free for the future. He turned to where Aura was trying to clean a smudge of soot off Juan's forehead with her handkerchief, to the boy's evident displeasure. "I agree."

Chapter Twenty-One

After Gregorio assured them that he would take care of Juan and the guests who remained on the docks, Aura asked Eduardo to take her back to her house.

Mr. Pulliam seemed to have taken charge, ordering his deputy to gather and guard the crate containing Aura's gold. It had been placed on her worktable, and the deputy gave her a kind smile and tactfully withdrew when she went to stand in front of it.

She was gazing down at the blank faces when she spotted a corner of what appeared to be an envelope tucked between the side of the crate and the newspapers wrapped around the figurines. Aura eased it out, aware that her heart had started pounding.

Her pulse sped up further when she recognized her father's handwriting. *For Aura*, he had written across the back of the envelope.

Hands steady, she used her sewing shears to open it and took out the pages that had been folded inside.

Earlier today, when I told you that all I needed was one last scheme and I'd never have to work again, I grew angry when you retorted by saying that I had never worked a day in my life. I have found it difficult to face up to many things, and none was more difficult than to face up to the fact that you were right.

I'm afraid I have entangled myself in something I shouldn't have. Having used your savings to purchase gold coins and a steamer ticket to New York, I was stymied by the sheer amount I would need for paying export taxes. I remembered that an old acquaintance worked at the Customs Office and approached him for help, thinking that perhaps he might appeal to the Customs Inspector or even a higher power to have the fees exonerated, as I'd heard some had.

Instead, he convinced me to take him on as a partner. He would make sure that I wasn't questioned or searched and in exchange, I would give him a portion of my earnings. It seemed reasonable to me, so I agreed.

It soon became clear, though, that my acquaintance at the Customs Office meant for me to continue working as his courier. His share of the gold would go toward the purchase of explosives that he intended to sell to the revolutionaries who have been making trouble since last March. Pulling the wool over the eyes of the Customs Office and the dreadful American who runs it was one thing, but I have no desire to contribute to the political instability in this country. I tried to refuse, but I had already transferred the deed to the house to his name—his way of ensuring I would go through with the plot.

I won't forfeit the house, not after all you sacrificed to purchase it in the first place. So I suppose I have no choice but to leave for New York in the morning. It'll all be worth it in the end, I'm certain of it.

I don't wish to alarm you unduly. However, if any-

*thing were to happen to me, be on the lookout for a
package from New York. My friend there has been
instructed to reach out to you with something I put
by for you and your siblings. And your mother, if she
should ever decide to accept anything from me.*

*I know I haven't given you much cause for believing in me. Trust that I have wanted nothing more in
my life than to provide for my family. The best I can
do now is to make provisions for you in case—*

The rest of the sentence was scratched out, and followed
only by the words, *Your affectionate father.*

Aura's heart squeezed inside her chest. He had put the
crate inside her wardrobe and he hadn't left the letter where
she could find it.

When her father had said, *Cambié,* he hadn't been telling her he had changed. He'd been trying to tell her that
he had changed his mind about going to New York. But
Aura couldn't help wondering if maybe he had done both.

By the time Eduardo returned with Aura to her house,
the situation there was well under control. While she
slipped inside, he remained on the sidewalk to speak with
the governor and William Pulliam and the captain of the
Civil Guard about what had just happened.

Felipe had stayed behind with them, and he was able
to confirm that the coins inside the clay figurines were
the ones that he had sold to Eduardo, who in turn had sold
them to Aura's father. Her legitimate ownership of them
established, the actions of the Marchenas were categorized
as theft.

Official imports had gone down in the wake of the US
government taking over Customs and with tax revenue

falling precipitously, Pulliam was coming down hard on smugglers. It was unlikely that the Marchenas would escape prosecution.

As for the other man, Eduardo was informed he was part of a smuggling ring that had seized the opportunity Eduardo had unknowingly provided by gathering every customs official in one place. Their intention in getting rid of them in a supposed accident had been to cause enough havoc for their activities to remain unnoticed, at least for some time. The authorities had been in pursuit of them in some time, and that night's events gave them what they needed to apprehend the ringleaders.

Eduardo told the captain of the Guard what he knew and what he had guessed about the purser's involvement, and left him to deal with the matter. The only person who could have told the full truth of what had transpired was no longer around to tell it—Eduardo could only hope that what they'd been able to piece together would be enough to satisfy Aura, who was the only person who truly mattered in this entire business.

He found her inside the house, seated at the large table in the front room. The crate was in front of her, and she was holding what looked like a letter, her grip so tight on the pages that their edges were crumpled.

Gently, he touched her shoulder. "Should we go home?"

For one heart-stopping moment, Eduardo thought she was going to send him there on his own. Then she nodded, and folded the letter.

Aura was quiet on the carriage ride back to the house, her gaze downcast as if she were studying the hands she had folded on her lap. She hadn't told him the contents of the letter, and Eduardo hadn't asked, though he was burning to know.

As if she had divined his thoughts, she said, "The letter was from my father. I think he wrote it meaning to leave it for me to find when he left for New York. Toward the end, he said he was leaving provisions for me and my siblings."

"Provisions?"

"I can only imagine what he meant by that—a lottery ticket, perhaps." The corners of her lips turned up in the most pitiful excuse for a smile he had ever seen.

He pulled her to him, and she rested her head against his shoulder.

"Also," she continued, "there was never any loan from Marchena. The transfer of the house's title was to ensure that he go through with it, as you guessed."

"If you want, we can present the letter to the magistrate and see if he can do anything about having the house restored to your ownership. I'm not acquainted with the relevant laws, but I doubt that Marchena will be allowed to keep it."

She nodded absently. "Yes, I'd like that."

Aura was silent the rest of the way home. The clock was striking eleven when they began climbing the stairs to their bedroom. He didn't know if it was exhaustion or grief or a combination of both that slowed down her steps. Stopping her with a murmur, he offered to carry her upstairs. To his surprise, she agreed readily, her arms curling around his neck as he lifted her easily and carried her all the way to their bed.

He laid her gently onto the mattress, toeing off his shoes and bracketing her with his body as she laid her face on her folded arms.

"Aura? What's wrong?"

She turned to him, raising an eyebrow. That simple gesture did more to reassure him than anything else would have. "Besides the harrowing few hours we just endured?" She sighed, and wrapped her arms around herself. "It was gold that the Marchenas were after. They claimed my father stole it from them, but he wrote that he purchased the gold with my savings."

"He did," he confirmed, and her gaze flew to his face. "I was the one who sold it to him."

She inhaled sharply. "You?"

"I didn't remember it until someone mentioned it earlier tonight. The coins belonged to my friend Felipe. He had fallen on hard times and all he had left was the gold, which had been collected by his grandfather. I bought them from him, intending to keep them until he was back on his feet financially and could repay my loan, but settling his debts was going to exhaust my personal finances and Leo was relying on me to provide half the capital to get our exporting venture off the ground."

She answered his explanation of her father's visit with a snort.

Eduardo concluded, "So you see, the gold was bought with your savings. It's legitimately yours."

To his alarm, Aura buried her face in her hands, rolling slightly in the mattress.

"The Marchenas told me he'd stolen the gold from them and I—I believed them."

He tugged at her elbows, only a little surprised when she allowed herself to be drawn into an embrace.

"I misjudged him." She tilted her head up so he could see into the warm brown pools of her eyes. "I misjudged my father."

"Aura…" It wasn't often that he found himself at a loss for words. He stroked her hair, trying to think. "After everything you've learned in the past several weeks, you'd have been justified in not knowing what to believe."

"I thought that because he was capable of smuggling… But that's just it, Eduardo—he wasn't. He changed his mind at the last minute. He wasn't going to go through with it, and he tried to tell me so just before he died. But I misunderstood him. I had been let down by him one time too many and I let my disappointment cloud my sympathy toward him."

"I'm sorry," he told her quietly.

Aura touched the knot of his tie. "It's too late for me to ask his forgiveness. But it's not too late for me to ask if you still want to be married to me."

"Of course I do. Aura, I'm sorry," he said in a rush. "I'm so sorry I was so beastly toward you. I should have told you about my parents—about everything in my past—but it was so easy to avoid thinking about everything…"

She laid a hand on his arm. "You should have," she told him. "And in the spirit of honesty, there's something I must tell you. Eduardo, I…" she began, and paused for the express purpose of giving him a heart attack. "I think I might be in love with you."

It was a good thing they were in private, because Eduardo strongly suspected that even if that hadn't been the case, he would have still reacted as he did.

"You *love* me? You love *me*?" He let a slow, flirtatious smile take over his mouth as he rolled over so that he was on top of her, crushing her under his weight.

"What the devil's gotten into you?" she asked with a creditable attempt at irritability that was unfortunately rendered unbelievable by the gleam of interest in her eyes. "You're wrinkling my dress."

"Did you really think I would react to a sentence like that with staid respectability?"

"Something like that—I thought you wanted nothing to do with love."

"It *is* extremely inconvenient," he agreed. "I wanted a relationship that was nothing more than easy and uncomplicated and I can't imagine why because you are neither of those things and we both know that what I really want is you. Because I *love* you."

He braced himself on his forearms, rising just enough to be able to brush his lips over his.

"I love everything about you," he said in between kisses. "And I'm beyond delighted that you feel the same way." He nibbled at her lip, then soothed the sting with his tongue. "Easy and uncomplicated are not enough to base a marriage on. But love is. As for the rest of it…we can figure it out, together."

"Do you really think we can? We haven't lost our chance?"

"I don't know much about sewing, but it doesn't ruin a garment to unpick its stitches in order to remake it, does it?"

She looked amused at the analogy. "Are you saying that being married is like sewing?"

"I have no idea what I'm saying. Clearly, I don't know much about marriage—except that it's hard work. And I also know that you've never been afraid of hard work."

"No." She looked thoughtfully into his eyes. "It has always meant safety and security. Without it, I won't be transformed into a society wife who attends yachting parties dripping in diamonds and pearls. Without it, I'll just feel like someone you rescued because you felt sorry for her."

"Sorry for you?" he echoed softly, the vulnerability in her eyes sending darts through him. "I admire you. You've been through much worse than I have and look how you turned out. As for the other part of that incredibly misguided sentence…if anything, you've rescued me."

He couldn't do it. He'd never been able to do it.

But if it was the only way of keeping her…

"I don't claim to have had a difficult life, just…a difficult time getting through painful patches. When my parents sent me away from New York, I truly believed they'd done it because I hadn't been useful enough to keep around. The experience on the journey back didn't help. I returned to the island a wreck, determined to be so useful that everyone would want to keep me around. My grandmother saw my pain and tried to help me, but she died less than a year later."

"Oh, Eduardo." She touched his jaw.

"Ever since then, I have drifted from amusement to frolic to party, not even knowing that I was searching for someone to brave the night with me. I actually believed that I liked being a bachelor," he scoffed. "And I thought my friends were envious of my freedom."

"Yes, well, I didn't think it was polite to tell you exactly how wrong you were."

He rolled to his side. "Are you sure you don't want to reconsider your options? There must be someone out there who will make you a better husband than a bonehead like me."

"Unfortunately for me, I happen to like boneheads," Aura informed him. "And honestly, all I want is someone who can set his own pride aside and let me work in the way I want to."

He threaded his fingers through hers and lifted her hand to kiss her callused fingers. "Aura, I love that you feel so strongly about your work. I'll respect your boundaries and your independence. Just…please let me help sometimes."

"I'll try to," she whispered. "I can't promise to be perfect, but I can promise to try."

"The same goes for me," he admitted. "You may not have noticed it, but occasionally I tend to be a tiny bit overzealous when it comes to giving others what I think they want."

"I noticed, all right," she said wryly. "But the truth is that I could learn a thing or two from you. You give so much of yourself. Your generosity is so unrestrained that it makes me uncomfortable because whenever I experienced that kind of abundance, it was always followed by disaster. But I don't want to be so bound by the past anymore. I want to give as freely as you do."

"You can start right now," he said with a wicked grin, letting his hand slip from her waist to the round curves farther down and kneading her firm flesh. "And I'll start by learning all the ways I can make you happy without reaching for my wallet."

"Oh, that's easy." Aura hooked her thigh over his to give his leg access between hers. "The bath you drew me, the day after our wedding. That was lovely—and that's what I like, Eduardo. Actions, not things."

"Actions, is it?" he asked with a contemplative look at the gathered silk covering her breasts. "I can do that. I can do that very well…"

"Don't you dare ruin this gown," she said warningly, though the thing was stained with soot and sweat and had lost half its delicate beading. "It's not mine."

"Then we'll have to get it off, won't we?"

Eduardo was nothing if not patient. Unfastening each of the half a million hooks running all along the side of her gray-and-silver gown took an eternity, at least. Another century was spent helping her out of bed and supporting her as she stepped carefully out of it so that not a single thread was snagged. Then came her corset, with so many hooks and laces that he could feel himself sprouting gray hairs.

It was an eon before she finally stood in front of him in just her stockings and linen underthings. And if he had changed in that time, so had she. Even before she removed the pins holding her hair in place, she had acquired a new openness that Eduardo found appealingly attractive.

"What about you?" she asked as she went to the dressing table to set down her hairpins because she was his careful, thrifty Aura and even at that moment wouldn't risk losing a single pin.

He gave her a crooked smile. "I'm not wearing a borrowed dress."

She made a noise that was half amusement and half exasperation and reached for his tie.

He had plenty of buttons and fastenings of his own, and Aura's clever fingers undid them all with swift grace. Being naked in her arms felt like releasing a breath he didn't realize he had been holding.

The lamplight touched the curves of her body the way he wanted to touch her. She was the one touching him, though, her cool, slim fingers gliding over his biceps and shoulders. Rising on the tips of her toes, she pressed a kiss to the scar on his collarbone that made his pulse leap.

He'd done enough waiting.

Clasping her by the waist with both hands, he walked her backward until they reached the whitewashed wall.

Her shoes were the same blue-gray silk as her dress, embroidered in silver thread and adorned with the same kinds of beads that had made her dress sparkle in the lamplight. Her stockings were silk, too, and so thin that he could see the brown of her skin through them. Easing them off, Eduardo showered her with kisses, each one more ardent than the last.

His fingers met the tantalizing heat between her legs,

and she nudged her thighs toward him, her eager murmurs falling into his mouth. He touched her gently, insistently, with urgency and affection.

Afterward, they lay in bed with their legs interwoven, the palm she pressed against his chest giving him the strength he needed to tell her everything she'd wanted to hear. About his childhood, and how abandoned he'd felt when his parents decided he would do better at home than in New York. About the year he'd had with his grandmother before she succumbed to her illness, reopening all the wounds that had begun to close under her nurturing. About how his grandfather had devoted himself to Eduardo, and how his cousins had grown fiercely protective about him and how he'd almost cost Gregorio his beloved because his cousin refused to leave him.

And as he did, he breathed in the fresh green scent of her, telling himself that this was only the beginning.

Chapter Twenty-Two

Aura's husband was doing some delightfully wicked things to her inner thighs when a knock sounded at the door.

He flung back the blanket covering him, looking annoyed. "They already brought a breakfast tray."

The knock came again, followed by a muffled voice. "Sorry to disturb you, but Don Gregorio insisted that you see this as soon as possible."

Eduardo groaned. "I can't wait for that man to get married and out of my house. I should toss him out right now and force him and Celia to elope like rational beings."

"The aunts will never forgive you if you deprive them of yet another wedding," Aura pointed out, pushing him away as another knock sounded through their bedroom.

"Just a moment," he called to the housemaid at the door as he got out of bed and tugged the sheet back over Aura.

For modesty's sake, he wrapped a discarded towel around his waist before going to open the door with a polite, "Yes?"

The girl's apologetic voice filtered past him to where Aura lay. "It's a package, Don Eduardo. From New York."

Aura's gaze flew to Eduardo's face as he shut the door and returned to bed. He was outwardly composed, but she could see the slight furrow between his brows as he looked down at the envelope.

In the ten or so days since her encounter with the March-enas, his private detective had found Aura's mother and siblings in Santo Domingo and delivered the letters she had written them. Eduardo had been slower in contacting his parents, though. He'd labored over several drafts of a letter before abandoning his efforts for the time being. As far as she knew, he hadn't finished the letter. Still…

"Is it from your parents?" she asked.

Eduardo glanced up. "Actually, it's for you."

Aura's heart gave a leap, and she took the package from him as he got back into bed beside her.

"The lottery ticket?" she said with a laugh, using the butter knife he passed her to slit open the heavy envelope.

It was stuffed with papers. Bewildered, Aura slid her thumb and forefinger inside and pulled out a sheaf of—

"Those look like savings bonds," Eduardo said. "A great deal of them."

Aura nodded mutely, unable to form even a scrap of coherent speech as she examined the papers, each of which was printed with the seal of the US Department of the Treasury and marked with an amount that while small, added up to a tidy sum. It was the best gift she'd ever received.

Thumbing through the papers for a second time revealed a piece of stationery, folded in half. A letter. And this one was addressed to *her*.

Aura scanned its contents quickly, then lowered the paper briefly, took a deep breath and read it again.

"My father's associate in New York is a *banker*." A wild giggle burst out of her. "He says they met when my father tried to sell him a hair tonic—and that my father was a good salesman, but he was a better one, and my father was the one who walked out of the meeting having made a purchase. They kept in touch, and over the years, every time my father had a windfall he mailed a check to the banker, asking him to keep the bonds in a safety-deposit box so that he wouldn't be tempted to cash them in." She lowered the letter. "I had no idea."

"Looks to me like you were right in believing in him," Eduardo remarked, stroking her forearm.

She nodded slowly. "I think I lost something when I stopped believing in my father. I convinced myself that I'd have an easier time if I kept my aspirations small and manageable. If I kept my dreams contained, if I didn't give my imagination free rein, then I couldn't possibly fail."

The store had been about feeling secure in her future. Now that she didn't need it, Aura was surprised over how much she still wanted it.

"I do still want my small store, Eduardo. But what makes sense in business doesn't make sense in love. I also want to love you without restraint. I want there to be no limits to the space inside my heart."

He took her hand and raised her fingers to his lips. "I will do everything I can to help you achieve your dreams, whatever they may be."

"I find it hard to believe that I didn't get the better end of the bargain," Aura said.

"Because of the bathroom?"

"Because of…" she gestured around her "…everything. A home and a family and…this. You."

"You're right, it's not a fair trade. You get all of that and I get you. I'd have to pile you with gold and jewels just to come close to restoring the balance. And even then…" Eduardo shrugged. "Even then, it's not enough. You're worth more than all of that. You're worth more than everything I've ever had."

She kissed his neck, and then his shoulder, her heart full of him.

Eduardo gathered up the bank certificates carefully, sliding them back into the envelope. When they had been secured on his bedside table, he rolled into her and pulled the blankets away, covering her with his own body as he pressed her back into the mattress.

Making a noise low in her throat, Aura arched into him.

"What are you going to do with your newfound fortune?" he asked in between kisses.

Aura hooked a leg around him. "Open the store, give some to charity..." She kissed the hollow beneath his ear. "I don't know, it might be time to finally indulge myself. A little."

"Why do I get the feeling that indulging yourself means a new set of sewing scissors or some bobbin thread?"

A laugh bubbled out of Aura as she moved her hips against him. "You know me too well. But I may surprise you yet."

"I have no doubt of that."

Gently but inexorably, Eduardo made his way inside her. Regardless of how often it happened, Aura's breath always caught in that moment. At the sharp pleasure of the intrusion, maybe. And marvel at the way her body stretched to accommodate him, just as her life had.

He'd made space for her, too. For the past ten days, he'd done little else—inviting her to have lunch with him at his desk when his duties grew too pressing to get away, he had filled her in on the details of his life without skipping over the difficult parts, like the move to New York and his grandmother Leonor's death.

And he'd made good on the rest of his promises. As he'd done on the day of María del Mar's party, he had introduced her to every woman of his acquaintance as his wife, who just so happened to be a dressmaker of exquisite taste and skill. The women all smiled at his overblown praise, but coupled with Lucía de Díaz's eager recommendations and the evidence of Aura's own beautiful wardrobe, most of them hadn't wasted any time in soliciting her services.

In a week's time, work would begin on her store. Aura had cautiously expanded her original plans to accommodate her new budget, though she was still careful to keep from spending more than the earnings she'd estimated for the first year. After seeing what Paulina de Linares had done in her own home, Aura had sought her help with the decoration, pleased to be able to support another working woman.

Her life was so much bigger now than it used to be. The day before, Eduardo had gathered up his friends and their children aboard the new clipper he had just purchased. They'd sailed out to a small cove where the land curved protectively around the Caribbean Sea, and they'd picnicked on the sand, underneath umbrellas as large as tents, watching the children run around as they searched for shells and threw pieces of seaweed at each other.

And even though Aura hadn't gotten any work at all, she had probably enjoyed herself more than everyone else.

Twining her arms and legs around Eduardo now, she made a subtle movement with her hips that indicated she wanted to be on top. Eduardo responded to her unspoken request immediately—his rhythm didn't falter as he rolled onto his back, keeping her hips firmly pressed against his.

Palms braced on his chest, she looked down at Eduardo's laughing eyes, now full of tenderness. His mouth was curled slightly at the edges with the hint of humor that softened his features and made him even more attractive than he already was.

She lowered herself onto her forearms and caught that mouth into a kiss. "How were you so sure that you were going to like being married to me?"

He cupped a hand around the back of her neck and kissed her again. "Because you're you," he said as if it was obvious, letting his lips brush her mouth as he spoke. "And because of that kiss in the garden—remember? I thought that anyone who kissed a near stranger with that much hunger and passion would probably be just as good in bed."

"You did not," Aura said, laughing despite herself.

"No, I didn't," he agreed. "But I *was* aroused and tantalized and intrigued and really, *really* eager to see you naked."

"Well, you've seen me now. Was it worth it?"

Eduardo's teeth closed gently over her bottom lip. "You're worth *everything*."

Returning his kiss, Aura gave herself over to the urgency that was building inside her, rising higher in pitch and intensity, carrying her in waves of pure feeling.

The sun was shining at full strength through the open shutters the next time they spoke again. Eduardo was lying on his side, tracing lazy circles on the skin over her abdomen.

"You'll think this is ridiculous of me, but given your aversion to fine jewelry, I—"

"Bought me a locomotive?" Aura said, only half-joking. "A fleet of ships? My own island?"

"Close." Grinning, Eduardo tumbled out of bed and went to his dresser, where he rummaged in the drawer that Aura knew contained his handkerchiefs and socks. "I made you something."

He turned around, holding aloft something that made Aura blink.

It was a flower made out of buttons and wire. In the center was the carved mother-of-pearl button that had been stolen from her crate.

"You finally did it," she said softly. "You found the one gift that I'd never refuse."

He lowered himself onto one knee, holding out the flower with his lips curled in an irresistible smile. "Aura Soriano de Martínez, would you do me the honor of being my wife?"

Aura tried hard to hold a disapproving frown between her brows. "Eduardo, you can't propose after we're already married."

"Why not? There hasn't been a single conventional thing about us from the moment we met."

"Are you trying to tell me that the men of your set are introduced to their future wives in ballrooms and drawing rooms and not when they attempt to foil pickpockets?"

"More fool them." Kneeling fully on the tiles, Eduardo propped both elbows on the bed and gazed up at her. "I love you. That's it, you know."

Arrested by the intensity in his eyes, it took Aura a moment to answer. Her hand drifted down to trace the curve of his ear and he captured it between both of his own and brought them to his warm chest. "That's what?"

"Why I married you."

The Martínezes, including Don Amable, began arriving the next day. Most of Eduardo's relatives stayed with friends, though he had guest rooms prepared for Gregorio's parents and a couple more of his aunts and uncles, and a handful of cots turned the upstairs parlor into a dormitory for six or seven of his youngest cousins.

Aura and Eduardo emerged from their bedroom on the day of the ball to find the entire house in a state of controlled chaos. Eduardo's grandfather had taken over the preparations for that evening's soiree with the air of a general getting ready for battle.

Horse-driven carts with enough plants and flowers to fill a botanical garden were crowded in the drive, while the dining room had been entirely taken over by freshly polished silver.

Stopping first by the terrace, from which his grandfather was overseeing the final touches that were being put on the dais at one end of the garden, Eduardo greeted his grandfather and made sure he had everything he needed. Then he seized his wife by the hand and escaped with her to his new yacht, where they spent a handful of pleasurable hours eating the lunch packed for them and crowding together into a wide deck chair to gaze up at the sky.

They returned in time to bathe and dress for the dance. They did it together, laughing as they splashed each other in the big tub and working on each other's fastenings in between refreshing sips of champagne from the bottle in the silver chiller Eduardo had carted up to their bedroom.

Aura's gown was a confection in black tulle, embroidered with white and cream rosebuds, with the merest hint in the tiny leaves that curled from the base of each bud. At the gathering point of each sleeve, she had sewn a modest cluster of seed pearls, from which dangled a black silk tassel.

Eduardo stepped behind her as she stood in front of the mirror, fussing with the sleeves, and wrapped his arms around her. "You look ravishing. In the sense that I feel like I shouldn't let you out of the room until I've ravished you."

"We'll be late for your grandfather's ball," she protested, squirming as his hand wandered up to her chest and he dipped a finger inside her bodice.

"No one will blame me when they see you," Eduardo said, but he retreated.

Downstairs, the musicians had finished tuning their instruments and were playing the first strains of a waltz, which probably meant that the first guests were starting to arrive. Night had long since fallen and the breeze that came in through the shutters, scented faintly with rose and citrus and the merest hint of salt, had cooled somewhat.

Eduardo opened his drawer to find the silk flower she'd made for their wedding day, intending to ask her to fix it to his lapel again. Next to it was the satin box he had gotten out of the safe earlier.

He took both out of the drawer, and pinned the flower on his lapel himself before going to her side and saying, "I was wondering if you wanted to wear these tonight."

The box had silver clasps that opened to reveal a slightly yellowed satin interior. Cushioned inside it were his grandmother's combs and pearls.

Aura touched the tip of her finger to the lustrous strands, a serious expression settling over her face. She had made herself a choker out of a length of black velvet ribbon and cream-colored rosebuds, each adorned with a seed pearl in its center and a miniature bow of the narrowest green satin ribbon. Untying it from around her neck, she said, "I would be honored to wear them, Eduardo. Thank you."

She turned around, scooping up the loose curl hanging down her back so that he could fasten the clasp. The pearls were warm from his touch when he put them around her neck, but the kiss he dropped on her nape was warmer still.

"Thank *you*," he murmured, and straightened. "My grandfather will be so pleased to see you wearing them."

"I'd do anything to make him happy." She placed her hands on his shoulders. "And you, too."

He inclined his head and she rose to meet him. Her lips were tart and cool from the champagne, an intriguing contrast to the warmth his tongue found when they parted. He licked at her lower lip, relishing in her taste and the delectable softness of her, breathing in her fresh river scent and wondering how he had ever thought her a path best left untrodden when she was the direction his entire life had been straining toward.

Letting out a soft noise that went like a dart to his chest, Aura ended the kiss but remained pressed up against him. "I was going to wait until tomorrow, but I think I had better ask you now."

Eduardo grinned. "I already proposed, Aura, you don't have to do it, too."

"This is a different kind of proposal." She twined their fingers together, looking serious. "It's about my father's gold. I met with the appraiser this morning, and the amount he believes the gold will fetch is much more than I ever dreamed of having, even after dividing it equally among my siblings."

"Good," Eduardo said, nuzzling her earlobe. "Because it's my turn to be plied with silk stockings and champagne."

She pretended to frown at him. "I would never do anything so recklessly impractical. I instructed him to set aside a percentage of my share for the store and for my own expenses. As for the rest… Eduardo, would you and Leo Díaz allow me to invest in your sugar exporting enterprise?"

He pulled away, raising an eyebrow. "When you said you wanted to do some charitable works, I didn't realize you meant me."

"I'm not being altruistic. With sugar prices the way they are, it's about as sure an investment as I can think of." As far as Aura understood it, the increased profitability of sugar had nothing to do with a rise in prices, but to an international agreement to withhold taxes on cane and beet sugar. "And I did ask Gregorio to help me draw up an agreement so you can be certain that it's fair and favorable to us both. And—"

Eduardo put a finger to her lips before replacing them briefly with his mouth. "I'll talk it over with Leo, but I have no doubt he'll accept your proposal. And I have one of my own—will you come with me to New York? I think it's time I saw my parents again. I don't promise that everything will be perfect, but…" He gave an embarrassed shrug. "The fact that I felt discarded doesn't mean that I *was*, as my grandfather pointed out to me when I spoke to him about it last night. I told him I would at least try to listen to what they had to say. And it does seem like a conversation better had in person rather than scribbled on a letter."

"Glad to hear that," she said softly.

"Also, I thought maybe you'd like to use some of your new fortune to purchase some stock for your store. I promise I won't meddle this time. Unless and until you want me to."

"I'll welcome your opinions," she told him, reaching up to adjust his white bow tie. "As long as you agree to curtail your spending. I won't have my investment squandered in silk stockings and champagne."

"But I really had my heart set on buying you a ship of your own," he pretended to protest. "How else are you meant to transport all your wares when your store grows so profitable that even Martínez & Hijos can't keep up with the demand?"

Aura had a hard time keeping her brow furrowed. "Behave yourself, Eduardo Martínez."

He lowered his head toward hers. "Make me."

It was another half hour before they went downstairs, flushed and breathing hard. As Eduardo had predicted, his family had turned out en masse, eager to get to know the woman who had captured Eduardo's heart. He showed her off to each of the relatives gathered, teasing her as she attempted to get everyone's names straight.

Glowing with happiness and champagne, Aura held her own among the Martínezes. He didn't know his admiration for her could be any higher, but he felt it grow as he watched her coax his grandfather into waltzing with her and advise his great-aunt on what colors suited her best and promise his youngest cousin to make him a stable's worth of horses out of felt.

How was it possible that he hadn't seen it before? After all the gifts she had rebuffed, all the luxuries she had scorned… this was what she'd truly wanted. Not money or influence or even a grand store to make her more than financially secure. She'd wanted to have something to belong to—and she had it now.

And if she wanted someone to belong to, well, she had that, too.

There was to be no formal dinner, only *picaderas* served by waiters circulating with trays of artfully arranged tartlets and *pastelitos* and miniature cakes. Eduardo's grandfather did call for a toast, though. Standing on the dais with a background of black-suited musicians, the old man raised a champagne coupe high in the air and beamed down at the gathering.

"*Estimados amigos, familia…* To the happy couple."

Epilogue

The painted shutters of Aura's new store had been thrown open to let in the faint sound of the municipal band playing in the distance. The music could barely be heard over the chatter of the dozens of people who had turned up to support her on her first day.

Eduardo's parents had sent a large, beautiful card from New York to offer their congratulations on the opening, and just that morning the postman had delivered a gossipy letter from Lucía in Vienna. A letter from María del Mar had also arrived, with postmarks from absolutely everywhere—and the woman herself had followed a handful of hours later, declaring that she didn't intend to miss one minute of the celebration.

She and Gregorio had been right—Eduardo's family had not just accepted her, they had embraced her. And they had turned out in full force for the opening of her store, bringing so many of their friends with them that close to forty people had spilled out into the narrow front porch and the sidewalk beyond.

Gregorio and his new wife stood among them, chatting with Gregorio's parents and Sebastián Linares. Celia and Gregorio had been so eager to start their new family that they'd begun by adopting Juan and his younger sister, who would no longer need to support herself by selling peanuts. Dressed in a gray suit and a frilly pink dress, the siblings were examining with obvious approval one of the felt horses Aura had made for Eduardo's six-year-old cousin.

Contentment built inside her chest as she oversaw her store, her nose perfumed by the small bouquet she had pinned to her shoulder, made out of flowers Eduardo had picked that morning from his grandfather's garden.

More bouquets had been placed on the polished wood and glass cases that displayed the sewing notions Aura had brought back from New York—large spools of ribbons in all shades and width, quantities of handmade and machine-made lace, delicate embroidery scissors and sturdy shears, and crepe paper for costumes in over a hundred brilliant hues.

A handsome wooden cabinet with pigeonholes held the more prosaic items, like papers of needles and pins, and next to it was a rack of fashion magazines. At the back of the store, under looped garlands, were the two gleaming sewing machines that served as models for the manufacturing company Aura was now representing.

The second floor was part storeroom and part workroom—the grand atelier Eduardo had suggested had become a much more modest space where Aura and another modiste received clients and sewed garments. Instead of hiring seamstresses, Aura had found it a better practice to partner herself with a woman who needed the space to do her work away from the chaos of the four young children she had at home.

Aura stepped out onto the porch, Eduardo at her side, to show his great-aunt the differences between the two shades of blue yarn she was considering. She paused in the middle of her sentence. Was the music growing louder?

The suspicion flaring in Aura's chest was confirmed when the glance she cast at her husband was met with a grin.

"I thought it was only proper to invite the municipal band," he told her. "Seeing as they were present when you and I first met."

A murmur was spreading through her guests as they turned to watch the band approach, Paulina de Linares bouncing the baby in her arms to the beat of the music. Aura smiled at them, emotion unspooling inside her chest as Eduardo slid an arm around her waist and gathered her close to his side. She was turning to him when she caught sight of something that made her freeze.

Was that—

Were those—

Her breath caught in her throat. And then, without any conscious thought, she abandoned all dignity and ran at full speed into her mother's arms.

The scent of camellias and freshly baked bread had once been as familiar to Aura as breathing. She inhaled it now, feeling something in her chest coming unraveled.

"I didn't think you would come," she said, her voice so muffled and thick with tears that she didn't think her mother had understood a single word she'd said.

Her mother pulled away far enough to peer into Aura's face. "How could we stay away? We've missed you so much."

We—she'd said *we*.

Aura stepped back and got a proper look at the pretty young women standing on either side of her mother. Her sisters had grown into beauties. And one of them... Aura took in the gold band encircling her finger and the slight swell at her midsection. Her sister nodded and drew Aura into a teary hug, whispering, "I'm so glad you'll be able to share in the joy."

"I'll be here for *everything* from now on," Aura said fiercely.

Aura squeezed her sister and stepped back, fumbling in her pocket for her handkerchief. That was when she spotted the boy hanging behind them. No, not a boy—a young man of fifteen in long trousers and a cap.

Her smile broadened.

And then it was time to introduce her family to Eduardo, who greeted them all with his usual easy friendliness, telling her that he had arranged for them to stay at the house for as long as they wished.

"You knew about this?" she asked, turning to him. "Why didn't you tell me?"

His smile was full of boyish mischief. "I was sworn to secrecy. And I thought you could use a good surprise, for once."

"It's a lovely one," she said, squeezing his hand.

Aura introduced her family to Eduardo's grandfather and cousins. Then she showed them around proudly, plucking ribbons from the displays for her sisters and consulting with her mother over the colors in her next embroidery project.

Champagne and rum punch were flowing freely, and dusk was falling by the time the last of her guests left the store. Eduardo, who had walked her family to the house so they could rest from their journey before dinner, came back to help her close up.

"Was it everything you hoped it would be?" Stepping behind her, he leaned his chin on her shoulder and wrapped his arms around her waist.

She reached up to stroke his arms. "More," she said, her voice charged with emotion. "Eduardo, it was so much more."

He turned her gently, tilting up her face with a finger

under her chin. Whatever he saw in it must have satisfied him because he pressed a kiss to her lips.

"We should be getting home," he said.

"Not just yet." Twining her arms around his neck, Aura drew him down again. "I haven't thanked you for all you did to make today such a success."

"That was all you, Aura. Your store is going to be a success because you are—because you're tenacious and hardworking and so incredibly beautiful."

"What has that got to do with it?" she asked, laughing.

He outlined her lips with his fingertip. "That one's just for me, I suppose. But true just the same."

"Come upstairs with me. You haven't seen the settee I got for my office. The upholstery is beautiful."

"The upholstery, is it?" He smirked. "Please, do show me your upholstery."

She swatted lightly at him. "Stop making fun of me and kiss me." She adjusted his tie, then trailed her fingertips around the rim of his collar, making sure to graze his skin. "You did promise me there would be kissing."

* * * * *

*If you enjoyed this story,
why not check out one of
Lydia San Andres's other great reads?*

The Return of His Caribbean Heiress
Alliance with His Stolen Heiress
Compromised into a Scandalous Marriage

HARLEQUIN
Reader Service

Enjoyed your book?

Try the perfect subscription for Romance readers and get more great books like this delivered right to your door.

See why over 10+ million readers have tried Harlequin Reader Service.

Start with a Free Welcome Collection with free books and a gift—valued over $20.

Choose any series in print or ebook. See website for details and order today:

TryReaderService.com/subscriptions